UNDER THE COCOON MOON

UNDER THE COCOON MOON

An Olivia Penn Mystery

THE OLIVIA PENN MYSTERY SERIES
BOOK III

KATHLEEN BAILEY

First hardcover edition: November 2023
First paperback edition: November 2023

ISBN (hardcover): 978-1-956270-10-5
ISBN (paperback): 978-1-956270-09-9
ISBN (e-book): 978-1-956270-08-2
ISBN (audio): 978-1-956270-15-0

Editing by Serena Clarke at Free Bird Editing
Proofreading by LaVerne Clark at LaVerne Clark Editing
Cover design by Robin Vuchnich at My Custom Book Cover

Published by:
Rhino Publishing LLC

www.kathleenbaileyauthor.com

For my Dad

The moon taught me that it's okay to go through phases.

CHAPTER 1

Olivia Penn cradled her cup of hot chocolate and gazed out the front office window of *The Apple Station Times*, softening her eyes on the delicate falling flurries transforming the town square into a life-sized snow globe. The forecast had called for temperatures to remain below freezing with little to no accumulation, but the anticipation of the season's first flakes had everyone giddy at the prediction of a white Christmas.

She sipped the steaming, maple-syrup-kissed Belgian hot chocolate, rating it a ten for decadence. The midday indulgence was courtesy of a surprise Friday holiday party thrown by the newspaper's editor, Ellen McCarthy. Cooper, her son and cub reporter, was detailing to those gathered how he'd slipped away to pick up the pastries and specialty drinks from Jillian's Cafe for the celebration.

She listened, captivated and amused by Cooper's

dramatization of his clandestine mission. Townsfolk hustled by outside, carrying shopping bags no doubt containing holiday gifts and goodies. A string of multi-color lights hanging inside the window twinkled as a reminder that Christmas was six days away, and she still had loads to do before then.

This was the first year in over a decade that she was in her hometown of Apple Station, Virginia, as a local and not a visitor. She had returned home seven months ago to spend time with her father, William Penn, before a planned move to New York to accept a job promotion. But after her dear friend Paige Warner was murdered, everything changed.

Two close calls with her own mortality had led to a reevaluation of what she wanted in her life. Connection with her father and friends. Days that were both fulfilling and easeful. And now, the undeniable warmth growing in her heart for Detective Preston Hills. Though not yet ready to attach *permanent* to her living situation, she had let go of using *temporary* as a constant crutch. She was in the in-between. What her life would look like on the other side remained unclear, but she sensed change was in the air.

"Liv, do you need another drink?" Cassandra said.

Olivia turned toward her friend and the newspaper's star reporter as she joined her by the window. "I'm still working on this one. Thanks, though."

Cassandra's eyes sparked. "It's snowing! Did it just start?"

Olivia nodded, glancing at Cooper, who was speaking with two other staff writers, Brad and Jeremy. "A few minutes ago. Do you know if anyone else is coming in for the party?"

"Rachel texted. She's coming in about an hour. Amanda should be here any minute. How long can you stay?"

Olivia sipped her hot chocolate and then set the paper cup on the window's ledge. "Not too much longer. I want to pick up a wreath from Gunns Farm and then get home. My dad has been helping with the test baking for the column, and we have a debrief in the afternoons about all that went right and wrong. The cleanup of his trials is a project unto itself."

Although Olivia didn't officially work for *The Apple Station Times*, she had agreed to write a hometown advice column once a week, answering what was foremost on the community's mind in exchange for an occasional lunch. The lopsided arrangement didn't bother her as she enjoyed coming into the office and catching up with everyone. The time spent there was therapeutic for her as well. Sitting at Paige's former desk fostered a connection to her friend, and for that, she could want no further compensation.

Ellen had conceived a novel feature for the paper this year: "The Twelve Bakes of Christmas." For the twelve days before Christmas, the column would highlight a holiday dessert, tips for making the recipe, and a feel-good vignette. It all sounded hunky-dory to Olivia, until she realized Ellen's intention was for her to be the baker and columnist. Though she puttered around with pies and cookies, nobody ever was going to nominate her as a contestant for *The Great British Bake Off.* But her mild protest was no match for Ellen's determination. And so, the folksy advice column morphed into a limited-time recipe extravaganza for the Christmas season.

"I'm making your yule log from day three on Sunday," Cassandra said. "I love a good chocolate sponge."

Olivia suppressed a smile as the one good sponge she and her father had managed came after four mediocre, three okayish, and two disastrous attempts. "It was a piece of cake to make."

"That's terrible," Cassandra groaned. "I revoke your writer card until you promise to stop with the baking puns."

Olivia held a hand over her heart, feigning her best shock-horror face. "My word. Where's your Christmas spirit? Don't you know life is what you bake it? Let's bake the world a butter place."

"Do you stay up at night thinking of these?" Cassandra said, cracking a reluctant smile.

"Bake me up before you dough dough."

"Please, stop."

"I can do this all day. But I won't, for my sanity."

"For *all* our sanity," Cassandra added. "Look, the flurries are picking up."

Olivia eyed the town square, where two children were

trying to make snow angels despite the flurries merely speckling the grass. "It's so pretty. The roads look okay." She glanced at Cassandra. "Do you have any other weekend plans?"

"I have a ton to do. Decorating, baking, wrapping. What about you?"

"Me too. I need to finish prepping for Christmas, and then there's all the other normal weekend stuff."

She hoped, at least. For the past four weeks on Saturday morning, at ten o'clock sharp, Olivia *just so happened* to go to Jillian's Cafe, when by chance, Preston *just so happened* to come for coffee as well. She always said she had errands in town. He always reciprocated with something about checking in to see if his mother, Beverly Styles, needed help with anything at the Apple Station Inn. Olivia never asked why he just didn't get his morning brew at the historic inn that Bev owned. She hoped the answer had to do with the ease of their conversations, the way time flew when they were together, and the friendly hug they had exchanged when parting ways last week.

"Liv, Cass, do you need anything?" Cooper said, striding toward them.

Olivia picked up her hot chocolate from the window ledge, and now that it had cooled, took several larger sips. "No, you better cut me off." She swirled her cup and polished off the rest. "This was a splurge, but it was worth every calorie."

"Time for me to go all in on those pastries,"

Cassandra said. She reached for Olivia's cup. "I'll throw that away for you in the bin near the goodies. It would be rude of me not to sample a little, or a lot, of everything."

Olivia grinned, handing her the cup. "Thanks. I need to go. Cooper, you surprised us with the party. Here I thought you'd hotfooted it out of the office because you had a juicy lead on a story."

He adjusted his Clark Kent glasses, beaming at the compliment. "I wish. But getting everyone together is a more-than-suitable substitute. There are stories to cover every day, but it's rare we're all in the same place at the same time."

Cooper had come a long way in his role at the paper over the last six months. Initially, his job had been to write the copy for the free item classifieds. Now, he was a staff reporter, contributing local interest articles. Olivia had taken over from Paige as a mentor for him, and they often talked shop while eating lunch together whenever she was in the office.

"Thanks again, Liv, for writing the recommendation for my school applications," he said.

"My pleasure. When do you expect to hear something?"

"Maybe in a couple of months."

After recently graduating from a community college, Cooper was now pursuing an advanced degree in journalism to further his career. He loosened the Windsor knot of his reindeer tie. Ever dapper, he never failed to dress the part of a budding journalist. Today, a festive red-and-green argyle sweater-vest topped his blue button-down Oxford.

"Good things are coming your way," Olivia said. "With your talent and determination, the sky is the limit."

"Ditto," Cassandra concurred, playfully nudging his shoulder. "You better remember us when you make it to the big leagues."

"I don't know about the big leagues. I'm not even in a program yet. Are you going to be around next week, Liv? I want to get your thoughts on an article I'm writing about the proposed cuts in the town's budget. Maybe we could talk over lunch one day?"

Olivia nodded as she pulled her black wool jacket, scarf, and beanie off the coatrack. "Of course. I took two weeks of vacation from work, so I'll be here." She slipped her jacket on and draped her scarf around her neck. "I want to pop in and say bye to Ellen before I go. Both of you have a good weekend."

Cooper and Cassandra returned her well-wishes, and then they set their sights on the table of treats while she headed for Ellen's office. She offered a wave to Brad and Jeremy, who were discussing the football playoffs over the first verse of "Rockin' Around the Christmas Tree," which was playing through a Bluetooth speaker. They saluted her with raised cups, and then she peeked around the edge of Ellen's open door.

"No, that won't work for me," Ellen said, speaking on the phone. She looked up and waved Olivia in.

"You've got to deliver on time. Christmas is a few days away."

Olivia tiptoed in as Ellen covered the handset's mouthpiece. She shook her head and whispered, "I don't mean to interrupt. Thank you for the party, and I'll see you next week."

Ellen held up a finger, silently asking for a second, and then put the phone back to her ear. "I'm still waiting. Do you know how much business I send your way?" She lowered it again and winked at Olivia, gleeful at her in-progress power play. "How hard can it be to ship a case of wine from Oregon?"

The ensuing silence muddled Olivia's assumption that the question was rhetorical.

"For heaven's sake," Ellen continued. "You'd think I'm asking for express shipping from the North Pole. Have a good weekend. I'll see you on Monday. Great job with the recipes." She repositioned the phone and spoke without hesitation. "Is this happening or not? Because if you can't … I thought you'd see it my way. Now, what are you going to add in with my order for all this hassle you've caused me?"

Olivia backed out of the office, congratulating her with a double thumbs-up. She always admired Ellen's tenacity and ability to get anyone to do just about anything she asked of them.

"See you, guys," Olivia said to the others gathered around the food, bantering about who had the worst handwriting.

"Weigh in, Liv," Brad said. "You're the tiebreaker. Who takes the title?"

"Definitely Jeremy. After all, you were pre-med, right?"

Jeremy raised his hands, celebrating the inauspicious victory as she turned and walked toward the door.

Outside, the refreshing, cool air chilled her cheeks, invigorating her dulled senses from the drowsiness induced by the overheated office. The season's first flurries were tapering, turning light and lacy, but the skies remained gray, making it seem later than four o'clock. She strolled along the sidewalk toward her Expedition, which was parked half a block down the street in front of Carol's Comforts. She still had a few holiday cards to buy from the boutique gift shop, but that would have to wait until another day.

A crew of workers was wrapping up construction of the displays for the Festival of Lights on the town square. The annual event would open tomorrow evening and run through New Year's Day. On Christmas Eve, carolers, a live nativity, and pictures with Santa would delight everyone seeking a last-minute fix of holiday cheer.

Though all who bustled by her seemed in a hurry, smiles and hellos came easily among strangers. Most of the shop owners had decorated their windows with lights or trees. For at least this week, Apple Station could give even the quaintest Austrian village a run for its money in Christmas spirit.

She donned her beanie, striding with sprightly,

contented steps. Maybe it was how the streetlamps warmly glowed, adorned by wreaths and bows, reminding her of Charles Dickens' *A Christmas Carol*. Maybe it was all the twinkling lights, dazzling and dancing, imparting good cheer to children and adults alike. Or maybe it was the anticipation of tomorrow's *just so happened* meetup with Preston. Christmas had a way of transforming all who were open to experiencing the joy and gratitude of the season. And this year, more so than any other in the recent past, she embraced the holiday spirit, smiling as if she'd won the lottery.

That is until she neared her Expedition. She had parallel parked dead center in the lined space along the curb, with ample room in the front and back for an easy exit. In her absence, a firecracker-red Jeep with dark tinted windows had blocked her in. The souped-up 4x4, equipped with an axe and shovel mounted on the roof rack, was parked over the line within her space, inches from her rear bumper. A quick estimate of three feet of room behind the Jeep made her wish she had a lump of coal for the inconsiderate driver.

You've got to be kidding me.

Now, she would have to delay her plans and wait for the grinch's return. It wasn't like she could blast a town-wide text, "Would the axe-wielder of the redder-than-red Jeep please move it so it's not blocking in my car?" Even if that was possible, she'd think better of provoking anyone who prominently displayed a potential murder weapon on their vehicle. Resigned to wait, she hoped a stroke of luck would bring a rapid return of the Jeep's driver.

As she rounded her front bumper, the driver's side door of the Jeep popped open, and a twentysomething, athletic man sprung out. His navy puffer, wraparound shades, and trucker's hat suggested an outdoorsy type who might well know how to fell a tree with his axe. But she didn't care if he was a camper or a glamper. She just wanted room to pull away from the curb and get on with her day.

"Hey there," he said. "Cool ride. Three-point-five-liter turbocharged V6 engine. That's got horsepower."

She was a wee bit thrown. Small talk this time of year tended toward the weather and not the specifications of her vehicle's power train. Still, politeness ruled as she scrambled to return the compliment. "Thanks … Nice axe."

He nodded with way too much pride and placed his hands in his puffer's pockets as if hunkering down for a marathon catch-up session with an old friend.

She glanced at her rear bumper. "Could you move your Jeep back a little? There's space behind you, and I'm blocked in."

His smile faded as he inspected the situation. "Oh, wow. I'm sorry. What an idiot I am to park that far over the line."

She reflexively tempered his self-criticism. "It's fine." *Not really.* "Everyone's in a hurry this time of year. Honest oversight."

"I'll move it right away."

She unlocked and opened her door. "Thanks, that would be great."

He took a few steps backward. "Yeah, I saw you leaving the newspaper's office. Do you work there?"

She paused, looking past him toward the paper's suite. *You saw me in your rearview mirror?* Wanting to be on her way, she dismissed the oddity. And rather than try to explain her complicated arrangement with the newspaper, she just went with it, "I do."

He opened his door. "Cool. Happy holidays."

"Same to you."

After settling in her vehicle and starting up its V6, she waited as he backed up. She switched on the satellite radio to a Christmas station and hummed along to a guitar strumming "Silent Night." When all was clear, she pulled away from the curb and drove out of town.

The lone stop on her agenda before going home was the seasonal tree stand set up near the frontage of Gunns Farm on Somerset Turnpike. Every year, the local farm sold their famed firs and spruces, as well as wreaths, trimmings, and pine garlands. When Olivia was a child, her mother always bought decorations from the stand for the holidays. Since her mother's death a little over ten years ago, Olivia had kept up the tradition, buying a wreath to adorn the front door of her father's house. That was the plan again for this year, and she made quick work of the task, slipping in and out amongst the families arguing about which tree would make their Christmas morning picture perfect.

Then she pulled back onto the two-lane country road and headed home. It was only five o'clock, but the early evening sky was pitch black, making it seem closer to bedtime than dinnertime. The cold front that had ushered in the afternoon flurries had left behind lingering clouds, ensuring there would be no sight of the moon tonight.

"White Christmas" played on the radio, and Bing Crosby's smooth vocals invited her mind to drift to thoughts of tomorrow morning as she drove along the road bordered by dense forest. There was no guarantee Preston would show. It wasn't a planned date. They had bonded through two traumatic experiences, and it was nice, for a change, to interact while doing something mundane like having coffee. She sensed they were both testing the waters, dipping their toes, but neither committing to jumping in. Last week he had arrived early, ordering her go-to Americano and half a dozen snowman sugar cookies, which they split.

Flashing high beams in the rearview mirror commanded her attention. She scanned all the mirrors and checked her speed. Though driving at the legal limit, she slowed, wary that the flashing lights were warning her of danger ahead. The vehicle behind her sped up, and she gripped the wheel tighter as the driver lay on their horn, honking with a staccato beat. Her eyes swept the mirrors again, looking for sparks, smoke, or fire, but all was clear. The vehicle inched closer and then veered into the empty, oncoming lane.

"What's your problem? Go around me," she said, glancing at her side mirror.

The vehicle did just that as it revved up and zoomed past her in seconds. Then the daring driver veered back into her lane and slammed on the brakes. Her foot floored the brake pedal, and she jerked the steering wheel to the right, maneuvering onto the shoulder to avoid a collision. The seat belt tightened, anchoring her in place. *What the ...*

The vehicle that had passed her pulled onto the shoulder twenty feet ahead and stopped. The driver jumped out of the car and hastened toward her.

She shifted into reverse, shooting back a vehicle's length. No other cars were approaching from either direction, and the closest well-lit area was the Stuff and Go self-storage complex a quarter mile up the road. The man slowed, holding his hands up high. She glanced past him at his vehicle, deciphering the outline of a Jeep with roof-mounted implements. When she hit her high beams, the man shielded his eyes and stopped.

"Wait!" he yelled. "I need to speak with you." He inched closer, raising his arms higher.

She reversed another five feet and revved the engine, hoping he would take it as a threat.

"Paige!" he shouted.

She froze, stunned at being called by her deceased friend's name.

"Paige!" he repeated. "I have information for you!"

CHAPTER 2

"Stay back!" Olivia yelled through the closed window.

The man's eyes narrowed as he shook his head. "What? I can't hear you. Open your window."

"Get back!" She pointed for emphasis, and he seemed to understand, coming no closer than the front bumper.

She cracked her window. "I'm not Paige."

He lowered his hands, dropping his shoulders in apparent confusion. "You said you work for the paper. I only saw two other women in the office. The older lady and the redhead. You don't exactly match the description I was given, but you were the closest of the three. Who are you?"

His references to Ellen and Cassandra were clear, but nobody who had ever met Paige would mistake Olivia for her. Paige was shorter and rail thin from a bizarre love of competing in 5K races. Olivia had blonde hair and was more of a swimmer than a run for fun type of gal.

"How do you know Paige?" she asked.

"I don't. I'm sorry about the aggressive driving, but I needed you to stop. I didn't mean to scare you. I thought you were Paige. Do you mind if I step closer to your window so we don't have to yell at each other?"

"No closer than the mirror," she said, keeping her foot on the brake and the gear in reverse. She turned down the radio, ensured her doors were locked, and set her phone on the center console, prepping to call the police if need be. "If you thought I was Paige, why didn't you give me your message in town?"

He scanned up and down the dark road as if concerned someone would pass by and see him speaking with her. "Too many people around. Do you know how I can get hold of Paige?"

She hesitated, mulling over how much to say to a stranger who had staked out the office and forced her off the road.

He thrust his hands into his jeans' front pockets and continued before she could answer. "My employer has information about the matter she asked him to investigate."

"You're not from around here, are you?" After he shook his head, she asked, "Who's your employer?"

He checked the road again in both directions. "Are you working with Paige on this?"

The oddity of the last ten minutes piqued her curiosity, and she'd already fallen down the rabbit hole by withholding from him that Paige was dead. She could leave it be, but then she would never know. Paige had been a stellar researcher and not one to sensationalize or waste her time on a wild goose chase. If she'd asked someone to investigate a matter, it must've been important to her. Whatever the story she'd been after, Olivia knew it had teeth.

She shifted into park, no longer feeling threatened by the young man who appeared earnest about his intentions.

Let's see what this is about.

"Yes. Paige and I are working together on it. Who's your employer?"

"John Mack, private investigator."

She nodded, playacting her part. "Right, of course. John Mack. And what did he find out?"

"He wants to meet with Paige. He's been trying to contact her for a couple of weeks, but she hasn't returned his e-mails. Can you give her a message?"

"Sure."

"Mack is coming through the area, and he wants to meet with Paige to give her the information tonight. Ten o'clock at Lake Crystal."

The mention of the local park lake, where less than two months ago Olivia had to fight for her life, was a sucker punch to the gut. She hadn't been back there since and had considered never setting eyes on one of her favorite childhood haunts ever again.

Setting aside her triggered queasiness, she fished for details, asking again. "What did your employer find out?"

The man removed his hands from his pockets and blew on them. A pickup approached in the oncoming lane, and he flipped up his collar and turned his back to the road. He watched and waited until the truck's taillights turned to dots in the distance and then looked back at her.

"I don't know all the specifics, but Paige was right about the local connection to the heist. There's a woman in town, Beverly Styles. She owns the Apple Station Inn. It seems she and her husband had a hand in covering up and profiting from the largest gem heist ever to happen in D.C. The funny thing is, and I swear I'm not making this up, their son is a cop in the local Podunk police department. That's all I know. Mack has more details."

She stared at him, speechless, sensing a prank. "Is this a joke? Did someone put you up to this?"

"Why would it be a joke?"

Bev? Paige was investigating Preston's family?

This was beyond absurd. Her thoughts reeled, recalling Paige's determination to uncover buried secrets. Her investigation of tax evasion by the former mayor of Apple Station had forced his resignation. Then there was what she'd dug up about A.J., Olivia's forever friend, who was like a big brother to her. Olivia's neighbor had adopted A.J. as an infant, and he knew nothing about his family history until Paige discovered the truth.

She refocused, evening her tone. "You must be mistaken."

Headlights hit the driver's side mirror, and they both looked at a vehicle barreling toward them in their lane. The man backed away from her window, retreating to his Jeep.

"That's all I know," he said. "Tell Paige to come alone."

She snatched the seatbelt buckle, released it, and cracked her door. "Wait! What's your name?"

He spun and hurried to his vehicle. She slid one foot out onto the running board but then thought better of it. The Jeep's brake lights glowed, and a cloud of exhaust shot out of the tailpipe in the frigid air. She pulled her foot inside and shut the door as the oncoming car zoomed by. Within seconds, the Jeep peeled back onto the road and sped away.

The cabin had cooled from having the window and door opened, so she dialed up the heat and flipped on the seat warmer. She sat still for several minutes, serenaded by line after line of "fa la la la la, la la la la." She spun the sparse details of the story in her head over and over, each time rejecting them. But the tightness in her throat and the tension in her neck proved that she couldn't let it go. When the playlist transitioned to "Blue Christmas," she turned the radio off, noting the time. Four hours remained until the requested meeting at Lake Crystal. There was even less time to make sense of what the stranger had divulged about the parents of the man she was falling for.

21

CHAPTER 3

Festive white lights welcomed Olivia home, twinkling like baby shooting stars waiting to be wished upon. Last weekend, she and her father had removed their Christmas decorations from the attic and sorted the indoor and outdoor light sets in the living room. Despite her efforts every year to store the strings in neat coils, they always tangled themselves in the off season, as if they'd played a game of Twister. After twenty minutes of straightening the sets, she draped the lights along the porch and shrubs while her father kept the strings away from her feet.

She had moved into her father's colonial-style home seven months ago, intending to eventually return to Georgetown to be closer to her job. But since being given the green light by her employers to write her syndicated advice column remotely, there was little incentive to leave. The living arrangement suited them both. As close as she had always been with her father, they had grown even tighter while sharing a home once again.

She pulled into the gravel driveway and parked behind her father's Escape. Her thoughts had been racing on the drive home. She would've outright dismissed the outrageous allegations had it been anyone but Paige linked to them. Olivia knew little about Preston's father, Joseph Hills. Preston had related only that he was a retired police officer when he passed away three years ago from a heart attack. She had pressed no further as it seemed both none of her business and too soon to be discussing such personal matters.

Bev, she knew well. Preston's mother was a savvy businesswoman, generous and gregarious to friends and strangers alike. She had played matchmaker for her son, inviting Olivia and her father to join her and Preston for dinner at the inn at least once a month. Although both Olivia and Preston had initially dismissed her efforts, the attraction that had sparked between them proved that mothers sometimes know best.

Still, she hadn't decided what to do about the meeting at Lake Crystal. Calling Preston was out of the question. She imagined the conversation. "Hey, Preston. Hoping to see you tomorrow morning for coffee. Quick question. Are your parents, by chance, jewel thieves?" A definite buzzkill for their fledgling romance. Following up on the claim wasn't the issue. The wild nature of the accusations gnawed at her mama bear instinct for Preston's family. Her qualms hinged on meeting Mack at

Lake Crystal. She was a writer who spent her days at a desk, not an investigative journalist conferring with confidential informants after dark.

She exited the Expedition and removed the wreath from the backseat. The smoky scent of cedar and pine burning from neighborhood fireplaces infused the cold, clear air and conjured images of cozy, glowing hearths. No remnants remained of this afternoon's flurries, but the frozen lawn crunched like crispy chips under her feet. As she opened the front door, a welcoming aroma of ginger and cinnamon spice heralded that her father had been busy baking.

Buddy, her father's beagle puppy, sprung up from his cushy dog bed by the Christmas tree. He trotted toward the door, greeting her with eager barks and an excited, high-waving tail. As he placed his forepaws on her shins, she leaned down, rubbing his head and chin.

"Hey there, Buddy. I missed you."

His attention shifted to the wreath. He returned to all fours, sniffing to inspect it while pawing at the red velvet bow tied to the bottom. She let him explore the wreath until he lost interest and wandered back to his dog bed. He curled up, lay his head down, and closed his brilliant blue eyes for a long winter's nap.

"Hi, honey," her father said, waving from the kitchen.

He was sporting a candy-red apron and matching oven mitts, neither of which, she knew for a fact, were Penn household possessions before she left this morning.

"Hey, Dad. What are you wearing?"

"Hold on. I have thirty seconds to go on this last batch of cookies." He turned, paced to the oven, and bent down, watching his creations bake to perfection.

She removed her jacket, beanie, and scarf, stashing them on the coat-rack by the door. The Christmas tree in the corner of the living room sparkled in her peripheral vision. Her father already had placed a few presents under the tree. Despite it being just the two of them, he insisted on using peel and stick "to" and "from" name tags. Fact: Buddy could sneak unmarked gifts amongst the others, mischievously wreaking chaos on Christmas morning.

She picked up a wreath hanger from an end table by the entrance.

"Time for a taste test," her father said.

She looked back as he entered the living room and walked toward her, carrying one gingerbread man cookie on a napkin in each hand.

"I picked up a wreath from Gunns Farm." She secured the hanger over the door and positioned the wreath to center the bow.

"That's pretty. Your mother would've loved that."

She smiled, satisfied, and closed the door. "I see more gifts under the tree. Either you or Buddy have been a busy shopper."

"It's a few small things." He held the cookies in front of her. "Taste both first and then give me your honest opinion."

She sampled each one twice. "They're both fantastic.

Maybe you've found a new calling. You could come out of retirement and set up shop in town. Penn's Sweets and Treats, or something like that."

He raised his eyebrows, tickled by the thought. "Now that's not a bad idea. I can't believe how much I enjoy baking. Until last week, the only thing I ever baked was an angel food cake from a box. I think I'm getting decent at this."

She nodded while sampling the cookies. "Yes, you are. It looks like you're dressing for the part too. Did you buy yourself an apron?"

"What do you think? Pretty nice, huh? I ordered it yesterday afternoon at three o'clock, and the package was waiting for me on the porch this morning before my second cup of coffee. I love shopping online." He brushed flour off the Star Baker design embroidered across the apron's front. "It came with matching oven mitts. Did you see them?"

"They were hard to miss."

"What about the cookies? Which do you like better?"

She finished each cookie before answering. "The second one had more warmth to it, if that makes sense."

"I knew it. I used Vietnamese cinnamon in that batch. It's spicier and makes the cookies far more aromatic and vibrant."

Never in a million years did she imagine he would school her in the nuances of cinnamon. She had to admit he was a quick study. His enthusiasm for helping her with the test baking this week had put an extra pep in his step that she hadn't seen in a while.

"Is it too late to adjust the recipe for the paper to suggest using Vietnamese cinnamon?" he asked. "I think it makes a difference."

She shook her head. "That's a simple change to make. I'm almost finished with the personal vignettes, so I only need to add your tips and tricks to the commentary on the recipes, along with the photos of the final bakes."

"I have the pictures of the best batch of cookies on my phone. Come see." He waved her on toward the kitchen. "What's your story for the gingerbread men?"

She followed him through the living room, anticipating at least thirty minutes of cleanup ahead. "I wrote about a Christmas craft fair in Middleburg that I went to with Mom when I was a teenager. There was a tent with displays of gingerbread houses made by pastry chefs from the local restaurants. It's one of my favorite Christmas memories with her. That's where we got the tree topper."

The crystal angel figurine was always the first adornment Olivia placed on the tree. After the holidays were over, she stored it in a sturdy cardboard box filled with bubble wrap for extra protection.

"Wow, it looks like you cleaned up in here," she said, stepping into the kitchen. He already had wiped down the counters, and there wasn't even a speck of flour on the floor.

"A clean kitchen is a happy kitchen," he replied. After picking up his phone and tapping the screen several times, he turned it toward her.

He had posed the gingerbread men as if they were sitting for a family portrait. Little did she know that the "Twelve Bakes of Christmas" column would transform her father into Paul Hollywood for the holidays.

"That's cute, Dad. I couldn't have done any better myself."

She selected another cookie from a cooled batch, stepped over to the counter, and looked out the kitchen's back window at her office. The one-room, cornflower-blue cottage near the rear of the property was where she wrote her columns for work. Her father already had turned on the multicolored lights wrapped around the arched wooden trellis framing the white door.

Olivia hadn't been sure if she'd still be needing an office until a few days ago. In late October, her editor, Angela, had warned that budget cuts mandated by their corporate bigwigs might lead to staff layoffs after the new year. She had encouraged Olivia to diversify her role with the paper in case things went sideways. All the worried whispers along the grapevine turned out to be rumors. She had received word last week that her position was safe, allowing her to look forward to a carefree vacation. The threat, though, motivated her to remain open to any new opportunities that came her way.

Her father set a baking tray and a wire rack on the counter next to her. "Are we having leftovers tonight?

Your chicken soup is great on the first day, but it's even more flavorful on the second."

She checked the time on the clock over the sink. It was near seven, and she hadn't decided whether to meet with Mack. Explaining why she'd be ditching their plans to watch TV and leaving the house at nine thirty wouldn't be easy. She had kept things from her father in the past regarding her involvement in two police matters so as not to worry him. But history had taught her honesty was the best policy, and she had vowed to keep him in the loop in future, no matter what.

"Honey? Is everything okay? You're staring out the window like you've seen a ghost."

She turned, facing him. "Just some things on my mind. Leftovers it is."

"Anything you want to talk about?"

She bit off her cookie's arms, peeking at the clock again. No need to say anything if she wasn't going. "Not right now. Let me start dinner."

"Okay. I'll get the rest of this stuff out of your way."

He cleared his baking wares as she prepped the table and meal. While they ate, Olivia said little, listening to her father detail this afternoon's adventures in the kitchen. Then he outlined his plans to make snowball cookies for the column's finale on Christmas Eve.

After they'd finished eating and were cleaning up, Buddy wandered into the kitchen, foraging under the table for any wayward dinner crumbs. Coming up empty, he whimpered in disappointment. Then he padded over to the closet, where they stored his food and treats. She spritzed the vinyl placemats with cleanser, then went to the closet and selected a dog biscuit from a resealable bag. Buddy plucked the crunchy treat out of her hand and trotted to his bed in the corner to enjoy.

"Did you get any gifts for Buddy?" her father asked, while washing the dinnerware in the sink.

She ripped a paper towel from the dispenser and dried the placemats. "I bought him a three-pack of red balls to play fetch with. You know, in case he loses one."

He turned, drying a soup bowl with a tea towel. "That's a practical gift. I wouldn't want him losing his favorite ball again, and then you go search for it and find *another* dead body."

"Yeah. Nobody wants that," she deadpanned.

"I'm sorry, honey. That's a too-soon joke."

"No. It's fine. It's not that."

"You seem to have something on your mind. A penny for your thoughts."

A not-so-subtle time check tensed her stomach as she saw it was nearing eight.

"Do you have plans to go somewhere? If you and Preston were getting together, don't worry about me."

"No. It's nothing like that." She had been open with her father about the close-but-not-yet relationship. He never interfered with her love life but always offered his opinion if asked. "Somebody told me something today about Preston's family, and it's not good."

He slid a chair away from the table. "It sounds like I should sit for this."

She sat across from him and related all that had occurred, omitting none of the unsavory details. To his credit and her surprise, he listened without interruption or conveying disapproval of her actions.

"You don't seem upset," she said. "Are you upset?"

He breathed in deeply, then extended his exhale, making peace with what she'd told him. "After everything you've been through since you moved back, this doesn't shock me. I understand why you don't want to tell Preston, but this is strange. The whole thing is weird. This guy mistakes you for Paige and then almost runs you off the road? I think you've got to tell him."

"It seems outlandish to me too. But before I say anything to him, I'm thinking maybe I should see what else this investigator knows. His employee sounded convinced there was evidence supporting the claim."

"Have you ever heard of this John Mack?" he asked.

She picked her phone up off the table and opened a browser. "No. Let's see if he even exists." She entered his name along with a few keywords into a search box, and the top result paid dividends. "Bingo. Here's his website … looks bare bones. He has a physical address in Winchester, and there's contact information, but that's it. No picture, no links, nothing much useful. I guess that's a private eye for you. He'll find out about you, but you can't find out about him."

"If he has a website, he's got to be legit," her father said.

She sometimes marveled at his naivete regarding the internet despite him following several podcasts aimed at keeping older folks safe from scams. One day last week, he had panicked her, texting that he bought four half-price baking trays off the dark web. She had rushed home to counter any cyberattacks, planning to run antivirus software and cancel the credit card he used for the purchase. Turned out his browser had switched into dark mode, and he hadn't been searching the shady side of the internet for the sake of a bakeware sale.

"Did Paige ever mention anything to you about him, or any of this?"

"No. Paige never talked about the stories she was researching until they went to print. I didn't even know she'd been looking into A.J.'s family. She had to be investigating that for months, at least. This claim about Preston's parents seems laughable. I think I know Bev pretty well, but I know next to nothing about his father. Did you ever meet him?"

He shook his head. "No. Bev told me some about him on the day we all went to eat after gathering at the cemetery with Sophia's family."

Sophia was Olivia's best friend, and every year her family celebrated Día De Los Muertos, honoring their deceased relatives on the first two days in November. This year they had honored Paige along with Olivia's mother and Preston's father, who were all buried at Saint

Luke's Cemetery. After their gathering at the church grounds, they all enjoyed a traditional Mexican feast at Sophia's parents' house.

"What did she say about him?"

"Not a lot. He was retired, of course. He had been in law enforcement his whole career. Good family man. He sounded like someone I would've liked to have known." He glanced at his watch. "You don't have much time to decide."

Buddy pawed at the kitchen door. She stood and went over to let him out into the backyard to do his business. He had a preferred location for his nightly outings, and she knew where to look in the morning to clean up. After closing the door, she sat back at the table.

"Now that you have a number and an address, you could call or visit this private investigator tomorrow," her father said.

"The thing is—he thinks Paige is meeting him tonight. If she doesn't show, then he'll wonder why and find out the reason."

"But *she* isn't going to show. Were you planning on pretending to be her?"

"No. But if he's prepared to tell Paige what he knows, maybe if I meet him in person and tell him the truth, he'd still be willing to speak with me. It's easy to say no over the phone, but face-to-face conversations can be more compelling."

Her father leaned back in his chair, crossing his arms

over his chest. "Okay. We'll go see what this John Mack has to say."

"We? No. *We* aren't going anywhere."

"You're not going alone. That's all there is to it."

Knocking at the front door spurred them both to look through the living room.

"Are you expecting someone?" her father asked.

After she shook her head, they stood and went to see who was visiting on a freezing Friday night after eight.

CHAPTER 4

"While you answer that, I'll get ready to go," her father said.

"You don't need to get ready to go anywhere." Olivia peeked through the peephole, smiled, and opened the door. "Hey, Sam. And Buddy?"

"I think this little guy lost his way," Sam said.

Buddy, wrapped in her neighbor's arms, licked Sam's cheek, and then tried to wriggle over her shoulder.

Sam, a former Marine, had moved into A.J.'s childhood home next door several years ago. Over the past seven months, Olivia and Sam had become fast friends. They often got together for weekend fun along with two other of Olivia's closest compadres, Sophia and Tori.

Sam lowered Buddy onto the floor and patted his side. He swayed his tail, then trotted over to his dog bed by the tree and lay down.

"He was pawing at my front door, and I thought he may have gotten loose."

Olivia shot Buddy a disapproving glare. "You rascal. I'm so sorry he bothered you. Please come in out of the cold."

She stepped inside, and Olivia closed the door.

"I let him outside for a minute because he needed to go. He usually does his business in one spot and then comes right back when he's finished. I hope he didn't go in your yard."

"Don't worry about it if he did." Sam glanced past Olivia and waved to her father, who was standing by the couch. "Hi, Mr. Penn."

"Hi, Sam. Good to see you," he said, joining them by the door. "I've got a great idea, honey. We'll take Sam with us."

"Dad, no. I'm sorry, Sam, for your trouble. Thanks for bringing Buddy back."

Sam's focus darted between them. "You'll take me where?"

Olivia held up a hand, dismissing the matter. "Nowhere."

"A private investigator is meeting Olivia at Lake Crystal in about an hour because he thinks Paige is coming."

"Dad! Stop."

Sam scrunched her eyes, puzzled by his explanation. "I don't understand."

"Oh, you've got to hear the whole story," he said. "Come, take a seat on the sofa."

She brushed past Olivia and settled on the couch. Her father chronicled his version of the story as Olivia plopped down on the recliner, feeling it was pointless to stop him now.

He was right about Sam, though. Sam worked as some sort of security consultant. She never went into details about her job, and Olivia never pressed. She had a hunch Sam's expertise leaned more toward tactical than IT. Sam had converted her garage into an elaborate gym, which included a large, well-padded mat for jujitsu training. She had invited Olivia to join in on a practice session once, but she declined, preferring to keep all her tendons and ligaments intact. Sam's training as a Marine meant she knew a thing or two about security and weaponry. Although Olivia wasn't expecting the need for that skill set in the meeting with Mack, she would feel safer if she knew Sam was there to watch their backs.

Still, it was a big ask. She glanced at the time on the cable box as her father's story stretched into a miniseries.

"Dad, could you stop for a second? We have less than an hour."

"I'm in," Sam said. She rose from the sofa, standing ramrod straight. "Your dad is right. You shouldn't meet this guy alone. And I'm right that the two of you shouldn't go there alone." She went to the door and opened it, then turned to face them. "Give me ten minutes, and I'll be back. Liv, you're driving. Mr. Penn, you'll be in the back-seat, and I'll be riding shotgun. We'll discuss the plan en route." And with that, she left the house, making it unnecessary for Olivia to give her the choice of opting out.

She and her father looked at each other as Buddy slept soundly, snoring under the tree's twinkling lights.

"I think we better follow her lead," she said.

He nodded. "I agree. Oh boy, what a day. Baking in the afternoon, and now a secret meeting under the cover of darkness." He wrapped his arm around her shoulder with a hint of a smile. "Life's gotten so much more interesting since you moved back."

CHAPTER 5

Sam outlined alternative plans on the drive to Lake Crystal, depending on whether they or Mack arrived first. In both scenarios, Olivia was to pull into the parking lot and U-turn, positioning their vehicle for a retreat should Sam scrub the mission after her rapid recon. If the meeting was a go, her father would stay in the car and move behind the wheel as the designated getaway driver. Olivia didn't know whether their makeshift tactical team was more akin to The Three Musketeers or The Three Blind Mice. Having Sam on board at least lent an A-Team credibility to the operation.

They were a few miles from the access lane leading to Lake Crystal State Park and fifteen minutes from the meeting with Mack. Olivia kept a firm focus on the road, distracting herself from the memories of the last time she'd been at the lake.

She peeked in the rearview mirror at her father and

then spoke in a low volume to Sam. "If he doesn't meet us in the parking lot, I'm not walking to the other side."

The eponymous lake was separated from the front side of the park by a dirt trail that cut through dense woodland. The lake's dock often served as a reference point for meetups and summer fun. When Olivia was a child, her parents often brought her and A.J. to the park for picnics and swimming in the lake. After almost losing her life there in October, she had considered never returning.

Sam unfastened her seatbelt and reached inside her black leather jacket. Olivia exhaled a deep breath, gripping the wheel tighter, and then heard a distinctive click well-known to her from watching far too many crime dramas. She turned her head quicker than the spread of small-town gossip and glimpsed a gun in Sam's hand.

"You brought a gun with you!" Olivia exclaimed.

Sam pointed at the windshield. "The road."

Olivia's focus shot forward, and she veered back into her lane. "I can't believe you brought a gun! No-no-no." She yanked the Expedition onto the road's shoulder and abruptly stopped, calling a time-out on their kooky caper. "Why did you bring a gun?"

"Because I knew you wouldn't."

"That's a nice-looking piece," her father said. "What is that, 9mm?"

Olivia glanced back at her father as he perched on the edge of the seat, admiring Sam's firearm.

"That's right. It's a Smith & Wesson. Do you want to see it?"

"No!" Olivia cried. "Are you out of your ever-loving mind? Do not hand him that gun. Is it loaded? Is the safety on?"

Sam secured the gun back in her jacket. "Relax, Liv. I've done this before. It's all good."

Her father slid back in his seat. "I haven't fired a gun since my National Guard days. Does that have much kick to it?"

"Not as much as a Glock. You should come with me to the range someday and fire off rounds with both. Then you could judge for yourself."

"That sounds like a good time," he replied. "I'm going to take you up on that."

Olivia yo-yoed her eyes between them in disbelief. "I don't mean to put a kibosh on you two planning a play-date, but is that gun loaded?"

"The gun is loaded, and the safety is on. And as far as what you said about not leaving the vicinity of the parking lot, you're right. That's our kill criteria."

Olivia glanced at where she guesstimated the concealed pocket was in Sam's coat.

"That's our turnaround point," Sam clarified.

"I knew that," Olivia said. "I didn't think you meant kill as in *kill*."

"If Mack is a no-show in the lot, we leave," Sam added.

Olivia stared out the windshield at the dark road

ahead. How had the afternoon, filled with holiday cheer, turned into a night with her driving an armed friend and her father to a dodgy confab involving Preston?

Sam grabbed Olivia's arm, giving her a light jostle. "Hey, Liv. Everything good? Time's a wasting."

She glanced at Sam and then at the console display clock. Ten minutes remained for them to get into position. "Yeah. Everything's wonderful. Please put your seatbelt back on."

Sam complied with the request, doing her best not to smile.

"I can't believe you brought a loaded gun with my dad in the backseat," Olivia mumbled under her breath. She shook her head, berating herself for not nixing her father's ride-along plans from the get-go.

After checking her mirrors, she pulled back into the roadway and drove the short distance to the park's entrance. She turned onto the gravel lane leading to the lake's lot, and as they rounded the last bend, a lone car came into view. A nondescript sedan was parked at the far end of the lot by the picnic pavilions. The park closed at sundown throughout the year, but that never stopped daring teenagers from coming after-hours to enjoy a moonlight swim. However, on a winter's night with temperatures dipping into the twenties, dollars to doughnuts, the car belonged to Mack.

Olivia executed her U-turn like a pro, shifted into park, and kept the engine running. Peering through her window, which paralleled the pavilion, she couldn't see hide nor hair of anyone in the car. Two pole-mounted sodium lights did little to illuminate the lot or inspire safety. The soft orange glow emanating from each lit only a small circular patch of ground around the poles' bases.

"I don't see anyone," Olivia said.

Sam unfastened her seatbelt. "Let me look." In a flash, she swiveled in her seat and climbed halfway across Olivia for a better view, peering through the driver's side window. "There. Someone is sitting at the picnic table under the pavilion."

Sam's maneuver pinned Olivia against the seat, requiring her to crane her neck for a second look.

"You think that's him?" Olivia asked.

Sam shot back over to the passenger side and popped her door. "Only one way to find out. As soon as we get close, Mr. Penn, move behind the wheel." She looked through the driver's side window again and froze as if spotting prey. "Whoever it is just got up. They're walking toward us. Let's go." She sprung out and hastened around the hood before Olivia had planted one foot onto the running board.

The disquieting stillness of the starless sky amplified the crunch and shifting of gravel under their feet. The night obscured familiar sights, and without light, the park seemed alien. As they neared the man walking toward them, Olivia discerned the outline of the playground by the pavilion. On sunny warmer days, adventurous kiddos frolicked there, chasing meandering butterflies, imaginary dragons, or wrinkled, hopping toads.

Sam quickened her pace, and when they were within twenty feet of the stranger, she stepped in front of Olivia and stopped.

"Are you John Mack?" Sam asked.

He slowed his approach, moving his hand toward his coat pocket. "Who are you two?"

Sam reacted, reaching toward the inside of her jacket. "Keep your hands where I can see them."

Olivia grabbed Sam's arm without taking her eyes off the man. Then she stepped out from behind Sam and stood beside her. "My name is Olivia Penn, and this is Sam. You're John Mack, and you've come to meet Paige, right?"

He nodded, lowering his hand. "That's right. Is she coming? Nolan told me someone passed on the message to her."

Olivia let go of Sam as they glanced at each other. "She's not coming," Olivia said.

"Why not?"

"Paige is dead," she replied.

Mack stepped closer, slack-jawed and deflated. "What? When?"

"About seven months ago."

He glanced to his side as if replaying a timeline. "That's terrible. I've been trying to contact her. I wondered why she wasn't replying. What happened?"

"She was murdered," Olivia said.

"Murdered?" He pointed at the ground by his feet. "Because of this?"

She shook her head. "No. It involved something else."

Mack rubbed his chin and adjusted his wireframe glasses. He appeared to be in his fifties, but the bags under his eyes and a day's worth of stubble may have added a few years that he didn't yet own. With no air of brokenness, sleaziness, or shadiness, he wouldn't cut it as a prime-time TV private eye. He could've been mistaken for an accountant, a pastor, or your next-door neighbor.

"I know I misled the man—I assume that's Nolan—you sent to set up this meeting. Paige was a dear friend of mine. I would like to know what you had planned to tell her tonight."

He shifted his weight from side to side and then looked past them toward her Expedition.

"Who's that in the car?"

Olivia drew her coat collar tighter around her neck, warming her skin from the drop in temperature. "That would be my dad."

Mack gave a thin smile. "Let me get this straight. You lied about Paige, and then you brought your dad and a bodyguard to meet me?"

Olivia peeked at Sam, whose steely stare hadn't deviated from Mack, though she had relaxed her arm from its ready-to-draw posture.

"That about sums it up," Olivia said.

"In all my years of PI work, I've been in some weird situations, but this is a first. The thing is, I don't know you from Adam. And your lie, although enterprising, makes me distrust you."

"Please, Mr. Mack."

"No need for the mister. Everyone calls me Mack."

His encouraging informality emboldened her. "Nolan relayed information about Beverly Styles and Joseph Hills. I know Bev, and I'm following up on what Paige started."

"Ms. Penn—"

"Please, call me Olivia."

"Olivia." He glanced at Sam, who inched closer to her side. "I'm sorry to hear about Paige. I didn't know her well. I only ever met her once, but she never mentioned you. How is it you know the Hills?"

Although nonthreatening, Mack's skeptical tone disclosed his suspicion. She proceeded with caution, matching his reticence to share. "I know of them. Bev Styles is the widow of Joe Hills, and she owns the Apple Station Inn. Their son is a detective in the local police department." When he offered no reply, she shifted strategy, playing the sympathy card. "Paige helped many people through her work. Maybe if I would've gone with her the day she was killed, she'd still be alive. You'd be telling her now what you came to say. Because she can't be here, I am. This information about the Hills was important to her, and if what you found can help someone, she deserves for it to be followed up on."

He blew on his hands and then placed them in his pants pockets. The tension furrowing his brow eased as he struck a casual stance. "You're right about her. She helped me out big-time a couple of years ago. That's how we first met. I needed a local connection in Apple Station for an investigation, and she dug up information I couldn't access. My client not only gave me a generous bonus for that job, but he also referred me to his associates."

"Did you work with her often?" Olivia asked.

He shook his head. "No. I rarely collaborate with reporters. After she helped me, I told her if she ever needed a favor, I'd do what I could."

Having him on a roll, she aligned her sights on the target. "What did Paige ask of you?"

"She contacted me a year ago and asked if I could look into any connection between Stuart Carter and a series of high-end gem heists along the East Coast."

The unfamiliar name threw her, and she tiptoed around the breadcrumbs, angling for details by keeping her queries to the point. "Why?"

"Paige said she was working with another reporter based in D.C., looking into the heists. She thought because of my unique contacts, I might find details that aren't accessible to the average person."

"Who was the other reporter?" Olivia asked.

"She didn't say. I got the impression the other reporter was the one investigating, and she was serving as a local connection because of Stuart. Before his most recent incarceration, he lived in Apple Station."

Olivia peeked over her shoulder at her vehicle. Her

father was leaning out of the opened driver's side window, watching them. *Oh, jeez.* She turned toward Sam. "Can you go over and let my dad know everything's okay? Tell him to close the window and stay warm. I don't want him breathing in exhaust."

Sam didn't budge. Rather, she pulled out her phone and sent a text. Olivia glanced back at the car as her father gave her a thumbs-up and closed the window.

"Thanks," she mouthed to Sam.

Mack removed his hands from his pockets, holding his car keys.

Before he unlocked his sedan, she pushed further. "What can you tell me about Stuart Carter?"

He puffed out a derisive sigh. "Too much. I'll hit the highlights for you. Stuart is your classic serial screwup. He's divorced with two grown kids and one granddaughter, whom he probably has never seen. His arrest record dates to when he was a teenager, but grand larceny was his forte and downfall."

This seemed to wander far off the trail leading to the allegations against Preston's parents. "How is this connected to the Hills?" Olivia asked.

"Three years ago on Christmas Eve, the Embassy of Greece held a gala at a posh hotel in D.C. A tycoon from Crete attended with his wife and his daughter, who had recently gotten engaged. As an engagement gift, he had given his daughter a necklace from the family's jewel collection. The centerpiece of the necklace was a three-hundred-fifty-carat sapphire, known as the Star of

Athens. It's estimated to be worth fifteen million dollars."

"Whoa," Sam blurted.

"Exactly," he replied. "The long and short of it is that someone stole the necklace from the daughter's hotel room before the gala. The story never made the news because it was an embarrassment for everyone involved. The family, the hotel, the police. The heist had all the hallmarks of a serial burglar who has been operating along the East Coast for almost twenty years. This guy is legendary and a complete ghost."

Olivia's skepticism outpaced her patience. "If he's a ghost, how is it he's connected to these heists? And how is it *you* know about all this? What's the connection to Stuart Carter?"

"In my line of work, I have many contacts, some of whom walk on the shady side of the fence. People talk, and anytime someone pulls a job off at scale, it's admirable in the criminal community. The connection between the heists is the pattern. Very high-end jewels stolen during glitzy galas and events in luxury districts where the wealthy play. Miami, New York, D.C."

"Cut to the chase," Sam demanded. "The connection to Carter and the Hills."

Olivia shot Sam a side-glance, certain this wasn't her first rodeo dealing with shifty characters.

Mack stared at Sam. "What did you say your last name was?"

"I didn't."

He nodded. "We should talk. I could use somebody like you working with me."

"Please, Mack," Olivia said, refocusing the meeting. "You were saying about Stuart Carter …"

"This guy pulling these heists—he's smart, well-organized, careful. He never even came close to being caught, until the night of the gala. Something must've gone wrong because my sources say a video camera captured him leaving the hotel, carrying a duffel bag. The police couldn't get a clear view of his face. But the investigators pieced together his movements using video footage from shop and traffic cams he passed when making his getaway. They traced him to a parking garage four blocks from the gala's hotel. Video shows him placing the duffel in the trunk of a Mercedes and then walking away."

"You can't be suggesting Stuart Carter was that man," Olivia said.

He shook his head. "No. Ten minutes after the guy dropped the duffel into the trunk, Carter stole the Mercedes and drove to Apple Station. My police source says he placed two phone calls that night from his cell phone—one to Stacey, his ex-wife, and one to Joseph Hills. On Christmas Day, the police arrested Carter at a motel in Luray. There was a BOLO on the Mercedes issued the day before, and the state police spotted it in the motel's parking lot. They found Carter passed out drunk in his room. In the trunk, they found the duffel, which contained burglary tools and the Star of Athens' storage case. I bet you can guess the punchline. No Star of Athens. Gone."

"What did he do with it?" Sam asked.

Mack singled out a fob attached to his key ring, signaling his intention to leave. "That's the fifteen-million-dollar question. My sources dried up, so I switched tactics. Carter, at the time of his arrest, was on probation for a previous conviction for grand larceny. They nailed him for the theft of the Mercedes, but the ironic thing is that the car was already stolen."

"He was convicted of stealing an already stolen vehicle?" Olivia asked.

"Those weren't the legal charges, but essentially that's what happened. He claimed to know nothing about the necklace. The prosecutors didn't have enough evidence to charge him with the theft. He received jail time and went to a prison outside of Richmond. Three weeks ago, he was released. I have it on good authority he's back in Apple Station, and I think there's a fifteen-million-dollar reason for that."

"You think he hid the necklace someplace?" Olivia asked.

"Or gave it to someone for safekeeping," he replied.

The humming of the Expedition running in idle faded as the implications of Mack's story became crystal clear. She swallowed hard, connecting the dots in her head. "That's the connection to Bev and Joe."

CHAPTER 6

Mack nodded. "I went to Carter's prison. It took me some time to get visiting privileges."

"Why would he agree to speak to you?" Sam interjected.

"Carter wasn't the target. I made a deal with his cellmate. I sent this guy's wife money, and in return, I fed him questions to ask Carter. The cellmate said Carter bragged about having a big payday coming upon his release. He wanted to make everything right with his family. He stuck to his story, doubling down on his claim of innocence regarding the necklace. But he admitted to stealing the car and then staying the night of Christmas Eve at a friend's cabin."

"Who was the friend?" Olivia asked.

"The cellmate couldn't get a name, only that he was a retired cop. I reviewed Carter's visitor log."

"How did you do that?" Sam asked.

"I greased the right wheels. The list wasn't long. Carter isn't a very likable character, and he doesn't have many friends. Besides regular meetings with his lawyer, he had only four visitors. His ex and son each came one time. A female reporter visited once. And so did Beverly Styles."

Olivia shook her head. "I don't understand what you're suggesting. This connection between the heist and the Hills seems very thin."

"Is it?" he posed. "How is it that the widow of a retired cop could afford to buy the Apple Station Inn at the full asking price, all cash? Does that seem thin?"

His rhetorical tone gave her pause. She knew nothing about how Bev had bought the inn, but the disconcerting question was how and why Mack did know. Gaps and missing details riddled the story, and his spin stunk of a hidden agenda. He might've been doing Paige a favor, but his motives seemed to extend beyond altruism.

"If Paige contacted you a year ago about this, why did you only reach out to her now?" Olivia asked.

"PI work isn't like you see in the movies. It takes time, a lot of digging. I have a full caseload of paying clients, so this wasn't my biggest priority."

An owl hooted from a bare branch of a towering oak tree nearby. Olivia looked up and then toward the trail through the trees leading to the lake. In winter, during the day, visitors could see the lake through the dormant forest. But at night, the poplars, oaks, and elms transformed into ghostly, jagged sticks. They reminded her of a nightmare she used to have as a child, in which she became lost by herself in a haunted forest.

The unease alarming her now was the same as when she would wake from that dream. As an advice columnist, she had learned that there's what's being said, and then there's what's *not* being said. A kernel of truth lived at the heart of even the strangest of stories, and this was what scared her now.

"For somebody just doing a favor, you've gone to a lot of trouble," she said.

Mack's eyes shifted between her and Sam, and then he unlocked his car with the remote. The double beep elicited a shuffling of dirt and gravel. A raccoon emerged from behind one of the sedan's tires and lolloped across the grass toward the forest, seeking a safer spot to rest.

"I have my reasons," he said. "I told you what I came to tell Paige. You have my condolences, Olivia, and Sam with no last name. Time for me to get on home and go to bed. It's been a long day." With that, he turned, got into his car, and drove out of the lot.

Olivia and Sam watched him leave as her father U-turned to come pick them up. Olivia wiggled her feet in her shoes, encouraging blood to flow to her numbed toes.

"What do you make of all that?" Olivia asked.

Sam sighed out a cloud of condensed breath as she zipped up her jacket. "I don't know. There's a lot of fact-checking behind that, most of which would be illegal. He knows more than he's saying. That's for sure."

"I got the same feeling. I don't think he came seeking a one-way flow of information."

"What do you mean?" Sam asked.

"I think he wanted to get more information from Paige than he was willing to share with her—us."

"You've become his local connection now."

"Maybe," Olivia replied. She glanced at Sam, caving to her curiosity. "Are you really a bodyguard?"

"No. I'm a security consultant," she said, as if reciting her name, rank, and serial number.

Olivia's father pulled up beside them and lowered the window. "What happened? What did he say?"

"A lot," Olivia replied. "Let's talk about it at home."

"Okay. Do you want to drive?"

"No. If you don't mind, would you?"

"At your service. Both of you get in and warm up."

As Olivia headed for the backseat, Sam grabbed the door handle for her.

"Liv, what you said about Paige—you know what happened to her wasn't your fault. There's nothing you could've done to prevent it."

"Yeah, I know," she said with zero conviction.

Sam opened the door for her. "Stop beating yourself up with what-ifs."

Olivia nodded. "I know. You're right. Thanks for reminding me. And for coming tonight. Mack would've been less forthcoming had my bodyguard not been with me."

"That's what friends are for," Sam said.

Olivia climbed into the backseat. "Especially those that bring their own firepower."

Sam patted her jacket, closed the door, and rounded the rear of the car to the front passenger side. She got in, and Olivia's father pulled out of the lot and drove home at a leisurely pace.

Olivia rested her head against the seat and stared out the window, allowing Mack's story to sink in. His motivation remained murky, and he'd stopped well short of drawing conclusions regarding Bev's role in his version of events. Insinuations and innuendoes, but nothing concrete.

Who was Paige working with? Had she investigated further on her own?

The questions kept coming, jostling each other for her attention until she had a splitting headache. By the time they returned home it was near eleven, and she'd be awake at least another hour recounting Mack's story to her father. A good night's sleep was out of the question, and tomorrow would come too soon. Her Saturday meetup with Preston loomed in the morning, and now she wavered on whether she should or even wanted to go.

CHAPTER 7

The night had proved as restless as Olivia imagined it would be. Tossing and turning had been her reward for meeting with Mack. She had resisted the urge, though, to scour the internet in the wee hours for evidence supporting his story. Her father, after hearing the gist of the conversation, had advised her to sleep on it. As preposterous as the allegations seemed, fresh eyes and a new day may help her see matters in a different light.

She woke at seven when Buddy nudged open her door and slipped through the slim gap to spend a few quiet minutes in her room. He padded to his pillow by the foot of the bed with his collar tags jingling like baby bells. After he curled up and lay his head down, his white-tipped tail twitched and flicked as he adjusted his legs. Within a minute, his breathing softened, and he settled in for a morning nap, drifting into his doggie dreams. She rolled to her side with heavy eyes, lulled by his carefree, serene slumber. *A few more minutes …*

"Honey?" her father said.

She pried her eyes open as he knocked on the door and poked his head into the room. Buddy had slipped away at some point, leaving only his displaced, rumpled dog pillow as evidence he had been there.

"It's nine fifteen. I wasn't sure if you were planning on—"

"Nine fifteen! Oh, no." She grabbed her cell off the nightstand, double-checking she'd heard correctly.

"Are you going to the cafe?"

She threw all the bed coverings off in one swoop and then sprung out of bed. He knew about her meetups with Preston over the past month. Their discussion last night of how she should handle this morning had concluded without a definitive decision.

"Yes. Thanks for waking me. I was up, but I fell back asleep. I'm going to be late now."

She grabbed a pair of jeans out of the closet and a black sweater off the top of her dresser. Last night before turning in, she had laid the sweater out flat to soften the fold creases and ensure it was free from stray strands of Buddy's hair. Preston had complimented the ensemble the previous Saturday, and though it was far from high-end fashion, she was keen to go with whatever worked.

"I've got to get ready," she said, hustling past him in the hallway.

"Need me to do anything?"

"No. I'm taking a quick shower and then bolting."

Twenty minutes later, she scampered down the stairs with her phone in hand. Sweat dripped down her back from using the highest heat setting on the blow dryer while the bathroom was still steamy. She grabbed her coat and then rushed into the kitchen for her keys and wallet. Buddy followed on her heels, revved up by her frantic pace, barking and flipping his tail as if he was going with her.

"That was fast," her father said. "What have you decided? Are you going to say anything to Preston?"

The unplanned snooze had thwarted any further debate over the pros and cons, leaving her time crunch as the determining factor. "Not this morning, but I will. Soon. Bev is collecting winter clothes for a local charity, and I packed up some donations from my closet last weekend. I'll go to the inn when we're done at the cafe and drop them off. I'll see if I can talk to Bev then."

Buddy stood on his hind legs, bracing himself with his forepaws against the wall. Then he reached with his mouth for a leash dangling from the hook.

She scooted over to him and bent down, guiding his forepaws to the floor. "Sorry, little guy. I can't take you with me today." She straightened, eyeing her father. "Can you make sure he gets out to do his thing? Put him on his leash. I don't want him to end up at Sam's again."

"Don't worry about it. I'll take care of him. What are you going to say to Bev?"

"I don't know. Maybe, somehow, I'll bring up Stuart

Carter's name and see what comes of it. As if that's not an awkward conversation starter. I've gotta go."

"Alright, drive carefully. Put everything out of your mind for the morning and enjoy your coffee with Preston."

"Thanks. I'll try." She kissed his cheek and dashed through the living room. After grabbing the bag of donations, she raced out of the house, hopped into her Expedition, and drove to town.

On the last Saturday before Christmas, cars always jammed the street parking along the storefronts, aligning bumper-to-bumper from block to block. She circled the town square once but deemed a second go-round too costly. The time was ten fifteen, already making her late for the non-date.

During the town festival this past spring, her father had shown her a secret spot behind the inn he often used to park. The space fronted a dumpster, and she assumed blocking it was a towable offense. With no time for second-guesses, she crossed her fingers and parked in the dubious space, hoping her vehicle would still be there upon her return.

Her feet hit the sidewalk in front of the inn within a minute, but weaving through the pedestrian traffic was harder than making headway through a mosh pit. Parents pushing strollers challenged harried shoppers laden with bags for the right of way. She slowed and slid by, shuffled and broke stride, until finally breaking free.

After scurrying around the town square, she perched

on the curb of Blossom Avenue, prepping to launch as soon as a station wagon passed by. Once safely in the driver's rearview, she jogged across the street and then walked straight into the cafe as another customer held the door open for her.

Patrons packed the local hot spot, occupying every seat and table. Christmas music played over mirthful chatter, loud laughter, and the espresso machine making drinks. She scanned the crowd, spotting Preston sitting on the bench side of a corner table. Her smile spread as he waved and held up a coffee cup, knowing it was meant for her. She vowed to arrive earlier and reciprocate next week, ordering his go-to vente bold roast with two packets of sugar and a quarter inch of cream.

She surveyed the cramped dining area. Customers sat side by side and across from strangers, sipping their specialty drinks. After plotting a route to the corner, she took one step before a tap on her arm held her in place.

"Olivia, good to see you," Dorothy Peabody said, sitting swiveled halfway in her chair. "It's been a while."

She shuffled closer so Dorothy didn't have to sit twisted in her seat like a contortionist. "Mrs. Peabody, good to see you too. How's your morning—" Words left her as she saw Dorothy's husband, Floyd, sitting across the table. He was wearing a holly-green sweater embroidered with a bucktoothed reindeer who had a blinking red nose.

The long-married couple was well-known in Apple Station. When the weather was pleasant, Dorothy and

Floyd would walk daily around the town square, talking to whomever cared to shoot the breeze. Dorothy heard and knew about everyone's business. Though not a gossip, her archival knowledge of the town's happenings and history made her a reliable source of offhand information. Floyd offered his opinions as facts without giving a hoot what others thought of that. His wardrobe usually leaned conservative, favoring shades of gray, brown, and black.

Olivia gathered herself and started over. "How have you two been?"

Floyd pointed to his sweater. "What do you think of this?"

Thank goodness he'd cut to the chase, because she wasn't sure whether politeness dictated saying something or pretending like it didn't exist. "That is …"

"Ugly!" he boasted, providing the precise word that was her first, second, and third choice.

She pursed her lips, restraining a grin. "It's certainly unusual. It's kind of cute?"

Dorothy intervened, saving her from grasping for anything complimentary to say. "Jillian is having an ugly sweater contest at eleven thirty."

"The winner gets free coffee for a year," Floyd added. "An entire year. I told the wife, go find something cheap online. What the heck? For free coffee, I'll wear an ugly sweater for a few hours."

Olivia laughed, and then peeked over her shoulder, wanting somehow to communicate with Preston that she'd be right over. The way he was looking at her with his broad, dimpled smile put her at ease, so she turned back to the Peabodys without feeling pressured.

"Please take this as a compliment, but I think you have a good chance of winning," she said.

"Dorothy knows what she's doing. That's why I keep her around." He added a teasing wink while toasting her with his coffee.

Dorothy reached across the table and snatched a blueberry muffin off his plate. "You old fool. This is mine now."

"Hey, come on. You know I was only kidding. Olivia, my wife is even more beautiful today than when we got married." He eyed his muffin, but Dorothy brushed him off with a sigh. "And she is the smartest woman I've ever known." He padded his compliment with a conciliatory smile, but Dorothy yawned, bored by the flattery. "And I'd be a wretched grump who wouldn't be able to take care of himself without her."

Dorothy reached out, patted his hand, and placed the muffin back on his plate. "That's for sure."

Olivia, amused by their playful sparring, peeked again at Preston. She always admired the companionship the Peabodys shared and often imagined what it would be like to grow old with someone so loved.

"Dear, I don't want to keep you from your boyfriend," Dorothy said. "When I saw you, I just wanted to say hi, since it's been a while."

"My boyfriend?"

"Bev's son," she replied, as sure as one plus one is two.

"We're not … no. We're just friends."

"Oh, my apologies," Dorothy said. "I saw you in here last Saturday with him, and it looked like you were getting along."

"Yeah, we just happened to run into each other." She hadn't noticed the Peabodys in the cafe last week. But if Dorothy said Godzilla had been there, too, she wouldn't have doubted it, as her attention had been only on one other person.

Floyd split his muffin into quarters and then took a bite, speaking as he chewed. "You could do worse. His father was a good man. It's a shame he died so young."

To Floyd, everyone seemed young, though he had the spirit of someone half his age. His reference to Preston's father piqued her curiosity, and the opening and opportunity were too good to pass up. "Did you know him well, Mr. Peabody?"

"Joe? Yeah, we went back aways. His boy takes after him. Joe was a hardworking family man. Everybody liked him, maybe except for the people he arrested. But I tell you what, he set many of those young ones straight. He helped some of them get jobs to keep them out of trouble, and he'd check up on them, making sure they were doing well in school."

Floyd wasn't one to suffer fools, and his judgment of Joe's character carried weight. Mack's allegations crept into Olivia's mind. She looked at Dorothy, knowing that asking her about random townsfolk wouldn't raise any red flags.

"Mrs. Peabody, you know a lot of people in town. Are you acquainted with Stuart Carter?"

"That's a name I haven't heard for a while," Dorothy said.

Floyd leaned his forearms on the table. "Stuart is in jail for stealing a car. He always was a troublemaker. His boy is just as bad. That apple didn't fall far from the tree."

"That's not true, dear."

"That's not what the paper said. The son—what's his name?"

"Dylan," Dorothy replied.

"That's it. He was scamming people. Getting information from their computers and then selling it."

"He's a phisher?" Olivia asked.

Floyd leaned back in his seat. "I don't know what his hobbies are."

Dorothy shook her head and sighed. "Not a fisher who fishes for fish, you fool. Don't listen to him, Olivia. Dylan's reformed. He's one of those white hat hackers now. He helps businesses improve their computer security systems."

Floyd smirked. "How dumb do you have to be to hire someone who already has an arrest record for stealing information from people's computers?"

"You don't think he changed his ways?" Olivia asked.

"No. And that's his father's fault."

"I feel sorry for his ex-wife," Dorothy said. "Stacey always had to work two jobs to support her kids because he was never around. Their daughter, Darcy, is the sweetest girl. She works at the Christmas shop and has a daughter, Kaitlyn. Cute as a button. It's so sad, though. Kaitlyn has some sort of rare lung disease, and I heard from Melissa Barns—you know her, don't you?"

"I do," Olivia replied. She'd become casual acquaintances with Melissa after helping her and her son Mikey during a murder investigation in October.

"Melissa tells me a new medication could improve Kaitlyn's condition, but it's expensive and Darcy's insurance won't cover it."

Floyd swigged the rest of his coffee. "How does a store stay in business by selling only Christmas decorations all year round?"

Though Floyd's comments were frequently off topic, he often had a point.

"I, for one, enjoy going in there regardless of the season," Dorothy said.

Olivia spied a chance to excuse herself as the Peabodys' banter turned to whether Christmas in July should be a thing. She wished them luck in the contest and politely took her leave. After Dorothy and Floyd bid her a good day, she shimmied and juked her way through the maze of seating to the corner table by the window. Though she now knew one hundred percent more about Stuart Carter than when she'd entered the cafe, she wanted to pretend not to care for the next hour.

CHAPTER 8

Preston stood as Olivia neared. "Good morning," he said with a smile spanning his square jawline.

"Good morning to you too. Fancy meeting you here."

"I wasn't sure if the crowds would keep you away."

She took a quick look-see around the cafe, whose teeming occupancy was pushing the fire code limit. "And miss the mass hysteria should the zombie apocalypse occur, or even worse, if Jillian runs out of coffee? Never. Sorry about being late. I was running behind schedule this morning."

"You're not late at all. I'm glad you came." He gestured toward the table. "Please, sit. I ordered your coffee. I hope it's okay." He slid back onto the bench side of the table.

"It's more than okay. It's fabulous. Thank you." She eyed the two chairs across the table from him. A herd of corralled shopping bags, presumably belonging to the family of four sitting a few feet from them, penned in both. His jacket hung over the back of one chair, so she removed her coat and placed it over the other.

"I hope you don't mind me sitting next to you," she said.

"That was my strategy for picking this spot."

The flirty comment stirred the baby butterflies in her stomach. After settling in next to him, she pointed at a blueberry muffin on a petite plate beside her coffee. "And breakfast too? You're my hero today."

He inched off the lid of his coffee cup, careful not to spill its brimming contents. "Just don't ask me to wear tights. That's where I draw the line."

"I'm sure you'd wear them well." *Argh. Filter.* She grabbed the muffin and chomped off a hearty bite, preventing herself from blurting out something even more awkward.

"Trust me. It's not a good look. You've never seen pictures of me in my singlet. I wrestled in high school for two years. When I stopped, I swore I'd never wear anything that tight again."

She took a long sip of coffee, imagining his broad shoulders and bare chest in spandex. "Hmm" was about all she could muster, hoping her eyes weren't hinting at the picture in her head.

"You look nice this morning," he added before she could conjure an innocent repartee. "That sweater makes your eyes pop."

She wasn't sure how a black sweater and her blue eyes aligned with color wheel theory, but now her first order of business after the holidays was to buy a backup black sweater ASAP.

"Did you do anything fun last night?" he asked.

And poof went her hope for an hour of reprieve. "Fun? Not really. What about you?"

He told her about building a shed beside his house to store his ever-increasing assortment of tools. His conversation and company charmed her, and she felt at ease, not having to contribute much.

As he was telling her about plans to expand his garden, she glanced out into the dining area, locking eyes with her good friend Tori.

Oh, please, no.

Tori poked and prodded Olivia about Preston every chance she got. And today, with the two of them sitting next to each other, her well-intentioned but meddling friend had all she needed to make a scene.

Tori waved like a hurricane flag and then beelined across the crowded cafe. Peeved patrons had to pause their conversations or stop mid-sip to scoot in their seats as she sashayed by. She bonked more than one head with her purse along the way, and a trail of coats littered the floor as casualties of her free-swinging shopping bag.

"Liv! What rock have you been hiding under? Detective, good day."

"Tori, good morning," he said. "You have quite a

talent for parting the seas. We could use you on crowd control detail for the next spring festival."

Tori lit up with an impish grin. "You. Are. Funny. Liv, don't toss this one back in the ocean like all the others."

Olivia silently gasped, feeling her cheeks go from warm to molten. "Tori, what are you doing here?" She meant it to sound innocuous, but it flew out too fast and stern to be judged as polite.

Tori slid onto the bench, bumping into Olivia with enough gusto to knock her against Preston. "Getting coffee, of course. Duh."

Olivia turned toward Tori, subtly shaking her head, and whispered, "Please, go away."

Tori's mischievous eyes widened. Then she scooched closer, forcing Olivia and Preston together, thigh-to-thigh.

Olivia glanced at him. "Sorry."

He tried to move over, but there was no room. "It's okay. Plenty of space for another."

"What are you two lovebirds up to today?"

Olivia jabbed Tori in the ribs with her elbow.

"Someone's a little sensitive," Tori said.

Tori was like a cat. You couldn't dissuade her from unwanted behavior. You could only try to distract her with something shiny.

"Where's Tyler?" Olivia asked. "Please tell me you didn't lose him on your way through the crowd." Tyler, her two-and-half-year-old son who had Down Syndrome, was her only child and the light of her life.

Tori broke off a piece of Olivia's muffin and then

leaned across her toward Preston. "She's funny," Tori said. "I get the attraction here." She popped the sample into her mouth. "Mmm … there's lemon in that. Sweet and tart. Just like you, Liv."

Olivia shoved Tori off her and then unleashed the death stare.

"My Ty is over at Soph's clinic." Sophia worked as a physical therapist whose office was down the street from the cafe. "She organized a motor playgroup this morning. It's like a madhouse over there. Kids, kids, kids everywhere. Which reminds me. She said something about a clothing drive, and if I saw you here, to ask you to stop by the clinic to pick something up, and then blah, blah, blah. Kids were screaming and running amuck, but that's the meat of the message."

Preston's phone rang, and he reached into his jeans pocket. "That's mine."

Olivia leaned away, giving him room, but as he pulled his cell out, he elbowed her arm.

"Oh, I'm sorry," he said.

"It's okay."

He looked at the caller ID. "It's the station. Give me a second." He held the phone up and answered it. "Hills … Hi, Jayden …"

Olivia turned toward Tori, giving him as much privacy as their thigh-to-thigh allowed.

Tori slid away. "My work here is done. Off to do more shopping. Enjoy the rest of your date."

"Thanks ever so much for your impeccable timing," Olivia said with a dollop of sarcasm.

Tori fashioned a faux frown and soft puppy-dog eyes. "Sorry. Not sorry." She winked and then continued. "You'll thank me later. Love you, Liv." She stood, grabbing her purse and shopping bag. "Toodles."

Despite Tori's incessant attempts to interfere in whatever was happening between her and Preston, Olivia knew she meant well. "Enjoy the rest of your weekend, Tori. Merry Christmas if I don't see you before then."

Tori offered a five-finger wiggle wave and then turned to go, parting the Red Sea of patrons again as she left the cafe.

Olivia inched away from Preston as he ended his call.

"I'm sorry," he said. "I have to cut today short. There's something I need to take care of at the station."

"Of course. No problem. I'm sorry about Tori. Sometimes she can't help herself." She slid farther across the shared seat and stood to let him out.

"Don't be," he said, rising from the bench and slipping his jacket on.

"I'll clean this stuff up," she offered. "Thanks for the coffee and muffin. Next week, it's my treat."

"Not if I get here first." Then he leaned in close, whispering in her ear. "I'd appreciate it if you'd keep the singlet story to yourself."

They exchanged a friendly goodbye hug, and she assured him his secret was safe with her. After he left, she cleared the table, grabbed her coat, and exited the cafe.

Though the sun was shining bright in the bluebird sky, a moody, gray cloud hung over her as she walked to the clinic. The morning had sputtered and fizzled before it had a fighting chance to begin. Now, with her agenda focused back on Bev, her gut grumbled that the day was about to get worse.

CHAPTER 9

The brisk air jarred loose Olivia's short-term hold on mulling over Mack's allegations. A whisper niggled that she should've said something to Preston. But the crowded cafe was far from an appropriate place to discuss delicate, personal business. After all, discretion was the better part of valor. That's at least what she told herself while passing a vacant suite on the way to Sophia's clinic.

Her day would've played out much differently had she not stopped to speak with Nolan yesterday. She'd be rushing about town like all those around her, anticipating joyful celebrations and buying last-minute gifts. Instead, her morning meetup with Preston had petered out, and now she faced an awkward conversation with Bev. Though it wasn't on her to make sense of Mack's story, Bev needed to know what he'd said. Olivia would pass the information along, but beyond that, she didn't want to be involved.

She stepped into the clinic's chaotic foyer as tiny tots and rambunctious kiddos were screaming, laughing, and chasing each other around. Toys and books lay strewn on the floor, along with two jackets, three socks, and four pairs of shoes. Sophia and Melissa were teamed up, deterring a pair of boys from using chairs to climb onto a table.

The clinic's ample foyer had once been the customer side of a bakery. When Sophia leased the suite, she reconfigured the space, designing the foyer as a waiting area with a children's play center in one corner. A long hallway connected the foyer to the back of the building, where remnants of the commercial kitchen remained. A treatment gym, several offices, and a bathroom were spaced along the hallway in between.

"Liv!" Sophia said. "I've never been so glad to see you in my life." She plucked a young boy off a chair and set him on the carpeted floor.

"Hey, Soph. Hi, Melissa. You've got a full house."

Melissa scooped up a toddler and carried him over to a toy kitchenette in the play corner. "Hi, Olivia. Welcome to the jungle."

"Thanks for coming," Sophia said. "I hope you don't mind. Tori mentioned she was stopping by Jillian's, and I thought you'd still be there with Preston. How'd it go this morning?" A plastic fried egg landed by Sophia's feet, and she turned, eyeing Tyler, who was throwing the play food toward the sofa. "Hold that thought. Tyler, stop that. The food stays in the kitchen."

Sophia's grandmother, Josefina, entered the foyer from the hallway, holding the hand of a young girl wearing a red velvet dress.

"Abuela, can you take control of the kitchen?" Sophia asked.

"Sí. Hola, Olivia."

"Hola, Abuela. How are you?"

Josefina waved her free hand, showcasing the room. "Ay, ay, ay. Esto es loco." She shuffled past Olivia and Sophia, leading the strawberry-blonde cutie to join Tyler in the play kitchen.

"Tori told me you were conducting a motor playgroup."

Sophia placed her hands on her hips as annoyance tightened her lips. "Yeah, and five people signed up. Then this morning all these parents of kids I work with came in and asked if they can drop off their little angels while they shop. I have twenty-five kids here now. Thank goodness Melissa stayed and that you've come."

"I thought I was here to pick up donations for Bev's charity drive."

"I told Tori I need you to cover story time until A.J. gets here."

"I don't know what that means."

"I'm breaking the kids into groups to make things easier to manage. I'm doing a motor group in the gym. Abuela is hosting cooking demos in the play kitchenette. My mom is handling coloring, and Melissa is making snowmen." She picked up a book from the sofa and thrust it against Olivia's stomach. "You're on story time until A.J. gets here."

Olivia grabbed the thin picture book before it fell to the ground. She flipped it over, recognizing the cover illustration of Santa sitting beside a large sack of toys. "Tori failed to mention that part." She fanned the pages. "Lucky for you, I'm a devotee of *'Twas the Night Before Christmas.*"

"Thanks. A.J. had planned to come later and assemble a jungle gym in the treatment room. But when he heard how swamped we were, he volunteered to show up earlier and help."

"He's been doing a lot of work around here recently," Olivia said.

"What's that supposed to mean?" Sophia shot back.

Olivia froze as if she'd pulled a pin from a grenade. "Nothing. It's just an observation. I didn't mean anything by it."

"What's the look for, then?"

"What look?"

Sophia pointed at her. "That look."

She shook her head, ready to swear on any Bible thrust in front of her. "There's no look. And I didn't mean anything by what I said. Should I have meant something by what I said?"

Sophia's mother, Maria, entered the foyer, carrying a crayon-filled container. She weaved through several children sprawled out on the floor. "Olivia, good to see you this morning."

Olivia glanced at Sophia, who shifted her eyes away. "Hi. I heard, or was supposed to have heard, from Tori that Soph needed an extra pair of hands."

Maria surveyed the foyer. "Can you believe this? Mija, I'll get a group started."

"Thanks, Mamá. Grab anyone and everyone who wants to color."

"I see Sophia has you leading story time," Maria said to Olivia. "That suits you. We're having lunch after all the children are gone. You're welcome to stay and recover with us."

"Thanks, but I'm only here until A.J. comes. I have a few things I need to do in town."

"Then how about joining us tomorrow for dinner, around seven?" Maria said. "Bring your dad. It will be Mamá, myself, and Sophia. Is A.J. coming?"

Olivia stole a side-glance at Sophia, trying not to give "a look."

Sophia peeked at Olivia. "He said maybe."

"I'd love to come. I'll ask my dad." *And what's up with the attitude about A.J.?*

"Excelente," Maria said. She rattled the crayons in the container, capturing the attention of two boys logrolling across the floor. "And now to create some masterpieces." She stepped over to the table, set her supplies down, and gathered children for the inaugural class of Holiday Drawing 101.

Tyler crawled over from the play corner to Olivia,

grabbed her jeans below the knees, and pulled himself up to standing.

"Hi there, Ty," Olivia said. She smoothed his ruffled hair as he giggled, bear-hugging her thigh. "He's getting taller, isn't he?"

"He sure is," Sophia replied. She unwrapped his arms, picked him up, and turned him to face the sofa. Tyler grasped the cushions with both hands and side-stepped along the sofa's length. "He's cruising now too. He'll go back and forth all day."

"You've done a great job working with him. When do you think he'll be walking by himself?"

"That I can't say for sure, but he'll get there. Listen, I'm sorry if I was short with you. Things aren't going as I planned this morning. I'm a little stressed."

"No worries. I know the feeling." She dismissed Sophia's defensiveness about A.J., giving her the benefit of the doubt.

Sophia leaned in toward her. "Things didn't go well with Preston?"

Olivia glanced at Tyler, who was holding on to the sofa's arm with one hand while reaching with every inch he had for the pint-sized stove in the play corner. "It's complicated."

Sophia stepped over to Tyler, picked him up, and set him on the floor next to her grandmother in the kitchenette. "When are things not complicated with you?"

"This is different. Something happened yesterday."

Sophia rejoined her, and they both sat on the couch for a brief reprieve.

"With Preston?" Sophia asked.

Olivia shook her head. "Not quite." She related an under five-minute skeleton version of her A-Team outing to meet Mack at the lake, trusting Sophia would keep the details to herself.

"As strange, scary, and creepy as that is, why am I not fazed anymore when something like this happens to you? You can't possibly believe any of that's true?"

"No. I don't think so. I'm not sure what to think. Can we swap lives for a while?"

"Preston isn't my type."

"I didn't know you had a type. Didn't you just re-up on your spinster club dues, anyway?"

Sophia sneered. "Ha-ha. Look who's talking. Pot and kettle, bestie. Besides, I have no desire to be involved in any murder investigations. And I don't fancy placing my life in peril. That's three strikes, and I'm out. You stay in your lane, and I'll stay in mine." She glanced around the room. "Unless you'd like to deal with this."

"Point taken," Olivia replied.

Sophia bent down and rolled a foam soccer ball back toward two children a few feet away. "The natives are getting restless. I'm sorry I don't have more time to talk about this now. Call me if you find out anything." She narrowed her eyes as if puzzling over a riddle. "I can't believe Sam took a gun with her. Do you think she's carrying concealed when we get together for girls' night out? Seriously, what do you think she really does?"

Olivia shook her head as they both stood. "She's going with security consultant. That's her story, and I'm not arguing with her if she wants to stick to it. I'll be wondering if she's packing heat every time we meet. You can't blame her. You know how rowdy the dinner theater crowds can get."

"Especially when the kitchen runs out of the early bird special," Sophia joked. "Are you talking with Bev after you leave here?"

"I'm dropping by the newspaper office first. I want to see if any of Paige's old files are still there. I'm sure she had records of her correspondence and notes about all this, but who knows where they are. After that, I'll head to the inn. I was planning to go there anyway to drop off some donations. Speaking of which, Tori said you had something for the charity drive."

"Yes. I have a bag. Let me get it from the storage closet."

Sophia turned and walked to the hallway, returning in less than a minute with an overstuffed shopping bag. "I'll leave this by the door. Thanks for taking it over."

Olivia nodded. "Where should I set up?"

"Any free space you can find." Sophia raised her voice. "Story time with Ms. Liv! Anyone who wants to hear about Santa, go to her!" She waved and mouthed "thanks" and then turned and headed for the gym.

Olivia plunked down on the floor as eight wide-eyed

kiddos gathered around. Two boys took turns reaching out to rip the book's pages, while the ponytailed cutie in the red velvet dress crawled across the carpet and into her lap. Mikey galloped over, sat cross-legged, and leaned against her side. She read the classic story, dramatizing Santa's lines with gusto. When she reached the end, her enchanted audience clamored for an encore. She undertook the second reading at half speed, and just as she was turning the last page, A.J. walked through the door.

"Hey, Liv. I didn't know you were going to be here," he said.

She lifted the little girl out of her lap and settled her on the floor next to a tyke wearing a blue sweater embroidered with a skiing polar bear. Then she unfolded her legs, stood, and handed A.J. the book. "That makes two of us. You'll find a wide variety of titles to choose from in the children's bookcase, but this one is a crowd favorite. Now that I'm relieved of my duties, I'm taking my leave."

"Will you be around today?" he asked, wrapping her in a friendly hug.

"Not too sure." *Depends on whether Preston's parents are accomplices in a fifteen-million-dollar heist.* "I have errands to run."

"I'll be in the office today and tomorrow if you want to stop by and catch up." A.J. owned a general contracting business, and his office was located a few suites down from the clinic.

"Why are you working over the weekend?"

He straightened, mimicking holding the lapels of a fine Italian wool suit. "There are no weekends when you're the CEO."

"Excuse me, and la-di-da," she replied, poking her finger through a small hole along the pocket seam of his work khakis. "Looks like Mr. CEO needs some darning."

"What the? This is a new pair too."

"You better fix that before it gives your business the wrong kind of exposure." She rose onto her tiptoes and playfully pecked his cheek. "Don't work too hard. It's Christmas, after all. I'll stop by if I have a chance."

With that, she said a quick goodbye to all, grabbed the bag of donations, and left the clinic. She crossed Blossom Avenue and walked along the sidewalk bordering the town square. The heavenly harmonics of the Tri-Church Choir serenaded an admiring gathering in front of the gazebo. Every year, the adult choirs from the Catholic, Baptist, and nondenominational churches joined for a performance on the last Saturday before Christmas. Though she was tempted to stop for a song or two, it was near noon, and she had one more stop before her dreaded conversation with Bev.

CHAPTER 10

Olivia crossed Cider Lane and strode back up the block to the newspaper suite. Typically, only Ellen and Cooper were ever in the office on Saturdays, and they always left by twelve. She quickened her pace as she got close enough to see the holiday lights in the window, hoping to catch whoever was still there.

Sleighs bells on the door handle jingled as she bustled through the entrance with her bag. Cassandra looked up from where she was sitting at a desk, wearing the second-ugliest sweater Olivia had ever seen in her thirty-plus years. It was grinch green with red-and-white striped sleeves. A tree with google eyes decorated the front along with the stitched claim, "I've been really naughty and a little nice."

"Hey, Liv. What are you doing here today?"

Olivia pursed her lips, perplexed yet again as to what politeness dictated under the circumstances. She went for a noncommittal, construe-it-as-you-like response. "Nice sweater."

Cassandra harrumphed. "Not nice enough to win."

Thank goodness they were on the same page. "That was for Jillian's contest?"

"Obviously. Do you think I would wear this for kicks?"

Olivia unbuttoned her coat and perched on the edge of the desk. "It's not a horrible look on you," she joked. "It's hard to believe anyone could top that."

"Floyd Peabody won—my sweater nemesis. A blinking reindeer nose did me in. Next year, it's going to be all about the tech. I'm thinking about lights and music. You're not even in the game wearing a plain old black sweater. Boring." She yawned, doubling down on her playful jab.

"I'll consult you next year, if I enter, as you seem to have a talent for finding ugly sweaters."

"One of my *many* talents," Cassandra replied.

Olivia laughed, then peeked at Ellen's closed office door. "Is anyone else here?"

"Nope. Just me. I was about to take off and lick my wounds from my defeat. I spent thirty-five bucks on this thing. I'll sell it to you for half price."

"I'd rather wear my plain old black sweater every day for the rest of my life."

"Your loss. I can stay longer to keep the office open if you have work to do. Looks like you've been shopping."

Olivia tilted the bag toward her. "No. These are

donations for the collection at the inn. I'm glad I caught you, though. I want to ask you something. I know Paige's mom collected her personal items from here, but what about any old work files? Did she have a file cabinet where she may have kept research?"

"Why do you ask?"

She hesitated, cautious of saying too much while knowing so little about Mack's allegations. "I can't go into the details right now, but Paige's name came up associated with something, and I want to see if she left behind any notes about it. I know that's horribly vague, but it's a sensitive situation."

Cassandra rocked in her chair. "Interesting. There's nothing of hers here. But you know Paige. She always was investigating something, and she was never without a notebook. I assume any research for stories she'd been working on, or whatever you're looking for, most likely was on her personal laptop or in one of those notebooks."

"Her mother probably has all of that," Olivia said.

"Or had, if she hasn't thrown it away. I helped June gather her personal effects from here, but it was mostly knickknacks."

"Have you ever worked with a private investigator by the name of John Mack?"

Cassandra steepled her hands. "This is getting intriguing. First you ask about Paige's research, and then about a PI. John Mack ... doesn't ring any bells."

"Paige had some dealings with him. He's based out

of Winchester. I talked to him yesterday, by a bizarre twist of fate—please don't ask right now. Did she ever mention to you she was working with a PI?"

Cassandra shook her head. "On what?"

"She had helped Mack one time, and he was returning the favor. Paige and another reporter were looking into something, and they thought Mack's connections could prove useful."

"Who was the other reporter?"

"I don't know. Mack didn't have a name. He only knew that they were from D.C."

Cassandra leaned forward, resting her arms on the desk. "That narrows it down swimmingly. Is there a story here?"

Olivia stood. "I hope not." But a doubt poked at her that there was. Mack had gone to great lengths to get the information he had. Though she couldn't verify much of it, too many details colored his story for it to be wholly fictional. He knew more than he had shared, and she feared something larger was in play. The timing of Mack's attempts to reach Paige and Stuart's release from prison three weeks ago wasn't coincidence. Her spidey senses tingled, warning that the allegations needed to be addressed sooner rather than later.

"I could use your help, if you have time," Olivia said. "You have a lot of connections and can access information that would take me twice the time to dig up. But you'd need to be discreet. This involves something that's very sensitive and important to me."

Cassandra nodded. "Okay. And I'm sure if there's a story here, I'll get first dibs, right? Kidding. How can I help?"

"Do you know Stuart Carter? He's from Apple Station and still has family here. Police arrested him three years ago for stealing a car in D.C. His prison sentence ended three weeks ago, and he's back in the area."

"The name isn't familiar. Stealing a car isn't a standout crime, even here in teeny-weeny Apple Station. Why are you looking into him?"

"It might be nothing. Could you see if you can find out anything about him? Maybe something about his arrest. Anything at all. His ex-wife's name is Stacey, and he has two children. A daughter, Darcy, who works here in town at the Christmas shop, and a son, Dylan, who's had his own run-ins with the law. It seems he's a computer hacker who's turned to the good side of the force and now works with companies to protect their IT security."

"You know a lot already, but that gives me some leads." She turned back to her laptop. "What are you going to do?"

Olivia grabbed the donation bag. "I'm heading to the inn to drop this off, and then I'm exploring another angle. Don't spend too much time on it. I know you must have a laundry list of things to do today."

Cassandra tapped away on the keyboard. "You don't have to ask twice. If this helps you, and it was important to Paige, I'm all in. Go do what you need to, and I'll get in touch when I find out something."

"Thanks. I appreciate it." With that, Olivia turned and left the office, heading for the alley leading to the back of the inn. After spotting her car still by the dumpsters, she offered a silent word of thanks to her guardian angels. She couldn't put off the dreaded conversation any longer, so she retrieved her own bag of donations. It was time to learn if Bev had been married to a conspirator in a fifteen-million-dollar heist.

CHAPTER 11

The inn's cozy lobby looked like a picture-perfect postcard depicting a charming destination for a holiday getaway. A fresh balsam fir towered by the door, standing straight as a soldier, wrapped in white lights, and bedecked by red satin balls. Two enchanted boys watched a four-car toy train circle a track around the tree. They hollered and hooted, imitating the caboose every time it loosed its high-pitched whistle. Gift boxes of all shapes and sizes, with shiny ribbons and bows, were piled high in every corner. Cinnamon spice infused the air from an amalgam of candles, decorations, and a basket of baked goods on a coffee cart by the lobby's sofa. Soothing piano melodies playing through wall-mounted speakers calmed all who entered.

Olivia walked to the welcome counter, carrying a bag of donations in each hand. She waited as the concierge recommended to an out-of-town couple the hot spots to shop and where to find the best pizza. Lively chatter and the aromatic air of country cuisine filtered out from the dining room just off the lobby. Pine garlands framed the restaurant's doorway, and an inviting ball of mistletoe hung over the entrance, enticing sweethearts to steal a quick kiss.

"Hello, ma'am. Are you checking in or dining with us today?" the twentysomething, freckle-faced concierge asked.

Olivia glanced at her gleaming gold name tag. "Hi, Zoey. Neither. I'm looking for Bev. Is she around?"

"Indeedy. I just saw her in the dining room. Would you like me to get her?"

"Please. Tell her it's Olivia Penn."

Zoey nodded, giving a smile that showed off her perfectly aligned, bright white teeth. She whipped around the counter and strode into the dining room as if on a most important mission.

Olivia set her bags on the floor, spying a crystal bowl of peppermint hard candies on the counter. She grabbed a few, stashing them in her coat pocket, as they always came in handy when a blood sugar plunge threatened. Then she wandered over to the balsam fir and tracked the train as it chugged along, whistling its hello and goodbye each time it circled.

"Olivia, how are you?" Bev said.

She turned and was startled by Bev's disheveled

appearance. Bev typically dressed neat as a pin, polished and coordinated from head to toe. She always matched her jewelry and shoes, with both complementing her stylish ensembles. Today, wayward strands of gray hair strayed from a loose bun, and a coffee stain blotted her white linen blouse. Her smile seemed forced, and the only color contrasting her ashen skin was the dark purple framing her lower lids.

"I didn't expect to see you here today," Bev continued. "It's always a delight. Are you here with Preston for lunch? The dining room is full, but I can make space."

"Thanks, but no. I'm here alone."

Bev's gracious smile faded as the energy charging it seemed to drain from her by the second.

"The inn looks lovely," Olivia said. "And I see business is booming. How are you?" She was stalling a bit. Small talk could be so darn uncomfortable when backed by an agenda.

Bev perked up, smiling while scanning the lobby. "I'm okay, dear. Kind of you to ask. It's a lot of work, but this is my favorite time of the year. Zoey said you were looking for me?"

"I brought some donations for your charity drive. There's a bag from me and one from Sophia's family." She pointed toward the counter. "I left them over there."

Bev glanced behind her and then took a deep breath. "Good. Thank you. I'll have Zoey take them to where we're storing everything until we deliver them."

A young couple holding hands bounded down the

steps from the second floor. Bev returned their greetings as they walked past, heading for the door.

"Those two are celebrating their first anniversary." Bev's eyes watered as she focused back on Olivia.

"I hope you don't mind me asking, but are you really okay?"

Bev pulled her shoulders back, straightening her slumped spine. "I'm fine. You're such a dear for worrying. No wonder my son thinks so highly of you."

But does he? Stop it. Focus. "You seem stressed."

"It's just the time of year."

Olivia hated to pile on to any of Bev's woes, but there was no sense in further do-si-doing around what she came to say. "I know you're busy, but can we talk for a few minutes? Someplace a little more private."

"Certainly, my dear. Come, we can talk in my office."

Olivia followed her to a window-paned French door at the rear of the lobby. Bev opened the door, and they continued through a hallway, passing several rooms until they came to her office. She flipped the lights on, revealing a cramped space furnished by a desk, three cabinets, a bookcase, and a pair of chairs. The neat desktop housed more outgoing than incoming mail in two mesh metal bins. A framed picture of Preston stood next to a lamp, and a red poinsettia anchored the opposite corner. Bev removed her phone from her back pocket, placed it on the desk, and lowered herself into a leather executive chair.

Olivia sat across from her and reached into her coat

pocket for one of the complementary candies, needing a bit of pep to get going. She untwisted both ends of the wrap and then placed the red-and-white swirled sweet in her mouth.

"What would you like to talk about?" Bev asked.

She tarried, moving the mint around until she found where best to lodge it before speaking. Then she repositioned herself in the seat and mustered the nerve to get on with it.

"I need to ask you a question, and I know this is coming out of left field, but something has come to my attention."

Bev remained still as a statue. "Is this about Preston?"

"No. It's about a man named Stuart Carter."

Bev's focus dropped to the desktop. She reached for an unopened envelope from the incoming mail bin and a pair of scissors. As she slipped a blade under the seal, the scissors fell from her hand, thudded off her keyboard, and clinked against a ceramic mug.

"Bev?"

She slid the scissors off to the side, stood, and adjusted her tucked blouse.

"Bev? Is there something wrong?"

"How do you know that name? Why are you asking me about him?"

Olivia chomped the candy into several small chunks as she scooted to the edge of her seat. She hadn't known what to expect when coming here, but seeing Bev agonized hadn't been her first guess. "The name has come up in connection to you."

Bev placed a hand on her cheek. "How did you find out? You're a reporter. Of course, you would find out. How could I expect to keep this from getting out?"

Olivia rose inch by inch, as if gravity had doubled under her feet. "First, you know, I'm not a reporter. I'm not sure—"

"Oh, Olivia. What am I going to do?"

Her thoughts spiraled, whirling all she thought she knew about Bev down the drain. Bev was on the verge of admitting something, and Olivia's pulse thumped, wondering if Preston knew. She wanted to replay the last twenty-four hours and walk away from Nolan without ever having asked him to move his Jeep. A stupid chance meeting that seemed insignificant had changed everything.

"I'm glad you know," Bev said. "I need to talk about this with someone. I'm about to burst."

Olivia shook her head. "No. Don't tell me anything. I don't want to know."

"It's not about the money. I'll pay the money. I'm worried about Preston."

That didn't quite make sense. *What money?* Tears brimmed in Bev's eyes. Olivia wrapped an arm around her shoulders and guided her back to her seat.

Bev sunk into the chair, plucked a tissue from a box on her desk, and dried her cheeks. "You hear about things like this happening to other people, but you never expect it's going to happen to you."

Olivia knelt in front of Bev and grasped her hand. "It's going to be okay. I'm sure we can figure this out."

"I never imagined someone would blackmail me."

CHAPTER 12

Olivia's a mile-a-minute train of thought hit a freeze-frame. She released Bev's hand and stood. "Blackmail? You're being blackmailed?"

Bev looked up at her. "I thought that's what you wanted to talk about."

"Why are you being blackmailed?"

Bev rose. "How else would you know about Stuart Carter? Why would you even ask me about him?"

"Stuart Carter is blackmailing you?"

"No. I mean, I don't know. He's in prison. Could he blackmail me from prison?"

"Stuart was released three weeks ago."

"Do you think he's the one blackmailing me?"

"I didn't even know you were being blackmailed!" This, on top of what Mack had alleged, was getting out of hand. "What's Preston doing about this?" *And why was he so flipping casual this morning when his own mother is on the edge of a meltdown because she's being blackmailed?*

Bev dabbed her eyes, looking like a kid caught with her hand in the cookie jar. She mumbled something, and Olivia asked her to repeat herself.

"He doesn't know," Bev replied.

Olivia gasped. "What? Why? He's your son. He's the police."

"That's exactly why. They said if I get the police involved, they'll expose everything."

"You have to tell Preston."

"Tell me what?" Preston said, tapping his knuckles on the office door.

Bev grasped Olivia's forearm with the ferocity of a mother giving birth to twins.

"Preston," Bev said, lighting up with a Cheshire Cat smile. "What a pleasant surprise. What are you doing here today?"

He stepped into the room and caught Olivia's eyes. "Hi, again." Then he looked at Bev. "I come here every Saturday morning to see you."

Bev's fingertips dug deeper into Olivia's skin.

"Hi, again, too," Olivia said. "Everything okay at the station?"

"Yeah. I had to sign off on some acquisition forms. I didn't know you were coming here."

"She dropped off donations for the charity drive," Bev said. "So very generous. Don't you think?"

He nodded. "I should gather some of my things and bring them here. What is it you were going to tell me?"

Olivia turned toward Bev. "I should go so you two can talk."

Bev squeezed Olivia's arm as if juicing a lemon.

"Olivia, dear as she is, came … to ask me … what your favorite dessert is because she wants to make a special dinner for you. She said we should tell you because you don't like surprises. Who doesn't like surprises? I like surprises. Olivia, you like surprises, don't you?"

Olivia wanted to shrink into herself, or perhaps spontaneously combust.

Bev loosened her grip a bit, encouraging her to play along. "Don't you?" she repeated.

"Yep. Love the surprises. Good times."

Preston looked back and forth between them as if deciphering who was telling the bigger lie. To his credit, or maybe as part of a good cop routine, he joined in the charade. "I don't mind surprises. I'm an apple pie guy."

"That's what I was going to tell her," Bev said. "Oh, well. Surprise ruined."

"It seems I interrupted the two of you," he said. "I came to see if you need anything fixed today."

Bev released Olivia's arm, stepped past him, and walked into the hallway. "Do I ever. Come, let me show you. There are two leaky faucets on the third floor." Her voice trailed off as she strode away from the office and down the hallway.

He turned halfway toward the door. "I should catch her. Good to see you again, and thanks."

"For what?"

"The dinner plans."

She forced a smile. "Right. Surprise." *For both of us.* "You better go."

"Can I get a raincheck on our coffee before Christmas?" he asked.

Her shoulders lowered at the chance for a do-over. "I would very much like that."

They exchanged a brief goodbye after agreeing to be back in touch soon about arranging another non-date. She plopped down in the seat, wondering what had just happened and conceding that dinner plans would now need to be in the works. Thank goodness apple pie was his go-to dessert rather than something as temperamental as a chocolate souffle.

After ten minutes, Bev hurried back into the office, carrying a plate of cookies and macaroons. She set the sweets on the desk, closed the door, and sat as if having dodged a bullet.

Olivia wanted to fume, but she couldn't. Bev was in something way too deep, and she would support her, even if it meant temporarily keeping things from Preston.

"Thank you for not saying anything," Bev said.

"I'm not saying anything to him right now, but he's got to know. Tell me what's going on."

Bev swiveled her seat and grabbed two bottles of water from a twenty-four-pack sitting on top of a short file cabinet. She placed one in front of Olivia and then opened hers, taking a sip before telling her story.

"About a week ago, I received a text that said to check my e-mail. I didn't recognize the number, but that's not unusual when I deal with so many people in running the inn. I checked my e-mail, and that's when I found it. Somebody wrote they had proof that my late husband was involved in a burglary. If I wanted to make the evidence disappear, I would have to pay ten thousand dollars. That's why when you mentioned Stuart Carter, I thought you knew. The blackmailer said that my Joe and Stuart were conspirators in the crime, and they threatened to expose the proof to the police and press."

Mack leapt to the forefront of Olivia's mind, served up on a silver platter as a prime suspect. He believed, though, that someone had hidden the Star of Athens in Apple Station, and compared to its value, ten thousand dollars seemed a paltry sum to demand.

"What about the e-mail address? Who sent it?"

"I don't know. I'm not computer savvy, but I have people helping me with that. So far, they can't trace it, but they're still working on it."

On any other day, Olivia would've called this out as a scam. She would have advised Bev to mark the message as such, and bin it along with the faux threats from those impersonating the IRS. But the timing of the blackmail coinciding with Mack's attempts to contact Paige suggested something more sinister was in play.

"What proof did they say they have?" Olivia asked.

"They attached a copy of banking records that showed a deposit into our checking account for two hundred thousand dollars."

The office door swung open, and they both jumped like frogs with springs on their legs. Preston stepped inside, all fired up in his no-nonsense cop mode.

"Sorry," he said. "I didn't mean to startle you. I got a call from the station. There's been an incident, and I need to go."

"We were swapping recipes," Bev blurted. "That's what we were discussing. Isn't that right, Olivia?"

Oy vey. Her focus ping-ponged between them as she debated whether neither confirming nor denying would be the same as lying.

"It must be important to have called you in on your day off," Bev continued, undeterred by Olivia's lack of backup. "What happened?"

"Do you remember the Carters?"

Bev narrowed her eyes as if searching for a memory from days of yore. "As in Stacey Carter?"

"Yeah. Two hikers found her ex-husband Stuart dead a little way from Dad's cabin."

"Oh, my. Stuart Carter … dead? That's awful. Stacey was a friend of your father's. Was he in an accident?"

"It doesn't look like it. We have deputies at the scene, closing off the area, but the nature of his injuries suggests otherwise. I'll come back later to fix those faucets, but it won't be today."

"Don't worry about them. Let me know if you find out anything."

"I will." He glanced at Olivia. "I'll call you about that coffee."

She managed a feeble smile as he said a hasty goodbye and then exited the office.

Bev shot up from her seat and scurried to the door. After closing it, she spun, looking at Olivia with enlivened eyes. "May all that is heavenly and holy forgive me for saying this, but Stuart's death might be the answer to our problem."

CHAPTER 13

"How can you say that?" Olivia countered, launching from her seat. "And what do you mean, *our* problem? Go tell Preston what's happened before he leaves."

Bev stepped toward her, gesturing for her to keep her voice down. "Shh … Let's see how this plays out."

Olivia jabbed her thumb at the door. "If you don't go, I will."

"Please, Olivia, wait. Come, sit." She rounded her desk, dropped into her chair, and lifted the plate of baked treats. "Cookie?"

"I don't want a cookie! You're not thinking straight."

"Don't you see? If Stuart was the blackmailer, now that he's dead, nobody ever has to know."

Olivia lowered herself onto the edge of her seat, leaning forward with her elbows pinned on the desk. "There are so many things wrong with what you just said. First, a man has died. Second, he may not be the blackmailer. Third, if he was the blackmailer, guess who becomes the prime suspect in his death."

Bev's face blanked.

"You! Because he was, maybe, blackmailing you!"

"Oh, dear." Bev plucked a tree sugar cookie with red sprinkles off the plate and snapped it in half.

"You better get your story straight of where you've been over the past few days, in case you need an alibi."

Bev bit off the top of the tree. "If I'm asked about a specific time, can I say I was with you?"

"No!" Olivia buried her face in her hands, a thousand times regretting not running after Preston and telling him herself.

"You've got to help me. Joe's reputation will be ruined. I could lose the inn. Preston might lose his job."

Olivia took a deep breath and uncovered her face, grounding her hands on the desk. "Stop. None of that can or will happen. You're catastrophizing. I can't help you." But she was already thinking of ways that she could. "The person you should talk to is your son, because he is the police." She snatched a chocolate chip cookie off the plate and chomped off a hearty chunk while leaning back in the seat.

"I will, but I don't know what to do. I'm just so scared."

Right now, the best Olivia could do was lend Bev an ear and try to put a small dent in the big picture. She finished chewing and then sipped her water before speaking. "Okay. Let's walk through this. What's the connection between the two hundred thousand dollars and the burglary?"

"The e-mailer said it came from Joe conspiring with Stuart to cover up a gem theft three years ago on Christmas Eve. I'm going to pay the money and make it all go away."

"You can't pay the money. As soon as you do, they'll ask for more. It won't stop." Bev's story lined up with what Mack had told her last night, but making sense of it was like solving a jigsaw puzzle with a flashlight. "Yesterday, I talked to a PI who told me a similar story." She related the bullet points of her meeting with Mack.

Bev listened as if hearing a tall tale not involving her. When Olivia finished, she shook her head, denying everything. "I've never heard of the Star of Athens. How could a necklace be worth that much money?"

"Your husband mentioned nothing to you about Stuart's connection to the heist?"

"No. It's true Stuart stayed that Christmas Eve at the cabin, but he left the next day."

Olivia tempered her tone. "I hate to ask you this, but do you think it's possible that Joe was involved?"

Tears welled in Bev's eyes, and she sat silent for a short while. "I can't believe it. But maybe it's because I don't want to believe it. My Joe was a loving husband. He was simple in the best kind of way. Money never meant much to him, other than providing for the necessities of life. He wasn't one to want anything fancy. He told me his most cherished possession was a pocketknife I had given to him as a gift. It wasn't anything special, but to him, it meant the world. He wanted Preston to have it. When Joe died, he said his father should never be without the knife, so we buried him with it."

Joe seemed very much like his son. She imagined him as an older version of Preston and couldn't accept that either man would ever be involved in anything as far-fetched as a high-end heist. She kept quiet for a moment, allowing time for Bev to collect herself before redirecting the conversation.

"Tell me about your cabin."

"It's way back in the forest, off Somerset Turnpike. Joe built it himself, and he'd go there on weekends a few times a month. Sometimes, his friends would meet him there to watch football on Sundays. I never go there anymore. Preston checks up on it occasionally, making sure nobody has broken into it. It needs a lot of work, but Preston does so much at his house, and then he comes here to help me. He thinks I should sell it."

"How did Stuart end up there on Christmas Eve?"

"That night, Joe and I were sitting around our Christmas tree, listening to music, as was our tradition. He received a call from Stuart, and he took it in the kitchen. I couldn't hear what Joe was saying, but he was angry. That wasn't like my husband at all. After Joe hung up, he came back and said he was letting Stuart stay in the cabin overnight."

"Why would he do that?"

"Stacey worked as an administrative assistant in Joe's

last police department. I've met her, and she's as nice as can be. But Stuart had issues. Stacey had asked Joe more than once if he could talk to her husband to straighten him out. Joe tried all sorts of things. He got Stuart involved in church groups and volunteer organizations. One time, he even helped him get a job. But Stuart never changed. Anyway, that Christmas Eve, Joe tried to convince Stuart to go back to his house, but I think by then Stacey had kicked him out."

"Why did Stuart need someplace to stay?"

"I didn't ask for details, and I thought nothing of it. As long as he wasn't coming to our home, I didn't care. Joe left around ten o'clock."

Bev's shoulders rounded as she slumped in her chair. She sighed heavily, glancing at the photo of Preston.

"Bev?"

"Joe left at ten. A round trip between our house and the cabin should take no longer than an hour. He didn't come home until almost two o'clock in the morning. I pretended to be asleep when he returned, but I know for a fact he was gone for over four hours."

"Where was he?"

"I don't know."

"You didn't ask?"

"It was Christmas morning, and Joe was his usual self, like nothing had happened. I asked him if everything went okay with Stuart. He said all was fine, and he'd be going back to the cabin probably the next day, getting Stuart to move along. I didn't know where he had gone for those hours. I thought maybe he and Stuart had talked for a while. I dropped it. I had lunch to prepare, and Preston was coming over. Later that afternoon after Preston left, Stacey called Joe."

Bev's phone buzzed. She tilted the screen, reading a text, and then spoke as she wrote a reply. "That's Zoey. I have a delivery I need to sign for. It'll take them ten minutes to unload."

Seeing the sand slip through the hourglass, Olivia pressed on. "What did Stacey want?"

Bev set her cell down. "Stacey told Joe that the police had arrested Stuart in Luray, and she asked him to find out anything he could about it. Joe knew he'd have to tell the police about Stuart staying in the cabin the night before. So, he left to do that. Then he called me later, letting me know he was at the cabin, and that the police were searching it."

"For what?"

"He didn't say. I assumed with Stuart it was something like guns or drugs. But they found nothing, and that was the end of the story with Stuart. He went to jail, and Joe never said any more about it. But what if they were searching for this stolen necklace, and the reason they couldn't find it was because Joe …"

Olivia held up a hand, stopping her from going any further. "Don't think that way. It doesn't seem like Joe was the type to get involved in anything like this."

Bev grabbed a tissue and dried her eyes. "But what if it's all true?"

"It can't be."

But it could be. Preston's veiled confirmation that Stuart's death wasn't an accident posed multiple problems. If Stuart wasn't the blackmailer, who would want him dead? If he was the blackmailer, then someone else other than Mack may have a stake in this. Regardless, the likelihood that Stuart's death and Bev's predicament were linked was better than a fifty-fifty bet.

"The banking statement the blackmailer sent—they must either believe the deposit came from selling the necklace or they're spurring you into action," Olivia said. "They could be watching you, thinking you still have it. Maybe they're waiting to see if you make a move and do something with it. I assume you've looked through all of Joe's personal things. What about a safe deposit box or any other storage units he may have used?"

"I went through all his things when he died. I wasn't looking for the necklace, of course, but surely, I couldn't have missed it. He didn't have many possessions. Everything he owned was in our house."

"Have you checked the cabin?"

"No. I haven't been there in over a year."

Olivia shifted in her seat. "I keep going back in my head to the ten thousand dollars. Don't get me wrong, it's a lot of money. But if someone believed you had the necklace, it's a small amount to demand."

"What do you think that means?"

"I'm not sure, yet." After taking a sip of water, she paused, thinking how best to word her next question. "I know this is personal, but it's relevant. How did you afford to buy the inn?"

The doorknob rattled, and they both jolted as if a battering ram was busting in.

"Yes?" Bev said with a raised voice.

"It's Zoey. We need you up front to sign for the delivery."

"Okay. Thank you. I'll be right there."

Bev stood, and Olivia followed suit.

"About two weeks after that Christmas, Joe received news that an uncle of his had died. This uncle, he barely even knew. I had never met him. His uncle, Joe told me, left him two hundred thousand dollars."

"So that's the deposit on the banking statement," Olivia said.

Bev picked up her phone, stepped to the door, and unlocked it. "I'm not sure. But back to the inn for a second. Two weeks after his uncle died, Joe found a large-acreage property for sale out near Hamilton & Sons General Store. He suggested we buy it with the money, so we did."

"How did he get the inheritance so soon?"

"I'm not sure, and I never questioned it. Joe handled everything. I saw when the money hit the account. It was a cash deposit."

"Two hundred thousand dollars in *cash*?"

Bev nodded. "I know. I trusted Joe. A month after we bought the property, he had a fatal heart attack. The following fall, a developer approached me with an offer to purchase the land. They quoted a price I couldn't refuse."

"Is that where all those new million-dollar homes are? That was your land?"

"Yes. I took the profit from the sale and bought the inn. The thing is, I never questioned that deposit. Joe hardly knew the man himself." She opened the door. "Come with me. I need to get my vendors on their way."

Olivia walked with Bev through the hallway and into the lobby. The blackmailer painted a compelling picture. Facts scattered amidst insinuation, suggesting connections between incriminating dots. The whole setup reeked of smoke and mirrors, but to what end? Weaving this together would require time, resources, and know-how. Mack topped her list of suspects for the blackmail, and perhaps now he may be a person of interest in Stuart's murder.

While Bev dealt with the delivery details at the lobby counter, Olivia stepped over to the balsam fir, pulled out her phone, and texted Cassandra. "Stuart Carter found dead on Somerset Turnpike. Foul play suspected. Police on scene."

Her cell buzzed with a reply of a shocked face emoji and, "Leaving now. Will get details. Back in touch soon."

When Bev finished, she joined Olivia by the tree. "Can you see whether the private investigator knows anything else? Maybe he didn't tell you everything. Do you think he'd talk to you again?"

Olivia leaned closer, keeping her voice discreet. "It's

possible. I'm following up another angle first. Can you try to trace the bank deposit? There has to be some sort of tracking information."

"I have people working on it," Bev replied.

"Who?"

"Two young people who've been staying here since mid-October. At first, I thought they were married, but they're not. They haven't been here the whole time, but they paid for three months up front. The guaranteed booking thrilled me, so I had no problem with them coming and going as they pleased. The day I got the threatening e-mail, I was beside myself. I was at the counter up front, trying to change the passwords on my accounts, but nothing was working. I was panicking, and this young lady, she's about your age, asked me what was wrong. I lied a little, only saying someone hacked me. She was very pleasant, and she knew right away what the problem was. It was something about firewalls and VPNs. I didn't understand any of it. I changed my passwords, and then we got to talking. Turns out, she and her partner do this kind of stuff all the time."

"I don't understand," Olivia said. "What kind of stuff? Computer security?"

Bev scanned around, ensuring no one was nearby. Then she whispered, "They're fixers."

"I don't know what that means."

"If you have a problem, they *fix* it."

"Like the mob?"

Bev shook her head. "They're actually lovely people."

"How angry do you think Preston will be when he finds this out?" Olivia asked.

"Please, let's see what they come up with. I need to get back to work."

Olivia waited to speak until a family of four had passed by, bundled up and walking toward the front door. "Before you go, one more thing. Why did you visit Stuart in prison?"

"After Joe died, Stuart contacted me and asked if I would come see him. I thought maybe he wanted to express gratitude for what Joe had done for him. I was so devastated after Joe's death that I thought hearing nice things about him would make me feel better. I drove all the way to Richmond, and when I got there, Stuart came into the room and sat on the other side of the divider. He asked me straight away whether Joe had said anything to me about that Christmas Eve night. I told him no, and then suddenly, he got up and called for the guard to take him back to his cell. I was furious. He never changed. I was a fool to think otherwise."

"I'm so sorry, Bev. That's terrible. I know you need to go, but promise me you'll tell Preston."

"I will."

"When?"

Bev squeezed Olivia's hand. "Thank you for helping me." With that, Bev turned and high-tailed into the dining room.

Olivia left the inn and walked around the back of the building, grateful her vehicle was still fronting the dumpster. It was almost one o'clock, and by now, Preston would be at the crime scene. She expected an unpleasant call from him at some point today, once Bev had kept her promise to come clean. Olivia had given her the okay to share with him the details of her meeting with Mack, knowing full well he would be upset that she didn't tell him this morning at the cafe. Between now and then, the most she could do was to reach out to Mack and try wrangling more details from him. First, though, she planned to play a hunch and go back to the story's source, where all of this had begun.

CHAPTER 14

The colonial-style house Paige grew up in was similar in design to Olivia's home, though it was on the south side of town. Her mom June, a widow of five years, lived there alone with Paige's cat, Willow. During the winter, her covered, full-length porch lacked pizzazz. In the spring, she would always have at least a half dozen hanging pots of purple, pink, and violet geraniums welcoming her guests.

When Olivia and Paige were in high school, they often came here after the day's dismissal bell to do their homework and hang out. They always did a little studying, a lot of laughing, and plenty of speculating on who liked who. Since Paige's passing, Olivia had visited June at least twice a month, musing each time about how quiet the home now was.

As Olivia walked up onto the porch, June opened her front door wearing a wide, warm smile.

"Hi, Olivia. I saw you pull into the driveway. What a pleasant surprise. Please come in."

"Thank you, Mrs. Warner."

"It's June. We've been through this," she teased as Olivia stepped inside. "Let me have your coat."

Olivia removed her coat and handed it to her. "Thanks. I hope I'm not interrupting anything."

"Not at all. It's great to see you. Can you stay for a while?" June closed the door and hung the coat on a wall-mounted brass rack.

"I was hoping to. How have you been?"

"As good as I can be. Please, have a seat on the sofa. Would you like something to drink? Coffee? Tea?"

Olivia settled on the pebble-gray couch, shaking her head. "Not right now, but thank you." She scanned the serene living room, searching for signs of the season. There wasn't anything red or green to be seen, and the corner normally housing her holiday tree stood bare.

"What's new in your world?" June asked. "Are you ready for Christmas?"

Willow sauntered over to Olivia, and she leaned forward, allowing the white shorthair kitty to sniff her hand. "Not too much." *Except for a blackmail-murder situation.* "I took two weeks of vacation from work. I still have some last-minute shopping to do." She stroked Willow's back and then brushed her fluffy cheeks.

"She likes you," June said. "She can be particular about who gets to dote on her."

Willow jumped onto the sofa and sat on the cushion next to Olivia.

"Willow and I are buds, aren't we? You're a cutie, little kitty." She rubbed the top of Willow's head, earning her appreciative purring. "I know how hard this Christmas must be for you. Do you have any plans?"

"A friend I met in my bereavement group invited me to dinner. He's a widower, and this past year, he lost his only daughter. Unfortunate common bonds. We're getting Chinese takeout and then watching a movie that we haven't yet agreed upon. I want this to be a low-key Christmas."

"I can understand that. It sounds like a good way to spend the day."

"Right after the new year, I want to visit my sister in North Carolina. My niece is having a baby any day now, and I'd like to be there. This is her first child, and believe me, she has no idea what those first few months are like."

Olivia laughed. "I can only imagine."

"Maybe one day you won't have to imagine. When that time comes, I would be more than happy to stand in as an honorary grandmother."

"That's a done deal because I would need all the help I could get."

"Then you shall have it," June said with a wide grin. "I'd like to stay with my sister for a while, maybe three months. The warmer weather and time with family would do me good. I can't wait to meet my new grand-niece or grandnephew—they want it to be a surprise for everyone. But I'm not sure if I can go."

"Why not?"

"It's Willow. I can't take her with me. My sister's husband is allergic to cats, and besides, Willow doesn't travel well. Even a ten-minute drive stresses her. I can't bear the thought of boarding her someplace with strangers. I also can't leave her alone in the house with someone seeing her only once a day. She's very social and needs to interact with people."

Olivia peeked at Willow, who had fallen asleep on her back with her front paws sticking up in the air.

"Is there any way ... you could watch her?" June asked.

Olivia straightened, feeling like she'd been caught off-guard by a pop quiz. "Oh, ah ... well, you know, I'm living in my dad's house right now, and we have a dog. I'm not sure how that dynamic would work."

"Willow is very quiet and not a bother at all. I'm sure she'd get along with your dog just fine. You could take all or some of her things from here to make her feel more at home—her cat tree, scratching posts, and toys. She minds her own business and is not in the least bit destructive. I'll give you all the food and treats you'd need. I know it's a lot to ask, but it would be a tremendous weight off my shoulders if I knew she was with someone I trust."

Olivia recalled seven months ago when Angela had tried to persuade her to adopt a Siamese cat. She'd considered it until reading a blog post that characterized the breed as evil geniuses. She glanced at Willow's black paws and plush white fur, feeling her heart melt and wanting to take her home on the spot.

"Aren't cats territorial?" she asked. "Won't the change in scenery bother her?"

June eyed Willow. "I'm worried about that, too, but she's comfortable around you. I know it's a huge ask, and I understand if you don't want to."

"It's not that. I want to help, but I'll need to check with my dad. It's his house. I think he'd be okay with it."

"That would be wonderful. She's very low-maintenance. She needs brushing and her claws trimmed when they get too long. I couldn't ask you to do the clipping, though. I'll give you the name of a groomer. Willow strongly protests anyone touching or trimming her death daggers."

Lovely. "I'll let you know soon, but I'll do my best to convince my dad." She paused for a second before redirecting the conversation. "Can I ask you something about Paige?" After June nodded, she continued. "Yesterday, something came to my attention involving her. Do you still have any of her old files or notebooks from work?"

"I kept everything. I can't bring myself to throw anything of hers away yet."

"Would you mind if I look through her files?"

June stood. "Not at all. Come. Everything is in her bedroom."

Olivia rose and followed her upstairs.

"Is this about one of her stories?" June asked as they entered Paige's room.

"She was collaborating with a reporter from D.C., looking into a series of gem heists."

June swung open the double closet doors. "That sounds like her. All her files are in these labeled boxes. Nobody organized like Paige. Last year, you should've seen it when she unwrapped a label maker I bought her for Christmas. You would've thought she'd won the lottery."

Olivia laughed as she knelt and surveyed the dated boxes. "The last time Paige visited me in Georgetown, she alphabetized my spice rack, bookcase, and cleaning supplies."

"That was my Paige," June said.

Olivia shuffled the corrugated boxes around until finding one from December of last year, guessing Paige had filed the notes under the date of her contact with Mack. She slid the box out of the closet and removed the lid. "This might be it."

"I'll let you alone to look through the files. I was about to make myself a sandwich. I bought a honey-baked ham yesterday. Paige and I always had one for Christmas. She loved it when I made her ham sandwiches with her favorite spicy mustard and sweet-hot pickles. I'm going to make one for myself and enjoy it for her. Can I interest you in one?"

Olivia stood, spying a laptop on Paige's desk. "That

sounds fantastic. Thank you. Is that her laptop? Can I look through that as well?"

"Of course." June stepped over to the desk and grabbed a small address book off the hutch. "All her passwords are in here. You'll need one to open the system."

"It also would be helpful if I could go through her e-mail. I wouldn't look at anything personal."

"You look at anything you need to. Please, you're like family to me. I didn't delete any of her e-mail. I just unsubscribed her account from junk sites and a bunch of retailers. Take all the time you need." With that, she turned and left Olivia alone.

She pulled the box across the carpet and sat in the desk chair. Leaning over, she worked her way through the files until finding one labeled "Gem Heist, Marco." She removed the folder, opened it on the desk, and turned on the lamp.

The file contained three pages of lined paper ripped from a yellow legal pad. Paige always wrote her research notes the same way, dating back to when she and Olivia worked together on the school newspaper. She would divide the sheet into two sections. On the right side, she wrote the facts of the story. On the left, she recorded her thoughts and opinions, circling keywords, phrases, or avenues for further research.

Olivia read through the notes, confirming much of what Mack had told her. A serial thief had committed a string of high-end heists along the East Coast, targeting moguls attending elite social events. Other than a partial print found at a heist in Miami, he had left no evidence. An FBI profiler had pegged him as an athletic, charming man with a background in building maintenance. His thefts were nonviolent, suggesting he schemed to steal while avoiding confrontation.

Paige had commented in the left column that someone called Marco had contacted her, seeking a connection between Joe and Stuart regarding the Star of Athens. Under that, she wrote a reminder for herself to call Mack. At the bottom of the third page, she weighed in with her verdict: "Involvement of Joe Hills unlikely."

A wee bit of relief washed over Olivia, knowing Paige had felt the same way. The lack of further follow-up hinted Paige hadn't taken the connection too seriously. She took photos of the pages with her phone as Willow nuzzled against her leg.

"Hey, little kitty. I didn't even hear you come in." She bent down and picked up a toy mouse that Willow had dropped by her feet. "Did you bring me a gift? Just don't bring me a real one if you end up crashing at my house."

She picked up the mouse and tossed it through the open doorway, spurring Willow to scamper after it.

"Whoa!" June said, dodging Willow as she entered the room. She set a plate with a sandwich and a bottle of water on the desk next to Olivia.

"Thank you so much. That looks fantastic."

"If you want more, let me know. I'll be eating ham

for at least a week. How's it going? Are you finding anything useful?"

"I came across what I was looking for. I'm checking her laptop next."

Willow sauntered back into the room, minus the mouse, and jumped onto the bed. A sprightly leap landed her on a dresser, which she then used as a walkway to access the window ledge.

"That's her favorite spot. Every day about this time, I know that's where she'll be. Take your time. I'll be in the kitchen if you need anything." June turned and left the room.

Olivia took a bite of her sandwich and booted up Paige's laptop. She spent the next twenty minutes searching the hard drive files for any research related to the heist, but there wasn't a single reference.

Then she opened a browser and accessed Paige's e-mail, scanning for any relevant correspondence, using last December as a reference point. The name Marco, matching that on the file, popped up, showing a thread of messages spanning two weeks. When she opened the initial message she recognized the sender, Marco Esposito, immediately. He was an award-winning investigative journalist who worked at her paper. Marco had gained acclaim for breaking stories involving corruption in the city's government and the cover-up of money laundering by a district judge. She didn't know him personally, but by the tone of his e-mails to Paige, it seemed that the two had been friendly.

After copying his e-mail address into her contacts on her phone, she turned her attention to the messages from Mack. They were as he said they would be—requests for a face-to-face meeting, saying that he had found information about what she'd asked.

After finishing her sandwich, she turned off the laptop and shut the screen. In coming here, she hadn't been expecting to find a smoking gun. Rather, she'd hoped to learn something to help fill in the gaps between Mack's and Bev's stories. If Paige were alive and had met Mack last night, she probably would've done more to follow up and collaborate with Marco. Mack's mention that another female reporter had visited Stuart in jail made Olivia wonder whether Marco was working with that person as well.

She stood and stepped over to the window, lingering for a minute as she imagined Paige sitting on the twin bed's quilted white duvet. She would encourage Olivia to keep digging for details. Then she would stage a no-holds-barred debate on the pros and cons of getting involved with Preston. So many days they had laughed together in this room, and now only memories remained. Willow had fallen asleep in the sun, serenely loafing on the ledge. Olivia stroked her back, whispering so as not to wake her. "Don't worry, Paige. I'll take good care of Willow for you."

CHAPTER 15

Olivia promised to get back to June soon about watching Willow. After they exchanged goodbyes, she returned to her Expedition and scooted behind the wheel. She entered Mack's address into the vehicle's GPS, backed out of the driveway, and headed west toward Winchester. The satellite system estimated a twenty-five-minute drive to his office, but she guessed it would be closer to thirty-five. The rural road between here and there was twisty and narrow, requiring a cautious pace, especially as the daylight was fading. While stopped at a traffic light, she paired her phone to the car's Bluetooth, called Cassandra, and spoke hands-free.

"Liv, hey. Great tip!" Cassandra chirped. "Thanks for the heads-up. Looks like a murder."

The light turned green, and she continued onward. "What's happening?"

"The police are all over the scene. They've closed off

the area and set up a checkpoint on either side. Only one car is getting through at a time. There's an ambulance, and your boyfriend—"

"Not my boyfriend."

"That's not what Cooper said. Is he wrong?"

"How do you know it was a murder?" Olivia asked, ignoring the irrelevant question.

"Everyone's favorite off-the-record police source, cutie-pie Deputy Cole Lee, told me Stuart was shot. Police located his car parked on the road's shoulder, and two hikers found his body nearby in the woods."

"Okay. I won't keep you from doing what you do. I'm on my way to speak with Mack again. Maybe I can get more out of him."

"You're going out to Winchester?"

"Yes. I should get there around four."

"Do you think he'll be there on a Saturday? Did you call ahead?"

Olivia dialed up the heat and closed the outside vents, feeling a chill in the cabin. "I don't think he'll speak with me over the phone. And I don't want to give him warning that I'm coming. Mack's interest in Stuart is suspicious for someone who was just doing Paige a favor. I bet by now he's aware Stuart is dead. If he isn't there, I'll turn around and come home. By the way, I found the name of the reporter who Paige was working with. Marco Esposito."

"Marco! I know him."

"How do you know Marco?"

Cassandra's voice turned breathy, as if she was hustling. "Sorry, I'm trying to get within earshot of Chief Payne while he's talking to some deputies. Looks like it's Jayden, Cole, and Burt. Preston is heading off into the woods with two EMS responders and the medical examiner. Pardon the play-by-play. Marco and I went to college together. He works at your paper."

Olivia slowed as a pointed buck crossed the road twenty yards ahead of her. She scanned the shoulder and the nearby tree line, looking for any of his friends. "Yeah, I know, but we've never met." Not seeing any other deer around, she ramped back up to speed. "Have you kept in touch with him?"

"It's been a few years."

"I copied his e-mail address from Paige's laptop. It looks like his personal address. It's not from our paper's e-mail system. I'll text it to you once I get to Winchester. Can you reach out to him?" Olivia knew she couldn't send Cassandra in blind. "He'd been investigating a series of gem heists. He had contacted Paige asking her about any connection between Stuart and Joe Hills."

"Hills? Any relation to Preston Hills?"

"It's his father."

"Oh. Wow. Liv, are you saying his dad was involved in these heists?"

"No. But there's a night in question three years ago on Christmas Eve. A fifteen-million-dollar necklace went missing."

"I knew it! I knew you were holding out on me. Wow,

okay. I'm all over this. I'll e-mail Marco and DM him on his socials."

"Thanks for doing this. Let's talk sometime tomorrow."

"Sounds good. Be careful."

They exchanged goodbyes as Olivia drove through downtown Winchester. The charming and quaint old town section boasted wide, welcoming avenues for pedestrian traffic. She had visited the area several times over the years during the annual Shenandoah Apple Blossom Festival. The GPS instructed her to turn south, and after driving four miles she arrived at a red brick building pinpointed as her destination.

Only a smattering of cars peppered the lot, hinting that few of the tenants kept Saturday hours. She parked and sent Marco's e-mail address to Cassandra. Then she entered the building, searching for Mack's first-floor suite. On the last door on the right side of the hallway, a gold-plated sign engraved with "Mack & Associates Investigations" confirmed she was in the right place.

Narrow windows on both sides of the door offered a preview of the office. Lights were on, showcasing a waiting room with a leather sofa, a coffee table, and two wingback chairs. As she opened the door, Nolan walked out of a back room and into a small workspace behind thick glass. He froze for a moment, looking like he had never planned to see her again.

"It's you," he said. "What are you doing here?"

She neared what appeared to be a reception desk,

guessing the heavy gauge of the dividing glass was bullet-proof. "Hi. It's Nolan, right? We missed the introductions yesterday."

"We also missed you telling me Paige was dead."

Touché. The workspace behind the glass was tidy, and only a sub, soda, and laptop sat on the counter. "Yeah, about that. I'm sorry I misled you."

"It's all good," he said with a wry smile. "I guess we're even for the whole ruse about blocking in your car. Do you know how long I had to sit outside the office to figure out who was who? Then you walked in, and I'd seen where you had parked. So, figuring you were Paige, I wanted to catch you before you left. I must've driven around that stupid square at least thirty times before the spot behind your car became available."

You could've just walked into the office and asked.

She glanced over his shoulder into the back room, spying a large monitor live-streaming a video feed from a black-and-white camera. "Are you an associate here?"

He appeared puzzled for a moment. "Oh, no. There are no other associates. Mack is a one-man show, but appearing as a larger firm is better for marketing."

"Gotcha. Is he here by chance?"

"Nope."

Pulling teeth would be hard from someone whose business involved evasion. "I spoke with Mack last night, and I came here wanting more information."

He picked up his sub and took a bite, speaking as he chewed. "I'm hungry. I hope you don't mind."

When he appeared content to let her statement hang without a reply, she cast out a baited line. "Did you speak with Mack last night?"

He sipped his soda, pondering the query as if she'd asked about something that happened five years ago. "Nope."

But he knew Paige was dead, so he was misdirecting again. Maybe it wasn't last night, but he'd surely talked to Mack after the meeting with her at the lake. She could question him, pinning down the exact time, but it didn't matter. His tight lips spoke volumes about his reticence to share.

"Is there a phone number I can reach him at?"

He wiped his mouth with the back of his hand and then took another swig of soda. "He's on a job right now. It's stakeout type of work. He doesn't like to be contacted unless it's an emergency because it could jeopardize his cover."

"How long will he be off-the-grid?"

Nolan raised his eyebrows and pursed his lips. "Your guess is as good as mine. Could be days. Could be weeks. You never know in these types of situations." He picked up his sub and took another bite.

She wondered whether Mack was standing in the back room, out of sight, listening in on their conversation. Leaning closer to the glass, she pointed over Nolan's shoulder. "You have a lot going on in there. Is that video surveillance for an active case? Wow. One, two, three, four computers. Is anyone else working here with you today?"

He backpedaled and slammed the door shut. "Nope."

"Are you the one who does the background checks for Mack's investigations?"

"I do most of it," he snapped, as if wanting credit for being the brains of the operation.

"Then you must know a good deal about Stuart Carter."

"Some."

"What's your impression of him?"

"He's a deadbeat. A bad dude who got what he deserved."

She wasn't sure whether the use of the present and past tense signaled an awareness of Stuart's murder. "Have you ever met Bev Styles?"

"Nope," he said without missing a beat.

She expected nothing else useful. After asking him to inform Mack about her visit, she left the office. Once inside her car, she checked for any missed messages. Preston hadn't called, and she wagered he was still at the crime scene. Certainly, Bev would tell him about the blackmail before the end of the day.

Though she had driven here to speak with Mack, her conversation with Nolan had proved productive. Mack's sudden absence piqued her curiosity in light of Stuart's death. The man who seemed to know the most about the gem heist and potential cover-up had gone missing.

Nolan knew more about Mack's investigation than he had let on yesterday. With all the research Nolan conducted, she wondered whether he would have the know-how to rummage around financial records.

Could Mack & Associates be two sides of the same coin? One person being the blackmailer, and the other the murderer? She started the engine and retraced her route, driving back to Apple Station. The sun was setting, and the sky stood ready to showcase its stars once twilight eased into night. She would take it slow on the way home, as the only light above the rural road was the rising, white glow of the nearly full moon.

CHAPTER 16

The Christmas tree's glimmering lights and the scent of cinnamon spice from a flickering candle welcomed Olivia when she stepped through the front door, drained by the day. The warm, familiar feel of a cozy home quieted the what-ifs whirling like dervishes in her head. She greeted her father, who was relaxing in his recliner, watching a sports talk show on ESPN.

"You've had a long day," he said. "How'd your talk with Bev go?"

She removed her coat and hung it on the rack as he stood and turned off the TV.

"It's complicated. I need something to drink. Let's sit in the kitchen, and I'll tell you all about it."

He followed her in and grabbed a beer out of the refrigerator as she poured herself a glass of water from a purifying pitcher. They both sat at the table, and she told him what she'd learned.

"This blackmail threat against Bev could be a scam," he said. "Some crackpot looking to make a quick buck."

"Maybe. But it doesn't look good. Now, with Stuart dead, there are two crimes in play. The question is if and how they're related."

"What's your gut say?"

"That they're connected. From what I gather about Joe, I don't believe he took part in any of it. I can see, though, how the facts might lead others to a different opinion. Stuart's death, assuming it was murder, and the gem heist are police matters. I'm more concerned about Bev. Preston is going to flip when he learns about the blackmail." She pulled her phone out of her pocket, checking if he had called or texted. "I expected to hear from either him or her by now."

"Do you think Bev will come clean?"

"She has to. She's his mother, after all."

He pushed back from the table. "That reminds me. I forgot to turn on your mother's—sorry, I mean your office Christmas lights."

She stood and looked through the kitchen window at the dark cottage. The pitch black belied the time, making it appear more like midnight than six o'clock.

"I better do that or else I'll forget," he said.

"Stay here, Dad. It's cold outside. I'll do it. I'll start dinner in half an hour, and maybe by the time we're done, Bev or Preston will have called."

She grabbed the office key off the hook rack, went out through the back door, and walked the short distance across the frozen yard. Once inside, she turned on the interior and exterior lights, bringing the cottage to life.

At the start of her two-week vacation, she'd vowed not to check any work-related e-mail. An automated reply would suffice for what could wait. Those who absolutely needed to get in touch always used her personal address, anyway. Still, she couldn't help but peek ahead in the calendar at her plans for the next ninety days.

She sat and slid her leather-bound agenda toward her from the corner of the desk. She flipped through January, February, and March, finding all the upcoming weeks looking the same. Columns, deadlines, and online chats sitting like ducks in a row. She enjoyed her work and had never given much thought to shaking things up until coming to stay back home. A voice had been whispering ever since that perhaps it was time for a change. Her heart wanted something more, and though unsure what that was, she believed it was here in Apple Station.

The glowing moon shone through the cottage's front window, still low and large in the night sky. She stood and gazed at the bright white light, thinking of a poem her mother had written for her when she was five. She stepped to the bookcase that housed all her mother's writings and searched for a volume of poetry from that year. After locating the binder, she pulled it out and turned to page eight, smiling upon seeing her mother's precise penmanship.

Olivia's nightmares about being lost in the haunted

woods had been a frustrating time for her parents. She would wake up in fright, keeping them up at night and insisting on sleeping in their bed. Her mother finally found the solution by writing a poem that eased Olivia's fears before she drifted off to dreams. Night after night, her mother's reassuring voice recited the lines until the nightmare disappeared. Though so many years had passed since then, in reading the poem again she still remembered the words to "The Cocoon Moon."

Sleepy little caterpillar, lay your head down,

dreaming of growing orange-and-black wings.

The sun must rest too, but the morning will come soon,

and you'll wake, smiling as the songbirds sing.

Though you can't see me, near you I'll always be,

watching you under the light of the cocoon moon.

The night is when other little ones rise and shine,

smiling as the moon wakes them for a new day.

Baby owlets hoot, hedgehog hoglets play games,

while wolf pack pups rumble, tumble, and bay.

Fox kits yelp, aardvark calves sniff for ants,

and whip-poor-will chicks chant their names.

Your friend the tadpole swims in the pond,

scared of the dark and the ravens croaking.

He zigs and zags, searching for his mom and dad,

but he can't see where he's going.

Soon he'll grow, sprouting lungs and legs,

safely jumping as a frog on land and lily pads.

Your friend the panda cub is born bare and blind,

pink as a pig and lighter than a bunny.

She wants to play and crawl but easily falls

because her legs can't hold up her tummy.

Soon she'll grow, eating shoots of bamboo,

and become a big, brave, black-and-white furball.

Sleepy little caterpillar, lay your head down,

dreaming of wildly flapping your wings.

You'll grow and change too, and someday soon,

you'll flutter among the flowers, blooming in spring.

Though you can't see me, near you I'll always be,

watching you under the light of the cocoon moon.

She closed the binder, smiling at the sweet poem that had soothed her and slayed her nightmare. Her mother always knew just what to do to make her feel better. Olivia had decided long ago that she'd read the poem to her own child every night before a fear of the dark ever developed.

After shelving the volume, she stepped back to her desk, wanting to organize it before leaving. She closed her daily planner, placed her reading glasses in their hard-shell case, and stored both in the desk's top drawer. In sliding her writing journal off to the side, she inadvertently nudged her mother's favorite blue fountain pen. It rolled off the desk, clinked off the chair's metal base, and landed on the wood laminate floor.

The barrel busted, separating from the section holding the nib. She panicked, picked up the pieces, and tried to reconnect them. But the deed was done, and the broken parts no longer held together. The special pen had been with her mother from Paris to Tasmania, and she'd written many stories with it along the way. Perhaps, too, her mother may have written the poem that had vanquished Olivia's nightmare with the pen's golden nib.

She chided herself with a few choice words for being so careless about breaking the one pen that couldn't ever be replaced. But a calmer voice soon prevailed, and she forgave herself, accepting it as an accident. She recalled what Maria had told her once—the only certainty in life was change. The pen was an object, a tool to be used that someday may no longer exist. It was, though, one of the few tangible things that meant anything to her. Breaking the pen felt like losing another piece of her mother.

After turning off the inside lights and locking the office, she hustled across the yard and back to the house with the busted pen in her hand. Without a coat, the chill cut through her, and by the time she stepped into the kitchen, her fingers and toes were almost numb.

"I was wondering if you got lost," her father joked, as he was setting the table. "I thought I would get a jump start. Are we having spaghetti?"

She set the broken pieces of the pen on the counter. "Yeah. Give me thirty minutes," she mumbled.

"You don't sound too enthusiastic about it."

She picked up the busted barrel and showed it to him. "I broke Mom's pen. I knocked it off the desk by accident. It hit some metal and came apart."

He stepped toward her, holding out his hand. "Let me see." After she gave him the pieces, he looked at the barrel, examining the break. "Maybe we can use some kind of glue. This looks like it's made of acrylic. I don't think we have anything besides superglue in the garage, and you wouldn't want to use that."

"I hope it's not ruined," she said.

He set the pieces on the counter. "I can take it to the watch and jewelry repair shop in town. They may be able to fix it. I think they work on more than just jewelry. I've seen clocks and vintage toys in the window. You want me to call them?"

She pulled out two pots from a low storage cabinet. "They're probably closed now, but that's a good idea. We need to be careful not to lose the end."

He opened a drawer, grabbed a quart-sized bag, and placed the pieces inside. "There. Safe and sound."

"Thanks, Dad. I'll have things ready soon. Which reminds me, Maria invited us to dinner tomorrow."

"That was nice of her. You go. It'll give me a free night to eat something unhealthy that you'd never make for me." He winked and then stepped toward the living room. "Hear that, Buddy? The boss will be away tomorrow. Treats for dinner!"

She turned, waiting for a pot to fill with water from

the faucet. "You better not, Dad! Make sure he eats his regular food."

"Don't worry, Buddy. I know where she keeps the good stuff. She'll be none the wiser."

Buddy met him in the living room, where they both rested until dinner was ready.

While they ate, Olivia raised the matter of watching Willow while June was away. After her father had a one-sided talk with Buddy about playing nice with their future guest, he agreed without reservation. During the rest of the meal, he talked about his plans to make snow-ball cookies for the final test baking tomorrow. She reminded him to take pictures and notes for the copy, which still needed her edits.

When they had finished cleaning up, her father settled on the sofa and turned on the TV. She rotated the handle on the kitchen window blinds and paused for a moment, eyeing the bright, round moon, now higher in the sky. Over the next month, it would go through phases, waxing and waning until the cycle was complete. Though ever changing, its nature was always the same.

She thought of what Bev had insinuated about Stuart having a rotten core. Did his plan to make amends with his family imply that he had changed his ways? Had prison been only one phase in his life, giving way and priming him for the next? Stuart wanted his wife back, and Olivia wondered how far he would go to make that happen.

Her cell had remained quiet on the counter through

dinner with no news from Preston or Bev. She closed the blinds and let the unsettling business rest. There was nothing more for her to do tonight, or maybe even going forward. The last thing she wanted was to be wedged between Preston and his mother. Her intuition cautioned her, speaking loud and clear: proceed carefully in the precarious days ahead.

CHAPTER 17

After waking on Sunday morning, Olivia showered and changed into a casual black blouse and jeans. She expected to find her father in the kitchen, tackling the paper's crossword puzzle. Instead, a note on the table bid her good morning and informed her that he had gone to the grocery store for vanilla extract and powdered sugar. The amusing specificity of the note begged the question of how many cookies he planned to make. They'd already packed every inch of free freezer space with bakes from the first eleven days' trials. Now, they were giving away gift plates of cookies and cake slices to all takers.

She'd never imagined her father would go whole hog when he volunteered to help with the test baking for the column. He'd immersed himself in the world of icing, batters, and doughs, buying two cookbooks and subscribing to every baking-related newsletter he came across. It still surprised her that he had plunked down money for the apron and matching mitts. He seldom bought anything for himself, unless what was being replaced had holes in awkward places. His wares were ready for his return on the counter, which reminded her to order a set of red silicone spatulas she'd seen online as a stocking stuffer for him.

She prepped her breakfast in a jiff, topping her oatmeal with blueberries and slivered almonds. A single cup of coffee today would wash down the largest gingerbread man cookie left in the storage tin. Signing her name to a baking column demanded continuous quality control. If that required morning dessert, then it was all part of the hard job she had to do.

As she ate her breakfast, a random thought crossed her mind. Maybe her father would enjoy developing his skills by attending professional classes. She picked up her phone to search for schools or restaurants offering lessons for amateur bakers. After she opened a browser, her cell buzzed with a text from Cassandra that read, "Check your e-mail."

Olivia opened her inbox, finding a message Cassandra had sent an hour ago. She reported speaking at length last night with Marco about the gem heists. There was too much to tell in an e-mail, so she suggested meeting today to exchange information. At the bottom of the message, she had attached a link to an online parenting magazine.

After clicking the link, Olivia skimmed an article

about how some insurance companies deny drug coverage for children with rare diseases. The author had interviewed several mothers with similar stories, including Darcy Carter. She explained how the medication that could help Kaitlyn had been FDA approved for certain conditions, but not for her diagnosis. Darcy's insurance company had used this guidance as the basis to reject her claim for the fifty-thousand-dollar per year cost of the drug.

After reading the article, Olivia texted Cassandra. "Thanks for the info. Office at eleven?"

Her phone buzzed with a thumbs-up emoji reply.

She suspended her search for baking schools and turned her attention back to the Carters. Darcy desperately needed money, and if the family knew about the connection Mack had drawn between Stuart and Bev, any of them could be the blackmailer.

There was still no word from Bev, so Olivia dialed her up. After the voice mail greeting, she left a message, asking Bev to return her call. Then she searched for Stacey's address through a reverse online phone directory and pinpointed the Carter home using a mapping app. The timing for a visit wasn't ideal, given Stuart's death, but the blackmail threat was a ticking clock and she wanted to gather any information that could help Bev ASAP. After cleaning up, she grabbed her coat and keys, and left to call on the Carters.

Stacey lived fifteen minutes outside of town in a small subdivision where all the modest-sized homes looked the same. Simple chain-link fences separated the sparse yards between split-level houses with white siding. She parked on the street at Stacey's address, double-checking that the number painted on the curb matched that on her cell's GPS. Snowmen, candy canes, and reindeer inflatables decorated the lawn, hinting that Darcy and Kaitlyn lived with her.

After getting out of her car, she walked to the three-foot-tall gate and pulled up the rusty latch. As she swung the gate open, the hinge squealed, spurring the neighbor's Jack Russell terrier to charge the fence separating the yards. The wiry white dog leapt at the top rail, barking and popping its front paws over. Undeterred, it darted back and forth along the fence, hotter than a pepper sprout under his collar. She whispered a word of gratitude for Buddy's congenial demeanor and made a mental note to give him some extra treats before the day was over.

Stacey's front window curtain parted and then quickly closed. Finding the screen door locked, Olivia knocked three times on its black aluminum framing. The muted bangs incited the terrier, and it tried vaulting the fence again. A bare path along the boundary suggested menacing the Carters was one of its favorite pastimes. She kept an eye focused on the tiny terror, readying herself in case it hurdled the rail.

She knocked harder three more times, and then the front door opened. A man in his late twenties with medium length brown hair and a Van Dyke beard answered.

"Hi. My name is Olivia Penn. I'm looking for Stacey Carter. Is she here?"

He looked over his shoulder and then back at her. "Now's not a good time."

"Are you Dylan Carter?" When he nodded, she said, "I'm very sorry about your father."

He stepped closer to the screen door, considering her more carefully. "How do you know about Stuart?"

Not wanting to reveal too many details and minding that he could be the blackmailer, she played her cards close.

"I'm a friend of Bev Styles, and I know her son, Detective Hills. I was with him when he received the call about your father."

That seemed to satisfy his suspicion, but he kept his distance, showing no inclination to invite her inside.

"Well, I'm not sorry," he said.

"Not sorry about—your father?"

"That's right. I hardly even knew the man."

The front door opened wider, and a woman in her fifties with graying auburn hair stepped beside him. "Dylan, who's here?" she said.

"Hi. Are you Mrs. Carter?"

"I am. What can I do for you?"

"My name is Olivia Penn, and I'm very sorry for your loss. I know this is a bad time, but can I speak with you for a few minutes? Bev Styles is a friend of mine, and

I know you worked with her late husband, Joe Hills, at one time."

Stacey stared at her with some suspicion. "Yes, that's right. It's been quite a few years, though."

Olivia eyed Dylan, gauging his reaction. "Bev may be in some trouble."

He stood unmoving, but Stacey unlocked the screen and pushed it open.

"Please come in," she said.

Olivia entered, stepping into a cramped living room furnished with a couch, love seat, and large-screen TV. Toys lay scattered about, and a four-foot-tall Christmas tree with a handful of gifts under it sat in the corner near a decorative mantle.

"Please have a seat," Stacey said.

Olivia sat, sinking deep into the well-worn sofa that had seen better days.

Stacey lowered herself onto the opposite end and turned, facing her. "This is my son, Dylan. My daughter Darcy lives with me, but she's at work right now. You're here about Joe's wife?"

"Yes. Something has come up that may involve your ex-husband, and anything you can tell me about him would be helpful." She glanced at Dylan, who was stewing on the love seat with his arms folded over his chest.

"What does Stuart have to do with it?" Stacey asked.

"I'm not at liberty to say. I know your ex-husband was released from prison three weeks ago, and he had been back in the area. Did he contact you during that time?"

Dylan launched from the loveseat. "How's that any of your business?"

"It's okay," Stacey said.

"We talked to the police yesterday," he continued. "We have nothing more to say to anyone about him. Who exactly are you again? Why are you here?"

He stepped toward the door, readying to usher her out.

Olivia repeated, "I'm a friend of Bev Styles, and she may be in some trouble." *And you're rather high-strung.*

"Dylan, either sit back down or leave us alone," his mother said.

She stared him down until he huffed, retraced his steps into the living room, and sat on the edge of the love seat.

Then she turned her attention back to Olivia. "Stuart and I divorced over two years ago. We've been separated for even longer. The police contacted us yesterday about finding him dead. To tell you the truth, it didn't surprise me."

"Did you know he got out of prison three weeks ago?" Olivia asked.

Stacey and Dylan glanced at each other before she answered. "Yes. He came here to the house."

"Do you mind me asking want he wanted?"

"Mom, you don't have to say anything to her."

"It's okay, Dylan. Joe helped me. It's the least I can

do to answer a few questions." She sighed, as if talking about her ex-husband sucked the life out of her. "Stuart wanted back in our lives. He said he had changed his ways. Then he carried on about how he was going to make everything right. He swore he had a plan. Stuart *always* had a plan. Get rich quick by whatever means. I told him to go away and never come back. I made my peace long ago with what he put us through, and I'm proud of who my children have become, despite having a deadbeat like him for a father. When he came to the house that night, I was scared he would ruin the life I've made for myself since our divorce. I didn't want him anywhere near here. He was only going to cause more problems. Stuart never changed."

"How'd he take it when you told him that?" Olivia asked.

Before she could answer, a little girl wearing a pink sweatshirt and khaki corduroys with teddy bears on the front pockets skipped into the living room, holding her arms wide and sputtering as if she was a twin prop plane.

"Kaitlyn, slow down," Stacey said.

Kaitlyn stopped in front of Stacey, placed her hands on her grandmother's knees, and jumped like a pogo stick. "Can I have a cookie, Grandma? Please-please."

Stacey enfolded Kaitlyn's hands, bestowing a loud kiss on her fingertips. "I'm talking to someone now. When I'm done, I'll check if you cleaned your room, and then maybe we'll get you a cookie."

Kaitlyn pulled her hands free, posturing them in a prayerful pose. "Please-please-please-please."

"Kaitlyn, you'll have to wait."

Though wishing to continue the conversation, Olivia didn't want to overstay her welcome. "It's okay. Thank you for speaking with me. I'll be on my way."

Kaitlyn tugged on Stacey's sweater sleeve. "Grandma, please! I cleaned my room. You can check."

Stacey stood. "I'm sorry I couldn't be more helpful."

Kaitlyn tried with all her might to pull her toward the staircase.

"Let go," Stacey told her. "My arm will need to grow longer if you stretch this sleeve anymore."

Kaitlyn giggled and released her sweater. "Your arm can't grow, Grandma. You're too old. Hurry!"

Olivia matched Stacey's smile as she stood to leave. "She's adorable."

Stacey grabbed her granddaughter's hand. "A real charmer. Now, take it slow on the stairs, Kaitlyn. My bones don't move as fast as your five-year-old ones. Let's go, so you can show me your room."

They walked upstairs as Dylan rose from the loveseat and stepped toward the door, with Olivia following behind. He opened the door and swung the screen out, holding it for her.

"You must think we're a strange family."

She stepped out onto the tiny porch and turned to face him. "In my line of work, I deal with a lot of diffi-cult family dynamics."

"Oh, yeah? Are you some sort of counselor?"

"Hmm … I never quite thought of it that way, but maybe. I write an advice column for a paper in D.C. I also do guest appearances for the paper here in town." She mischievously smiled, hoping to ease the tension by schilling her own column. "Don't miss the hard-hitting, much-anticipated grand finale of my special feature, 'The Twelve Bakes of Christmas,' in *The Apple Station Times*. The final recipe runs on Christmas Eve, and I'll give you the exclusive scoop. It's for snowball cookies. Maybe you can make them with your niece for Christmas Day."

The suggestion seemed to hit a soft spot as he relaxed his stance. A spark appeared in his eyes at the mention of Kaitlyn. "She's a special little girl. I'd do anything for her."

"I bet she's enjoying her school vacation."

"Kaitlyn can't go to school because her condition makes her susceptible to infections. Even a common cold can hit her hard. The school sends out a teacher a couple times a week, and she leaves lesson plans for my mom and sister to use with her. It's working okay now, but she'd rather be with her friends."

"I can understand that. I hope that happens soon for her." Seeing a small opening, she moved in before it closed. "Can I ask you something?"

"Okay."

"Did a private investigator by the name of John Mack ever visit you?"

He paused for a second, then glanced over his shoulder and stepped out of the house, closing the door behind him to a crack. "Yes. He came to talk to my mom."

"What did he want?"

Dylan slipped his hands into his front pockets. "He brought up a bizarre story about Stuart stealing an expensive necklace, and then he flat out asked my mom whether she had it or sold it. You tell me, does it look like we're rolling in dough? My niece needs medical treatment that my sister's insurance won't cover. If my mom had money, she'd put it all toward Kaitlyn. I don't know where he got that story from, but I wouldn't put it past Stuart to do something like that. He was upsetting my mom, so I asked him to leave."

"Were you here the night Stuart visited?"

He shook his head. "I wasn't, but my mom's fiancé was."

"Do you mind giving me his name?"

"Edward Graham. He goes by Ed. He works as a mechanic at Jed's Auto Body."

"Did he tell you anything about that night?"

"Ed said Stuart was all worked up about seeing him here. Stuart stood here on the porch, yelling about how much he loved my mom. After fifteen minutes, Ed had all he could take. He grabbed Stuart by the collar and threw him down into the yard, warning him never to come back, or else."

"Or else? What do you think he meant by that?"

"Nothing, really. Stuart had zero chance of ever getting back with my mom. Ed is a great guy. He loves her, and he treats her well. Darcy and I both like him. I'm not sorry Stuart is dead. The only thing that upsets me is that we're stuck planning a funeral for him right before Christmas."

Olivia didn't know how to respond to that, and so she simply thanked him for his time, got into her car, and left to meet Cassandra.

There was obviously no love lost in the family for Stuart. Despite Dylan's initial reserve, he hadn't been shy about his true feelings. He'd admitted to knowing about the theft, but offered no clues to whether the family was aware of Bev's connection. After Mack's visit with Stacey, Dylan could've hacked for details, putting two and two together. The blackmailer's demand for ten thousand dollars wasn't enough to cover the cost of Kaitlyn's medication, although a common strategy would be to start low and then keep increasing the amount. All the Carters could be involved, but Olivia didn't peg any of them as murderers. Instead, she mulled over Stacey's concern that Stuart would ruin her new life. Could his murder be unrelated to the blackmail, and should the police be questioning Ed Graham?

CHAPTER 18

The newspaper suite was dark and locked when Olivia arrived at a quarter past eleven. She was about to text to say she'd arrived when Cassandra stepped out of Ellen's office. Olivia tapped on the pane, catching her attention, and Cassandra walked over and unlocked the door.

"Sorry I'm late," Olivia said, stepping inside.

Cassandra flipped the lights on, illuminating the back half of the workroom. "Don't worry. I've only been here five minutes."

"I spoke with Stacey Carter and her son, Dylan. They have an interesting family dynamic."

Cassandra raised her eyebrows, reading between the lines. "Your *interesting* sounds dysfunctional to me."

Olivia followed Cassandra to her desk, where a laptop sat next to an opened file containing pages of handwritten notes.

"Maybe when Stuart was still in their lives," Olivia

said. "They seem to be better off without him, but not because he's dead." Stuart's and Joe's names were highlighted in yellow on the top sheet. "What are you working on?"

Cassandra fanned the papers across the desk. "These are notes from my talk last night with Marco."

"Are they all about Stuart?"

Cassandra pulled her chair closer, sat, and turned on her laptop. "Him and the gem heists. This is juicy stuff."

Olivia rolled Cooper's chair over and sat across from her. "Did you learn anything else yesterday at the crime scene?"

"Cole let it slip that Stuart had been shot in the back. So, I think we can go with murder. The police most likely won't release a statement today, but I'm going to the station anyway to question whoever is there."

"Could it have been a hunting accident?" Olivia asked.

Cassandra contorted her face like a pouting child. "Why do you have to be so logical? It's a bit of a buzzkill. You could be right. I don't have any idea what animal you can shoot with what type of weapon this time of year —legally, of course."

"I don't think it's open season for anything, but that wouldn't stop a poacher. Either way, we're looking at murder or manslaughter. Do you know anything about the location where the hikers found him?"

Cassandra slid a pocket-sized notepad across the desk and flipped it open. "Not too much. The police wouldn't allow me near the scene, but it didn't seem like a trek to get there. I watched the EMS crew go in with a stretcher, and in less than fifteen minutes, they returned with the body. About a quarter mile down the road from where the police located Stuart's car, there's a trailhead. That's where the hikers who found Stuart had parked."

"Did you speak with them?"

"Please, do you take me for an amateur?" Cassandra teased. "Of course I did. The police kept the couple at the scene for a while, and Cole pointed them out to me. As soon as he cleared them to leave, they walked back down the trail toward their car, and I high-tailed it after them. They had little to add to what I already knew. But they told me the trail they were hiking parallels the road about fifty yards into the forest."

"With Stuart's car being found nearby, the murderer could've shot him roadside and then dumped him in the woods," Olivia said. "Or he could've been out in the woods looking for something. Maybe he was being followed."

"And by looking for something, you're talking about the Star of Athens."

Olivia hesitated, reluctant to cast a shadow on Joe's involvement and dead set on not revealing the blackmail threat against Bev.

"Don't worry," Cassandra said. "I know all about it, including the connection between Stuart and Preston's family. I assume Joe Hill's cabin is in the vicinity. Marco knew Stuart had stayed at Joe's cabin, but he didn't have any information on its location."

"Wow, Marco is good. He already knows a lot of details."

"You don't know the half of it. I had trouble writing fast enough when I was taking notes last night." She spun her notepad around toward Olivia. "Look at this scribble. I almost can't read my writing. By the way, he knows you. He asked about you."

Olivia swiveled her seat. "What about me?"

"If you were seeing anyone."

"What did you say?"

Cassandra cracked a thin smile and leaned forward, resting her forearms on the table. "What do I know? I only hear rumors and apparently, they're wrong. Deal with your love life on your own time. Focus, Penn. So, back to dearly departed Stuart. Maybe he recovered the necklace while someone was following him."

"If that's the case, the police may never find the necklace or the murderer. Maybe he didn't find it, but somebody thought he knew where it was. Or maybe it has nothing to do with the heist. Stacey's fiancé threatened him. His own son despised him."

"Those are all possibilities," Cassandra replied. "Jealousy, anger, revenge—all motives for murder." She spread her notes from the file in front of her. "Let me walk you through what Marco shared with me. He's been following these heists for several years, but his research goes back almost two decades. The last theft fitting the

MO was the burglary at the gala. Marco's sources have dried up, and there haven't been many leads in identifying the thief since."

"Maybe this guy moved or gave up his life of crime and is now enjoying the high life on a beach somewhere," Olivia said.

Cassandra skimmed her notes before replying. "Marco has sources in high places, including in police departments and the FBI. He told me they have a profile of this guy. He's not thieving only for the money. It's also an adrenaline rush for him. The Star of Athens theft would've been his biggest job to date. Some think it was a planned farewell, a coup de grâce, and one last thumbing his nose at the police. If that's the case, holding the gem in his greedy hands and then losing it would be a bitter fifteen-million-dollar pill to swallow. That's not something easily walked away from."

"But this all happened three years ago," Olivia replied.

"Marco said thieves who operate at this level will sit on stolen merchandise for years before trying to fence it. Extremely valuable stolen goods are difficult to unload when the job is fresh. Police have their informants on the shady side of the fence, no pun intended, and they're on the lookout whenever something like this happens. Our thief is patient. One heist linked to him involved a twenty-five-thousand-dollar ring stolen from a high-rise luxury hotel in New York. Five years after that theft, a random raid on a fence turned up that ring, which someone had sold to him the previous week."

Olivia took a deep breath before speaking. "He sat on the ring for five years. So, waiting three years for a fifteen-million-dollar swan song is conceivable. That means he may be here in Apple Station." She stood, removed her coat, and tossed it onto a nearby desk. "This is more than I was expecting, and it looks like you still have more to share. I need a drink. Do you want something?"

Cassandra started typing on her laptop. "Diet soda, please. Thank you."

Olivia walked to the back of the office, grabbed a bottle of water and a can of soda from the fridge, and rejoined Cassandra at her desk.

Cassandra turned her laptop around to face Olivia and then popped the can tab. "That's the Star of Athens. It's not a great shot. I pulled it from the social media feed of a Greek newspaper that had covered an event in Elounda. That's a town on the northeastern coast of Crete. The woman in the picture is the wife of the tycoon who owned the necklace."

Olivia took a sip of water while drawing in closer to the screen. "My, oh my. That's a stunning necklace."

"No kidding."

"How could you even sell something like that? Who would buy it? You could never wear it in public. That's an identifiable, one-of-a-kind piece."

Cassandra turned her laptop back around. "I asked

Marco the same thing. You and me—great minds think alike. He said people who buy stolen jewelry often keep it in private collections. Sometimes, fences will break down jewelry and sell it in pieces. That diminishes the value, but it's easier to offload that way. One of Marco's sources said a buyer would likely remove the diamonds from the necklace and sell them individually. They're of high karat weight and exceptional quality. They could go for five thousand dollars a pop. There are forty diamonds on the necklace, so that's a nice payday. The sapphire is a different story. The combo of the color and cut is very rare. A fence would sell that to a private collector."

The possibility that the thief could be in Apple Station added to Olivia's list of blackmailer suspects. If he was the blackmailer, the paltry ten-thousand-dollar demand confirmed that the threat wasn't about the money. If she accepted that premise, then what was his agenda? Stuart had been in town for three weeks, so he may have been the thief. The ghost Mack described could've been waiting, watching for Stuart to make his move.

"What else does the profile reveal about him?" Olivia asked.

Cassandra scanned her notes. "A man between forty and sixty with mechanical skills. The investigators nick-named him the Tuxedo Bandit because he blends into the social scene of those he robs. It's a thing to give criminals nicknames to publicize the perps in the media to generate leads. He's meticulous, smart, and patient. The police don't have any photos except for a fuzzy shot of someone dressed as a maintenance worker leaving the hotel the night of the Christmas Eve theft. They have a partial print from a heist in Miami that they believe he committed."

"We're looking for a ghost who's also a chameleon," Olivia said. "He shouldn't be hard to find at all."

"There's so much more Marco told me last night."

"Did he speak with Stuart while he was in prison?"

Cassandra shook her head. "He didn't say. Then again, I didn't ask. But I think he probably would've told me if he had. He was open with me about everything."

"Mack told me one of the few people to visit Stuart in prison was a female reporter."

Cassandra took a sip of soda, staring for a moment at her laptop screen. "Hmm … could it have been Paige?"

"No. Paige may have contacted Mack so she wouldn't have to visit Stuart in jail. I don't think she was too enthused about getting involved. Prison interviews don't strike me as her cup of tea."

"I wouldn't blame her," Cassandra said. "I'd let Mack do that dirty work for me too."

"I'm with you on that. I wonder if Marco is working with anyone else."

"I'll ask him next time we speak," Cassandra said. "Stuart's death has stirred the pot, and Marco is contacting his old sources to see if there's any new chatter about the Star of Athens. We're talking in a day or two, depending on what we both turn up."

Olivia finished her water, aimed the plastic bottle at a nearby recycling bin, and swished her shot.

"Nothing but net," Cassandra chirped.

"Luck."

"Then maybe today is your lucky day. I hope I have luck at the police station getting something I can use for the paper."

Olivia stood and grabbed her coat. "Remember, you can't mention anything about a connection between Stuart and the heists."

Cassandra held three fingers up, promising with a Girl Scout's salute. "Yes, ma'am. What's next for you?"

Olivia slipped her coat on and straightened the collar. "None of the Carters I've talked to so far are shedding tears for Stuart. Stacey's daughter, Darcy, is working today at the Christmas shop, and I thought I'd go there and pick up a new ornament." She decided not to tell Cassandra about her planned pit stop at the inn. Though she trusted Cassandra, the blackmail was Bev's personal business.

"And if Darcy is around?" Cassandra asked with a knowing grin.

"I'll express my condolences. Then perhaps I'll have a little conversation with her about Stuart. Thanks for talking with Marco."

Cassandra gathered her papers and stacked them together in the folder. "If there's a connection between Stuart's death and the heist, it's big. If this pans out,

Marco wants to collaborate with me on a piece for his—your—paper."

"That would be great for you." *But maybe not for Bev.* "Good luck with the police."

With that, Olivia turned, waved goodbye, and walked toward the door. She'd check in with Bev at the inn before visiting Darcy at the Christmas shop. Preston must know about the blackmail scheme by now, so why hadn't Bev returned her call?

CHAPTER 19

"Hi, Zoey," Olivia said, approaching the inn's lobby counter. "We met yesterday. I came in with a couple of bags of donations."

Zoey lit up with a perky grin, supercharged by the steaming brew in the oversized mug she was holding. "I never forget a face." She leaned forward, peering over the counter's edge. "Did you bring more goodies?"

"No. I'm looking for Bev."

"I haven't seen her recently. She may be in her office. Let me check." Zoey set her cup down, picked up the desk phone's handset, and dialed. "Hi, Bev. I'm up front in the lobby. There's someone asking for you." She lowered the phone. "What's your name again?"

"Olivia."

"Bev, it's … Oh, okay. Will do … Yeah, it's totally packed. The waiting list is about twenty minutes. I'll tell the kitchen. Bye-bye." Zoey replaced the handset. "She heard you. She's in her office. You can go right on back."

After thanking Zoey, Olivia walked to the rear of the lobby and proceeded to Bev's office. She paused before entering, first peeking inside. "Bev? Are you busy?"

"No. Come in."

She stepped in, shutting the door behind her. "I called you earlier and left a message. What happened yesterday? How did it go when you told Preston?"

Bev gestured toward the chair across from her desk, waiting until she sat. "Now before you say anything—"

"Please tell me you told Preston."

"Let me explain," Bev said.

"You didn't tell him, did you?" She would've wagered a year's pay on the answer.

"I didn't hear from him after he left yesterday morning. This situation would've only distracted him. I first wanted to see if you had spoken with the private investigator again."

Olivia wiggled out of her coat, letting it fall haphazardly behind her in the chair. "What you're calling a *situation* is a serious crime. I learned a lot, the most pressing matter being that you may be in danger."

Bev sunk in the seat with her eyes at half-mast, looking like she hadn't slept a wink in a week. "The blackmailer threatened to expose information about my family, not physically harm me."

"I don't think the blackmail threat is about the money.

There are a lot of moving pieces here, but I'm not sure how they connect yet. The only two people who know what happened that Christmas Eve are dead. Joe's missing hours from that night leave room for speculation. I don't believe he was involved, but there are those who think the stolen necklace still is in Apple Station. Stuart's death, the heist, and the blackmail are all related somehow."

Three loud knocks rattled the door, spurring Olivia to silence.

"It's probably Zoey," Bev whispered. "Can you come back later?" she said with a raised voice. "I'm in a meeting."

The door swung open and Preston stepped inside, along with another man who was wearing a charcoal suit, white-collar shirt, and burgundy tie.

Bev dialed up her natural charm. "Preston, what a delightful surprise. I didn't expect to see you here."

Preston paused for a second upon seeing Olivia and then closed the door. The stranger appeared to be in his fifties, and his buzz-cut hinted he was in law enforcement or had a military background.

"Mom, I need to speak with you."

Bev acted genuinely surprised. "Oh, about what? If it's about the faucets, I told you those can wait."

"No, it's not about the faucets."

The mystery man reached into his suit jacket inside pocket, pulled out a black case, and opened it, showing Bev a badge with an ID. "I'm Special Agent Paul Allen with the FBI. I would appreciate a few minutes of your time."

Olivia understood his no-nonsense glance at her as an invitation to leave. "I'll go."

"No," Bev said. "I would like you to stay."

Allen placed his ID case back into his pocket. "I prefer we speak privately."

"I think I know what this is about," Bev said.

Allen looked at Preston and then back at Bev. "Mrs. Styles, what do you think this is about?"

"Stuart Carter. And Olivia knows the whole story."

That's a gross overstatement.

Preston stepped closer to his mother, placing his hands on his hips.

Allen looked down at Olivia. "Who are you, and what's your connection to this?"

Preston answered for her. "This is Olivia Penn. She's a friend of the family. I'd like to hear her connection to this as well."

"Preston, there are two chairs in the room next door," Bev said. "Please bring them in so you can both sit."

He kept his jaw set as he glanced at Olivia again. He left the office, then returned in a blink with one chair and positioned it beside Olivia. After closing the door, he crossed his arms and remained standing.

Allen removed his black overcoat, draped it over the back of the seat, and sat with a friendly lean toward Bev. "Mrs. Styles, why would you think I'm here to speak with you about Stuart Carter?"

"I know Stuart is dead, and the police found him in the general area of my husband's cabin."

"Had you spoken to Stuart recently?" Allen asked.

"No, I haven't." He nodded, then questioned her about the night of the heist. Bev repeated the story she'd told Olivia, minus the doubts about Joe's involvement.

Allen listened without taking notes, seemingly already aware of the sequence of events. When she finished speaking, he pulled out a metal case from his pants pocket, removed a business card, and placed it on her desk. "If there's anything else that you can remember from that night, call me."

Olivia caught Bev's eye and subtly tilted her head toward Allen. If Bev insisted on keeping mum, she would do the talking for her.

Bev cleared her throat while folding her hands on the desk. "Agent Allen, I might be involved with something relevant to Stuart's death."

He glanced at Preston. "What would that be, Mrs. Styles?"

She picked her cell up off the desk and swiped through several screens. "A couple of days ago, I received this text."

She gave the phone to Allen, who then passed it to Preston.

"I don't understand, Mrs. Styles."

She gestured for Preston to return the phone to her. "I checked my e-mail and then saw I had received this." She handed the phone back to Allen.

He read the e-mail, scrolling up and down the screen several times before passing it to Preston. "Did you know about this, Detective?"

Preston seemed to read much faster, and in a flash, he reacted. "Why didn't you show me this?" He held up the phone to Bev. "Somebody's threatening you, and you keep it to yourself? What were you thinking? You were going to deal with this on your own?"

She kept her eyes focused on her desk, speaking in a muted tone. "I have a team helping me."

"What are you talking about? You're being black-mailed, and you have a team? This is a crime, and I am the police!"

Allen stood and put a hand on Preston's arm. "Detective, I think you need to take a moment."

"Tell me everything right now about what's been going on," Preston insisted. Then he glared at Olivia. "And let me guess. You knew about this and said nothing."

The question had been asked and answered. He'd caught her off guard, as keeping it from him hadn't been her motive.

"Detective, calm down," Allen said.

Preston rubbed his face with his hand and then blew out a full breath of steam. "I would like a few minutes alone with my mother."

Allen weighed the request for a moment before answering. "Okay. But I'll need to know what she says."

After Preston nodded once, Allen and Olivia left the room.

Preston shut the door firmly as she and Allen waited in the hallway. She'd never seen Preston nearly as upset, though she understood his point of view. Since his father's passing, he had felt extra responsibility to look after Bev, even to the point of moving to Apple Station to be closer to her. The conversation from inside the office was muted, but she imagined the tenor of it was that of a loving son's concern for his victimized mother.

Allen stepped to stand opposite her, casually holding one hand in the other. "Is Detective Hills right? Did you know about the blackmail threat against Mrs. Styles?"

"She told me yesterday, and I tried to get her to tell him. That's why I'm here now—to see if she did. But surprise on me, she didn't."

He nodded with empathic eyes. "Ms. Penn, what is it you do for a living?"

"I work for a newspaper."

"A reporter?"

She shook her head. "Advice columnist."

"I see." He placed his hands in his pants pockets. "How well do you know Mrs. Styles?"

Her defenses shot up, sensing she was being questioned. "A little."

The office door opened. "Thank you for giving us a moment," Preston said. "Please come back in."

Olivia followed Allen, and they both took their seats.

"Mrs. Styles, this information you've shared with us

changes matters," Allen said. "I need a copy of that e-mail. If you don't mind, I would like to forward it to myself right now." After Bev handed him the phone, he continued. "I'll have someone look at this and try to trace it. We'll need to deal with this threat." He sent the e-mail to himself, then set the cell on the desk.

"I'll post a deputy on the premises for extra security," Preston said.

"That sounds advised. Mrs. Styles, don't worry. I'll pool my resources with the local authorities, and we'll sort this out."

Olivia glanced at Preston, who hadn't once looked at her since she reentered the room. Wanting to mitigate any doubts he felt toward her, she had no choice but to come clean. "Agent Allen, there's something I can add that may be useful."

He turned in his seat to face her. "What would that be?"

She gave a censored version of her meeting with Mack, keeping her father's and Sam's involvement out of the story. She would tell the full tale to Preston in private later. She trusted him but didn't have an angle on what Allen would do with the information.

Allen listened without a hint of emotion. "That's valuable, Ms. Penn. I'll need to investigate John Mack's background. He could be involved with the threat Mrs. Styles received." He stood, grabbed his overcoat from the back of his chair, and put it on. "Mrs. Styles, thank you for your time." He turned halfway, then paused. "One more thing. Where were you on Friday night between ten p.m. and midnight?"

"I was at home, sleeping. I always go to bed around ten."

"Was there anyone else there with you?"

She glanced at Preston. "Of course not."

"Do you own any guns?" Allen asked.

Bev paused, perhaps realizing the question's intent, as she had just admitted to lacking an alibi for the presumed time frame of Stuart's death. "My husband did. I still have them."

Allen addressed Preston. "We'll need to test those guns. I can send someone—"

"I'll get them myself," he growled.

"Detective, I can't let you do that."

Preston straightened. "I'll have a deputy come. Is that satisfactory?"

Allen buttoned his coat. "That'll be fine." Then he turned toward Olivia. "I may need to speak with you again. Where can I reach you?"

She provided her cell number, which he recorded in his phone's directory. After thanking her, he left the room with Preston following behind.

Olivia shot out of her seat and darted into the hallway. "Preston, can we talk for a second?"

Allen eyed them both. "Go on, Detective. I need to liaise with my team regarding this development. When I have something solid, I'll get in touch." He glanced back and forth between them, then turned and walked toward the exit for the lobby.

Preston watched and waited until the door closed behind him, and then turned to Olivia, his eyes dark. "You knew about this and didn't tell me. I find out my mother is being blackmailed only because an FBI agent shows up. Explain that to me."

"I'm so sorry. As soon as Bev told me, I pleaded with her to tell you."

"My mother tells *you* and not me," he said, his voice strained. "She could be in danger. Did you ever think about that?"

"Yes."

"And you were okay with that?"

She shook her head. "Of course not."

"Did you know about this yesterday morning when we met?"

"No."

"Olivia, I don't even know what to say." He took a slow, deep breath.

"Preston, you're getting the wrong impression. I—"

"What were you thinking, stopping on the side of the road at night to talk to some stranger?" He holstered his hands on his hips, his jaw tight. "You could've been killed. And then you meet a PI alone at Lake Crystal? Of all places. Didn't *something* inside you say that was a bad idea? Why didn't you call me?"

There was so much racing through her head. *I wasn't alone. I didn't want to be at Lake Crystal. Every bone in my body said it was a bad idea.* But this wasn't the time for a detailed explanation. She just needed him to calm down. "I know you're upset, but please understand, your mother told me yesterday that she would tell you. I tried to get her to talk to you."

That burst a fuse, and he pointed a finger at her. "Well, you didn't try hard enough. From now on, stay out of my mother's life." With that, he turned his back and walked away.

CHAPTER 20

"He's mad at me, not you," Bev said, standing in the doorway of her office. "I'm sorry. I couldn't help overhearing. He didn't mean it." She stepped out into the hallway and handed Olivia her coat. "I'm sorry I put you in this position."

"Don't be," Olivia replied. "He has a right to be angry. He always means what he says." She grabbed her coat from Bev and slipped it on. The sting from his sharp tone blurred her eyes, and she dabbed the corner of one, determined not to let it show in front of Bev. "I'm going. If I find out anything useful, I'll get in touch."

She offered Bev a terse goodbye, strode out into the lobby, and left the inn. Outside, she stood on the sidewalk in front of the French doors, looking at the unlit displays for the Festival of Lights in the town square. During the day, the decorations were indiscernible contortions of steel and wire. At night, the twisted metal transformed into whimsical holiday scenes. Twinkling candy canes, snowflakes, and holly wreaths accompanied animations of snowmen swaying, fire-breathing baby dragons, and reindeer leaping over the moon. She always walked through the lights when she was home for the holidays, usually spotting one addition to the familiar displays each year. Her favorite was the traditional grand finale: a ten-yard tunnel animated like a sparkling diamond snow shower.

A group of six revelers split in half and maneuvered around her to enter the inn. She didn't budge and hardly noticed, still pained by Preston's pointed words. She had implored Bev to tell him. *What else was I supposed to do?* Bev had put her in the middle of this, and for a mother trying to play matchmaker, she had a hell of a way of bringing them closer.

A young mother with a stroller stood in front of her. "Excuse me. Can I get around you?"

She snapped out of it, stepped aside, and opened the door for the woman and her daughter. A faint whiff of cinnamon wafted out from the lobby, soothing her sour mood. At least now the police would ensure Bev's safety, but her concern for Preston was growing. She didn't believe Joe had taken part in the theft, but someone clearly did. If they linked Joe to the heist or to aiding Stuart, the press or police might implicate Preston. Accusations of a local detective protecting his parents in a fifteen-million-dollar theft would be prime fodder for media accusations of a cover-up.

Preston had ordered her to stay out of his mother's life, but as a friend of Bev's, that was a no can do. At least, for now, he hadn't said to stay out of *his* life. If she proceeded with caution, perhaps they could rewind the morning's ill will and begin anew. After shaking off the bite of his heated words, she continued with her intended afternoon agenda.

The year-round Christmas shop was at the opposite end of town. She wasn't a regular at the store and never went there in the offseason. Most of the ornaments decorating the Penn family tree every year were ones her parents had purchased when she was a child. A few newer baubles appeared here and there courtesy of mother-daughter outings to local craft fairs.

She kept pace with the Sunday shoppers, strolling past the unlit newspaper office. Cassandra was most likely at the police station demanding answers from whoever had the afternoon shift. As she neared Daisy's Feed and Saddlery, a familiar face lifted her spirits, prompting her to wave.

"Hey, Sawyer," she said.

Sawyer Weston stepped toward her and brushed her cheek with a warm, welcoming kiss. Sawyer, a longtime friend, worked part-time repairing tack at Daisy's. His full-time gig had him doing a little of everything at his parents' ranch in Berryville. From giving riding lessons to training horses, he was involved in every aspect of the business. He worked at the saddlery mostly as a favor to Daisy, who paid a hefty sum to board her three mares at their stables.

"Merry Christmas, in case I don't see you before then," he said.

"Same to you. Are you working here today?"

He adjusted his black cowboy hat and then dipped his fingertips into the front pockets of his dark denim jeans. "Sort of. This is the busiest weekend of the year for Daisy. She asked me to come in for a few hours to help answer questions. Customers want to buy gifts for friends and family but don't have a clue about what to get." He jabbed a thumb at his chest. "That's where I come in. Daisy says I'm a lucky charm around the ladies."

His wink and twinkling smile spurred a full, heartfelt grin from her. Once upon a time, she and Sawyer had dated after high school. They had attended colleges on opposite coasts, leaving too much distance and too many years between them. They remained good friends, and it had all turned out for the best. If they had tried harder, Olivia may have never left Apple Station, and perhaps now she would be married to her hometown sweetheart. Her life experiences over the intervening years, though, had made her strong and independent. And that was something she wouldn't trade for the love of anyone.

"Are you going to pop inside and shop for a saddle today?" he joked.

"Maybe, as long as you throw in the horse and all the upkeep for free."

"Daisy has a special for twenty percent off feed, but

that's about the best I can do. How about instead, you come up to the ranch next week and we go riding?"

"Deal—as long as I ride Gypsy."

He opened the door for two women entering the store. "Of course. She's been asking about you."

"Really? And what exactly does a mare say?"

"Gyps looked me straight in the eye—you know the way she does when something's on her mind—and said, 'Where is that Liv Penn who always likes to stirrup trouble?'"

She chuckled. "I walked into that, didn't I? Please let her know I miss her and can't wait for next week." They stepped aside for a pair of customers exiting the store. "I better let you go so you don't waste all that charm on me."

He tipped his hat. "Never a waste on you. Hey, what are you doing for New Year's Eve?"

Though she was only in her early thirties, it had been several years since she'd stayed up to watch the ball drop in New York's Times Square on TV. "I haven't given much thought to it. I'll probably stay home with my dad."

"Why don't you come out to the ranch? My family is hosting a New Year's Eve party. We're having barbeque and bringing in a band to play in one of our barns that we're clearing out. Bring a friend. The more the merrier."

She knew of a plus one who definitely wouldn't be attending. Though celebrating anything was the last thing on her mind, she thanked Sawyer for the invitation, promising to get back to him, and then they parted ways.

After walking another block, Olivia neared the Christmas shop. The store's holiday window display changed every year, in a small-town version of Macy's Herald Square at Christmas. Groups always would gather around the window, waiting turns to take selfies or family portraits for next year's greeting cards.

A gingerbread mansion with royal icing icicles dripping from the roof shined as the centerpiece this season. It was flanked by two five-tiered gingerbread cakes with matching white drizzles, green wreaths, and silver bows. A mantel and a fireplace with fake embers backdropped the showcase scene, and multiple strands of lights framing the window shone bright enough at night to make the sidewalk glow.

She stepped inside the jam-packed specialty shop, not sure of where to begin. Densely staged display trees made the store seem like the Bavarian Forest, and tables piled high with merchandise were in every nook and cranny. Loud, lively music inspired buying while drowning out second thoughts of impulse purchases. Red aprons and tasseled elf hats distinguished the employees from the shoppers.

A young woman identified by the Santa tag on her sweater as Elf Chloe approached, carrying a gold tray of snowflake sugar cookies. "Would you like one?" she asked. When Olivia declined, she asked, "Can I help you with anything?"

"I'm browsing right now."

"Okay. As you can see, we've got an ornament for everything, so if you're looking for something special, just ask."

"Thanks. Do you know if Darcy is working today?" She already knew the answer, but hadn't seen Darcy in the store yet.

"Yep. She was gift wrapping at the counter in the back the last time I saw her."

"Perfect."

Elf Chloe turned to the next potential buyer, hawking her cookies, as Olivia maneuvered her way to the back of the crowded store. She had to sidestep and stop several times, allowing customers with bags and children in tow to pass by between cramped tables. A life-sized, robotic Santa shouted "ho, ho, ho" every few minutes, spurring her to imagine how annoying that could be 365 days a year.

As she neared the gift wrap counter, she spotted Darcy chatting with an older woman while fashioning a red satin bow around an ornament box. Stepping closer, she feigned interest in a fake Douglas fir next to the counter. She eyed the ornaments with no real interest until spying a figurine of a puppy and kitten embracing. She unhooked it from the branch, deciding it was time for an addition to the Penn family collection. When Darcy finished wrapping the box and the customer walked away, Olivia slid over, aiming to catch her alone for a moment.

Darcy pointed to the ornament in Olivia's hand. "Aw, that's so cute. Would you like it wrapped?"

"I couldn't resist, but I don't need it wrapped. Do you have a minute?"

Darcy glanced toward the front of the store, and with no one else waiting in her line, she shrugged. "Yeah, I guess."

"My name is Olivia Penn. I met your family this morning at your house. I'm very sorry about your father."

Her perky smile flatlined. "Oh. Thanks. How do you know about my father?"

"I have connections with the local newspaper. I'm also friends with Bev Styles. She was married to a police officer who was a friend of your mother's and had some dealings with your father. Bev is the owner of the Apple Station Inn."

"I've been there a few times to eat." Darcy allowed her customer-friendly face to take a break.

"I met your daughter this morning. She's adorable."

She smiled as she removed her elf cap. "She's everything to me. That's why I'm working today. You must think it's odd that I would be here after what happened to my father."

Olivia shook her head. "Not at all. Your mother and brother were very forthcoming about how he hadn't been involved in your lives for a while."

"That's true. We've had little contact with him over the years."

"Did he ever meet Kaitlyn?"

"Once, when she was about six months old. Of course, she doesn't remember him, but it's normal for her not to have a grandfather. Much like me growing up. I always felt that I was raised by a single mother."

Olivia followed Darcy's focus and saw a man walking toward the counter with a basket full of gifts. She leaned over the table, taking a shot before her window closed. "Your mom told me about the night your father came to the house after he got out of prison. Were you there?"

"Ah … yeah. Why do you ask? Why are you so interested in my father?"

Olivia kept her voice low. "He may have been involved in something that has placed Bev Styles in danger."

Darcy glanced over Olivia's shoulder. "I wouldn't know anything about that. We had nothing to do with him."

"Your mother's fiancé threatened him."

Darcy's face brightened as she spoke to someone behind Olivia. "I'll be right with you, sir." Then she looked at Olivia, donned her elf cap, and lowered her voice. "I need to get back to work. Are you sure you don't want the ornament wrapped? It's free."

Olivia eyed the figurine. "No, thanks. This one is for me. I appreciate your time."

Darcy nodded. "Hey, you know, sometimes people say things they don't really mean when they're angry."

Olivia offered a polite smile, and after paying for the ornament, she left the forever Christmas store.

Darcy didn't strike her as a blackmailer, but desperate mothers could do desperate things to protect their children. Though Olivia couldn't rule out Darcy as a suspect in the blackmail scheme, her active role in the caper seemed dubious. Her brother wasn't shy about expressing his disdain for his father, and he, too, would do anything for Kaitlyn. The Carters knew about the connection between Stuart and the stolen necklace, thanks to Mack's spilling the beans. Did Darcy and Dylan have it in them to concoct the blackmail scheme to get money for Kaitlyn's medical treatment? Both children had exonerated Ed lightning quick. Was that to protect their mother or to cover up something her fiancé did?

Olivia crossed the street, aiming for where she had parked near A.J.'s office. His truck was now behind her Expedition, hinting that he was inside handling his weekend business. She decided to pop in and say hi, keeping her promise to drop by. Besides, after speaking to the Carters and not turning up a solid lead, she was unsure if there was anything else she could do at this point to help Bev.

CHAPTER 21

The blue neon "open" sign A.J. had installed last week inside his suite's front window shone bright, welcoming weekend walk-ins needing home repairs before the holidays. Olivia tripped a motion sensor as she entered, triggering a double chime. A.J. stepped out of the back storage area, wiping his hands with a towel.

He was a few years older than Olivia, but they'd spent much of their childhood as best buds playing together between their neighboring homes. Summer nights often saw them camped out in a tent in Olivia's backyard, sharing stories, secrets, and dreams under the stars. A.J. was tall and athletic, and as a teen, he always wrangled her into playing pickup games of soccer and football with his friends. They were as close as could be, and no one was dearer to her except for her father and Sophia.

"Hey, Liv," he said. "Now, my day is looking up. How are you doing?"

"I'm fine."

He tossed his towel toward a desk but came up a few feet short. "Air ball. That didn't sound fine. Maybe you didn't see my sign."

She glanced around, wondering what she'd missed.

"The open sign," he clarified. "Isn't she a beauty?" He grabbed her hand, dragging her to the window. "Come, take a closer look."

"It's a sign. I saw it last week when you put it up."

He held his face up to the glowing glass tubes, filling in the middle of the "O" with his head. "It's not just a sign." He stepped back and gestured with his hands as if showcasing a cinema marquee. "It says—I'm open."

She matched his theatrics, holding her hands under the sign. "Do you also have one that says—I'm a moron?"

He rubbed his chin like a philosophy professor contemplating the Socratic method. "I never thought of that. Your knowledge is vast, and the force is growing strong within you, young Jedi."

His wisecrack lightened her mood. "It's a very nice sign, Mr. Entrepreneur. I'm proud of you."

He gathered her in with a side hug. "That wasn't so hard, was it?"

"Will I have to compliment your sign every time I come here?"

"For the first six months, definitely." He grasped her

hand and pinky swore for her. "There. Now you're obligated."

"Or what?"

"Something terribly cosmic and catastrophic will happen. I wouldn't risk it if I were you."

"Oh, well, in that case. I don't want to be the cause of parallel universes colliding."

His eyes glazed as he pretended to be stunned like a deer in headlights. "That's way deep and over my head." He beamed a smile. "I love you all the same. Here, give me your coat."

"I wasn't planning on staying long. I came into town earlier, and I was heading out when I saw your truck parked outside."

"Since you're here, can you lend me a hand?"

She nodded, unbuttoning her coat. "Of course. Or should I first ask what for?"

"Trust. That's the word I'm meditating on today." He helped remove her coat and then laid it on a nearby desk.

"Thanks. When did you start meditating?"

He formed a mudra with his hands and closed his eyes a moment before he spoke. "Soph showed me an app she uses. I'm getting into it." Then he waved for her to follow him. "Come with."

She walked with him into his back shop, which also served as a storage area for equipment. The normally neat space was in disarray. Groupings of similar tools dotted the floor, while piles of trash lined the wall near the rear exit.

"What on earth are you doing in here?" she asked. "And perhaps more pertinent, what am I lending you a hand with?"

"I'm reorganizing."

"I can see that."

"I could use your expertise with this." He picked up a bucket of nuts and bolts and set it on a workbench next to a pair of empty plastic containers. "I need you to separate the nuts and bolts into two boxes."

She eyed the full bucket. "Me? You need *me* to do this?"

He wrapped an arm around her shoulders, pleading with a plaintive smile. "I love you, Liv." When she didn't even twitch, he begged, "Please?" He reached to his side and pulled over a high stool. "You can even have a seat."

She sat, laughing at herself for being hoodwinked. "Wow, you make it hard for a girl to say no. This seems an awful lot like busy work."

"It is. That's why I don't want to do it. I was fixing cabinets at the Peabodys' one day last week, and every time I'm there, Floyd shows me his garage. He has tools up the wazoo that I'm sure he never uses anymore. He has a beautiful, almost brand-new miter saw—"

"Wait," she said. "I've heard the name, but don't know what it does."

"Pardon, madame. I forgot you're a *writer.* It's a circular type of saw for making precision angle and cross cuts. It's great for carpentry work. Anyway, as I was saying before today's tool talk, Floyd keeps everything.

He's a complete pack rat, and when I was there, he asked me if I wanted this random collection of nuts and bolts. Apparently, Dorothy has been on him to clean up the space, and he thought giving me the bucket would help the cause."

"I'm sure that's exactly what she was thinking about when issuing that directive." Olivia changed her tone, impersonating Dorothy. "If he would just get rid of that bucket of bolts, everything would be so much neater."

A.J. clapped. "Bravo! I'm impressed. For a minute, I thought Dorothy was right here with me." He tipped the bucket, rattling the contents around. "It was very nice of him to give these to me. Sometimes I need odd sizes or extras, and having stock like this comes in handy. It's even handier when they're separated."

She nodded. "I get it. Say no more. I'm your gal." She began her task, guesstimating she'd be done by dinnertime. "Why are you keeping the office opened today?"

He heaved a heavy box off the floor and carried it past her. "You never know. Somebody buying a last-minute gift for a loved one may suddenly remember they need a ceiling fan installed. Who doesn't want to support the local hometown handyman during the holidays? Or perhaps somebody is looking for a unique present. Nothing says Merry Christmas more than a gift certificate for roof repair." He set the box on the floor next to a tool chest and walked over to the tall table, examining

Olivia's work. "Excellent technique. Have you done this before?"

She jabbed his ribs in jest. "I'm buying you that moron sign for the front window. Customized with your name."

His eyes lit up as he folded his hands in a prayerful pose. "Oh, please!"

"I can never win with you," she teased.

"As soon as you accept that, the better we'll both be. So, what brings you into town today? I'm sure it wasn't for nuts and bolts."

Where to even begin? Though she trusted A.J. with her life, it wasn't her place, nor was it the time, to bring him into all that had happened over the past two days. "I had some business at the inn, and then I went to the Christmas shop."

"When you came in, you looked—don't get angry—a little stressed. Just saying."

She plinked down several bolts with extra oomph. "What would make you think that?"

"Come on now, those bolts never crossed you. Take it easy on them."

"How's the playground construction going?" she asked, spinning the conversation on end.

"I see what you did there," he replied. "Classic Liv Penn technique. Change the subject so quickly you think I didn't even notice. But I'm clever."

She grabbed a handful of bolts and stood, smiling. "Extraordinarily clever." Then she pulled the collar of his flannel shirt away from his neck and dropped the fistful of bolts down inside.

A.J. jumped back. "Oh, you—I can't believe you did that!" He untucked his shirt, letting the bolts fall and clink on the concrete floor. He held up his hands in mock surrender. "Truce. I'm totally afraid of where you'll try to jam the nuts."

She sat back on the stool, laughing as he picked the bolts up off the floor.

"The playground, since that seems to be a safe topic, is coming along," he said. "My contractor has finished clearing the site, and Soph is consulting with the designer on the equipment and access the playground will need. My lawyer is handling the legal stuff with the town government."

A.J. was working with local authorities and subcontractors to build a special needs playground on a piece of property he had inherited last May. His lawyer had devised a deal that would have him donate an acre of ground to the town with provisions for the use, insurance, and funding of the land. A.J. had hatched the scheme one day after talking to Sophia about the lack of playgrounds nearby that were accessible and safe for children with special needs. After he negotiated a mix of private and public funding, the town council had agreed to the deal. He had kept his plans secret until the contracts were signed and then surprised his friends, revealing the project at Sophia's family's Día De Los Muertos celebration in November.

"What about your house?" she asked.

A.J. told her about the timetable and construction of the home he was building for himself on the same property, as she worked her way through the bucket like a pro.

"Do you ever talk to the woman who bought that acreage on the far end of the property?" she asked.

"No. I've never even met her. The lawyers handled everything. I see trucks coming and going on the road that winds up to the site, but I don't go back there. They're not causing any problems, and it's no longer my property."

Twenty minutes into her task, she dropped the last bolt into the box and brushed her hands together. "There you are. All done."

"You're better than sliced bread, Liv."

She swiveled on the stool to face him as he stepped toward her. "I'm not sure everybody thinks that."

He held her eyes for a moment. "Something you wanna talk about?"

She glanced off to her side. Without the distraction of the mechanical task, her thoughts shot straight to Preston's pointed words, feeling as though she'd just heard them for the first time.

"Look, you don't have to say anything. If it's none of my business ..."

"No, it's not that. I had a dustup with Preston this morning."

He pulled another stool closer and sat next to her. "What about?"

She pinned her elbow to the table and rested her chin on her hand. "I can't talk about the details. Sorry. It's an active police investigation."

"Liv, are you mixed up in something again?" He grabbed her hand. "Please tell me you're not putting yourself in danger."

She shook her head, giving his hand a slight squeeze. "No. It's nothing like that. I can't go into it, but his mother is involved."

He blew out a slow breath. "That's tough. Coming between a mother and her son. I thought Bev was in favor of you and Preston sitting in a tree, k-i-s-s-i-n-g."

She withdrew her hand from his hold and playfully whacked his arm.

"Sorry," he said. "I'm such a child sometimes."

"Bev's not the problem. Preston is angry about what he feels is me overstepping into his mother's life."

"Is he right?"

"It's complicated."

"That's why I try to live a simple life, so that we balance each other out." A.J gave her a sympathetic smile as they stood. "Whatever happened, give it time. Sometimes when men get angry, present company excluded, they can be oafs and say things they regret later."

"I don't think this is going to blow over."

"Remember my word for the day—trust. I don't know Preston all that well, but I saw the way he was looking at you when we were together with Soph's family last month. I know you, though, and it's been a while since I've seen you as lit up as when you were talking with him that day. With you, what you see is what you get. You weren't faking then, and I don't think he was either."

She wrapped her arms around him, settling in for a hug. "Thanks. You're the best."

He gently pecked her cheek. "No, you are. Because there is no one else in my life who would separate a bucket of nuts and bolts for me."

"That's what friends are for," she replied as they released each other.

A.J.'s cell rang, and he turned toward the back door where his coat hung on a rack. "Excuse me. Let me get that. Could be a million-dollar contract."

She walked out into the front of the office, giving him privacy, and sat on the edge of the desk, considering her next move. She had discovered a few pieces of the puzzle regarding the blackmail threat. But they were like the bucket of nuts and bolts—all jumbled up, without knowing which parts fit together. The link between the blackmail and Stuart's death remained unclear, but one suspect who had a motive for both was Ed. Could he be the connection tying them together? And were the Carters conspiring to cover for him?

She picked up her coat and reached into her pocket for her phone, wanting to contact Cassandra to see if she'd wheedled any more details from the police. Finding the pocket empty, she checked the other one, coming up zero for two.

She dove into both pockets again, only finding a few of the candies she'd swiped from the inn's counter. "Oh, no." Her eyes scanned the floor, and then she lowered onto her hands and knees, searching under the desk.

A.J. walked out into the office. "Liv, what are you doing?"

"I can't find my phone." She stood, muttering a frustrated grunt. "Shih tzu. It's not here."

"When do you last remember having it?"

"I put it in my coat pocket this morning. Before I came here, I was at the Christmas store, but I didn't use it there. I was also at the inn. You know what? I took my coat off in Bev's office, and it could've fallen out in there."

"You want me to call to see if they have it?"

She slipped her coat on. "No, I'll run over and check. Besides, you have a lot of work back there, Mr. Entrepreneur. How'd the million-dollar contract pan out?"

He growled a throaty pirate "arrr." "Blimey. It was only a return call from a supplier. But the day is still young, matey."

She stepped backward toward the door. "Good luck, Jack Sparrow."

"Thanks. Be careful and don't get yourself into any trouble. Remember, trust."

"Will do. Love you." She held up her pinky, pointing at his window sign. "And I love that you're open."

He chuckled, holding up his pinky too. "You always say the sweetest things. Love you too."

CHAPTER 22

Zoey brimmed with a bubbly grin, greeting Olivia as she approached the lobby's counter. "Hiya. Let me guess, you're here to see Bev."

"That seems to be happening a lot recently," Olivia replied. "But no. I was in her office earlier, and I think my phone may have fallen out of my coat pocket in there."

Zoey's peppy smile plummeted as her green eyes rounded, grasping the gravity of the situation. "Wait here. I'm sure we'll find it. Don't panic." She whipped out from behind the counter and scurried through the lobby, weaving between a father toting four suitcases and two grandmothers struggling to corral his three children.

Faint chatter drifting from the dining room hinted that the lunch crowd had thinned. Olivia meandered toward the entrance and looked inside, focusing on a rustic round table near the fireplace. She recalled a day last May when Bev had wrangled her and Preston in here, dragging them both reluctantly to that table where they shared their first meal.

So much had changed over the course of the year. Last December, she was nearly engaged and living in D.C. During a weekend visit with her father before Christmas, she had brought Buddy home, bundled in a basket, to give to him as a gift. Now, they couldn't imagine their house without their loyal beagle in it, and she didn't miss her previous life in the city one bit. Her former relationship had ended without bitterness or regret. And perhaps on that afternoon in May, a new romance had been kindled at that round table, with a little nudging from Bev.

She turned as Zoey raced toward her, holding out a phone at arm's length. "Is this it?" she asked.

Olivia recognized the paw-print sticker on the case. "You saved the day."

Zoey handed it to her. "I get it. There was one time when I lost mine for two *whole* days, and it wasn't pretty. It was like being hangry on steroids."

She placed the phone in her pants pocket for safe-keeping. "Thanks for finding it."

"Right-o!" Zoey said, scooting around the lobby counter.

As Olivia turned to leave, Bev's boisterous laughter bellowed out from the dining room. She glanced inside, thinking about saying hi, and spotted Bev chatting with a patron who was eating alone at a table for two near the entrance. Bev stepped to the side, still speaking with the diner, and Olivia froze upon seeing John Mack.

She withdrew from view ninja-quick, hoping Mack hadn't noticed her just a few feet from him. She counted to ten-Mississippi like a tired tortoise and then poked her head around the corner. Bev and Mack were bantering and laughing like bosom buddies. For someone supposedly investigating off-the-grid, Mack was suddenly rather easy to locate.

Bev said something to him, and then she turned and stepped to a nearby table, greeting a party of five. He picked up his phone and tapped out either a brief message or a note to himself. After finishing, he set the cell on his napkin, took a sip of his drink, and surveyed the other patrons in the room. Olivia backed away from the entrance and padded to the lobby desk.

"Hi, Olivia!" Zoey chirped, as if it had been weeks since they'd last seen each other.

Olivia leaned over the counter, keeping her voice discreet. "Can I ask you for another favor?"

Zoey drew in close, matching Olivia's hushed tone. "Do you want me to get Bev for you?"

"Please. Thanks. You're a mind reader."

Zoey nodded and whispered, "I know." Then she turned and zipped into the dining room as Olivia walked toward the rear of the lobby.

Within a minute, Bev emerged, and Olivia waved her over to where she was waiting near the staircase leading to the second floor.

"Olivia, I want to apologize again for Preston's behavior."

She cut Bev off. "That's not why I'm here. You were talking to a man in the dining room who was eating alone."

Bev paused as if rewinding the past ten minutes. "Yes."

Olivia kept one eye on the dining room entrance, readying to bolt up the steps should Mack walk out into the lobby. He was unaware of Olivia's close connection to Bev's family, and for now, she wanted to keep it that way.

"Do you know who he is?" Olivia asked.

Bev nodded. "His name is Joseph, but he goes by Joe, just like my husband. He's been coming in here off and on for about a month. He travels through the area often, and he said he saw a five-star review for our restaurant, so he wanted to try our menu. He's been here at least half a dozen times and is always very pleasant to talk to. He's a big fan of our country ham and apple crumble."

Olivia drew in closer. "His name isn't Joseph or Joe. That's John Mack. He's the PI who I spoke with."

Bev's eyes went blank. "What? I don't understand." She glanced at the dining room and then turned back to Olivia. "Why would he … He lied to me?" She lowered her voice to a whisper. "Do you think he's the blackmailer?"

"It's a possibility."

"I can't believe he's been lying to me all this time. But

he was so nice to me. He said this was his favorite place to eat. He called himself by my husband's name. Why would he do that?"

"To get you to like and trust him. It's not your fault. He's been playing all of us. What have you two been talking about?"

"Nothing important. Mostly small talk about the town and our families. He was interested in the inn's history, so I told him a good deal about that. I gave him a tour one day when it wasn't busy. He asked me how much it cost to insure the inn, and that struck me as odd. Zoey came in and pulled me away for something, so I never answered him."

"Does he always come alone?"

Bev nodded. "Except once. He met a younger colleague for lunch last week."

Ten to one, his acquaintance was Nolan, and the true target of Mack's off-the-grid investigation and stakeout was Bev.

"What should I do?" Bev asked.

Olivia glanced at the door. "Act normal. If he comes back or you speak with him again, don't let on that you know who he is. He's done nothing wrong other than lie about his identity to you. I don't think your son is going to be too enthusiastic about hearing any theories from me right now about Mack's motives. Let me handle Mack. Do this. Go back and mingle around in the dining room as you normally would. When Mack leaves, text me. Do you think you can do that?"

Bev nodded. "Yes. Act normal."

Olivia gave her a quick hug. "You've got this."

"Be careful, Olivia."

They said a whispered goodbye, and Olivia hurried out of the inn. She rushed across the street and cut straight through the town square's light displays to her car. After hopping inside, she pulled away from the curb, U-turned by the dumpsters behind the inn, and then parked halfway up the narrow alley. If anyone needed to get past, they'd be out of luck because the car wasn't moving until Mack left the building.

She hastened to the sidewalk, crossed the street, and sat on an empty bench in front of the bookstore. The vantage gave her a clear view of the inn's entrance while she waited for Bev's text. A steady stream of pedestrians moseyed by, helping her blend in as a Sunday shopper. On Friday night, in the dark, she hadn't thought to note the color, make, and model of his sedan. He could've parked anywhere, and she spied three cars along the street that all looked like his. She didn't have time to circle the square, hoping to guess correctly. Instead, she would wait until he left the inn and, fingers crossed, walked straight to his sedan. Then she would turn the tables, tailing him to his next off-the-grid location.

CHAPTER 23

The wrought-iron bench's frozen slats cut straight through Olivia's jeans. An overhead awning helped to obscure her from a distance, but it cast her in a chilly shadow. She hadn't dressed this morning for a stakeout, sitting in the shade on a thirty-degree day. If Mack milled around town, her plan may need rethinking.

A few minutes passed like she'd been ice fishing for an hour on a frozen Minnesota lake. Her phone buzzed once. She kept her head bowed, anticipating Mack's exit at any second. She watched and waited, prepping to spring from the bench once he showed his face. Half a minute went by, but there was no movement in or out of the inn. Her phone buzzed again, and then she glanced at the screen, discovering both messages were from her father. The first was a picture of snowball cookies piled together, forming an igloo. The second was a caption identifying the photo, as if it wasn't self-explanatory. She thumbed a quick reply, remarking on the marvel of his culinary creations.

Hoping Mack wouldn't linger much longer, she wiggled her fingers and toes, encouraging blood flow to her extremities. She mulled over Mack's murky motivation to distract herself from the windchill factor. The connection between the blackmail and the murder remained fuzzy. So, too, was whether Mack had the opportunity and means for either crime. Like the nuts and bolts, deciphering which pieces of the puzzle fit together would be easier if she could separate them. All her suspects mingled in a catchall bucket, and she needed to create two piles: potential blackmailers and potential murderers.

She blew on her hands, promising her frigid fingertips it wouldn't be much longer. She looked at her messages, opened her last thread with Cassandra, and texted, "Ed Graham, Stacey's fiancé, mechanic at Jed's Auto Body, threatened Stuart. Might be worth looking into his background."

The reply came double-quick, proving Cassandra was never far from her phone when a juicy story was in play. She replied, "Interesting. Good lead. Will check it out. Nothing new from the police. TTYL."

Olivia kept her cell in hand while huddling with her coat buttoned all the way to the top. Locals and visitors passed by with rosy red cheeks, carrying shopping bags or steaming cups of warming drinks. Christmas was a few days away, and she still had gifts to buy and wrap. The intention of her two-week vacation had been to relax, spending time with friends and enjoying the slower pace of the season. Instead, she was knee-deep in another murder investigation, and the prospect of downtime was dwindling.

The idea of retreating to her office to write fiction was increasingly appealing. She had tabled her manuscript after her near-death experience in October and had given little thought to doing anything with it since. After the new year, she planned on revisiting whether publication was still on her long-term agenda.

Her phone buzzed with a text from Bev, confirming Mack had paid for his meal and was preparing to leave. She leaned forward and fiddled with her shoes, lowering her profile to lessen the chances of being seen.

Mack exited the inn, strolling down the sidewalk in the opposite direction from her. He crossed Cider Lane, rounding the rear bumper of a run-of-the-mill silver sedan parked between two SUVs. She stood and went to the top of the alley. Then she opened her phone's camera, focused on Mac's vehicle, and magnified the view. He got into the sedan and started the engine, shooting out a white stream of exhaust from the tailpipe.

She turned and bolted to her car, hopping in quicker than a hungry fox chasing a hare. By the time she pulled out to the street, Mack was already over two blocks away. She pushed her speed right to the town's snail-paced limit and made rolling stops at two intersections when no cars or pedestrians were in her way.

He drove a circuitous route out of town and wound up on Somerset Turnpike, traveling in the direction of where the police had found Stuart's car. With no other vehicles between them, she maintained a healthy distance, figuring he kept one eye glued to his rearview. She lost sight of the sedan as he went up and over a hill about a quarter mile ahead. After cresting the peak, she hit the brakes, watching as he pulled over onto the shoulder fifty yards from her.

A few salty words escaped her, but she carried on, determined to finish the pursuit she'd started. After checking her mirrors, she veered off the road and parked within ten feet of his bumper. As she unfastened her seat belt, he stepped out of his car, sporting a friendly smile. She waited until an oncoming car passed by and then slid out of her seat, closed the door, and met him halfway between their vehicles.

He gestured toward the grass. "Should we take this someplace safer?" After they moved farther away from the road, he continued. "Where's your bodyguard today?"

"She's working off-the-grid. Maybe you'll run into her, since that's where you're supposed to be right now, Joseph—Joe—John, whatever you go by on Sundays."

"You have chutzpah for stopping on the side of the road. For all you know, I could be a murderer."

"Are you?" she asked in a beat.

He cracked a wry smile. "No. By the way, next time

you follow someone, use a car that's less conspicuous. Nolan said you were looking for me."

"Why are you continuing to investigate the Star of Athens heist?"

He shrugged his shoulders while adjusting his glasses. "I'm not the bad guy, if that's what you're thinking. Why? Simple. This is a treasure hunt. I believe the necklace is still someplace in your charming town."

Though her hands were cold, she kept them out of her pockets, holding both up in a subtle self-defense stance. "You're trying to find the necklace, and then what? You could never sell it."

"I wouldn't want to. There's a substantial reward for its return."

"What makes you think that it's still here?"

He placed his hands in his pockets, casually standing as if talking to a buddy. "I believe that's why Stuart returned to Apple Station. It was all part of his plan to turn his life around. He retrieves the necklace, fences it, and then wins back his family with money."

"Did you speak with Stuart after his release?" she asked.

His cell buzzed, and he removed it from his coat pocket, checking the screen. "People like Stuart never change."

She ignored his evasiveness, knowing whatever he said had to be taken with a grain of salt, anyway. "Why have you been staking out the inn and chumming it up with Bev?"

"That's what I do. I investigate."

She glanced over her shoulder, hearing a car coming from behind, and spoke as it passed. "Do you think Joe Hills was involved?"

He shook his head. "That's the fifteen-million-dollar question."

"What about Stuart's family? You talked to them. What's your impression?"

He flashed a thin grin. "Are you sure you're not a PI? You're asking all the right questions, and if I were you, I would be skeptical of me too." He blew out a full breath. "The Carters. I should ask you the same. Someone in the family is involved. Maybe the entire lot of them, excluding little Kaitlyn. If I had to place money on it, I'd say the son tops the list. Like father, like son. That apple didn't fall far from the tree. He's as much of a hothead as Stuart was. It's no secret Dylan hated his father."

"I've met Dylan, and although what you say about his feelings is true, he's nothing like Stuart."

Mack smirked. "How can you say that? You've never met Stuart, and you've talked with Dylan how many times? He's had his run-ins with the law, just like his father. Look at him now. A white hat hacker? Give me a break. He's probably stealing information from the companies he's supposedly protecting. Dylan is so smart that they wouldn't even know it. Getting paid by the people he's hacking. What a gig."

Mack had a point about Dylan, though his expertise seemed more in line with blackmail than murder. The fact he had mentioned nothing specific about Bev suggested he was hiding something or may not be aware of the blackmail threat.

"Do you really think somebody in Stuart's family would kill him?" she asked.

"Stuart was a scumbag. I'm sure he had a lot of enemies besides those in his family. Who knows how many others he could've ticked off in the three weeks since his release. His son hated him. His mother's boyfriend threatened him. What do those two have in common? Who are they trying to protect?"

She followed his logic, unable to argue with his deductions. "Stacey. You think she was involved with his murder?"

"What did Shakespeare say? Something like there's no greater anger than a woman scorned. You look incredulous. Believe me, it's not as far-fetched as you think."

A pickup whizzed by as they both stood silent for a moment. Mack's targeting of the Carters wasn't off base, and yet her instinct niggled that he was still withholding information.

"I hope I've answered your questions," he said. "I'm not the bad guy here. I'm trying to return a piece of stolen property to the rightful owners."

"You've been lying to Bev about who you are. Using her husband's name to charm her is underhanded."

His cell buzzed again, and he peeked at the screen. "Demanding clients." He pocketed his phone. "PI work involves stretching the truth sometimes. Not everyone has the stomach for it, but it seems you do. Bev is nice, and I did nothing other than tell her a story. Nobody is who they say they are. I suppose you'll blow my cover now. It's a shame. I enjoyed the country ham and apple crumble. Now, I need to go. Something has come up."

"Stay away from Bev and the inn," she said.

He lit up with a Mr. Rogers smile. "No problem. I've already learned everything I wanted to know from her, anyway. I don't think you need to be following me anymore. Have a Merry Christmas." He turned and walked back to his car, and she did likewise without saying a word.

Once inside, she started the engine and dialed up the heat. She watched as he pulled away, using his blinker for safety, even though nobody was coming his way. Mack was a storyteller by trade, spinning the evidence to construct the narrative he wanted others to believe. He divulged enough facts for his story to make sense, but the connecting dots were missing, and therein lay the misdirection.

What Mack had wanted from Bev was unclear. Though he didn't have a solid motive for blackmail, there wasn't anything to exclude him from Olivia's suspect pool for Stuart's murder. When Allen had questioned Bev, he insinuated Stuart had been killed between 10:00 p.m. and midnight on Friday. Had Mack arranged the meeting at the lake at that odd time to construct an alibi? They had talked for only thirty minutes, and he could have murdered Stuart before or after. She bet that Mack, as an experienced fibber, could easily weave a web accounting for the time he wasn't with her.

Mack had targeted the Carter family, and she couldn't disagree with his assessment. Her work as an advice columnist had taught her that dysfunctional families can treat strangers better than kin. She fastened her seatbelt and thought about the brains behind Mack's operation, wondering if hackers like Dylan and Nolan traveled in the same dark web circles.

CHAPTER 24

Olivia glanced at the time on the console display as scattered flurries fell, melting in slow motion as they landed on the warm windshield. Though it was only half past three, sunset was less than two hours away. With low gray clouds streaming in, the daylight was rapidly waning. If Mack was truly on a treasure hunt, locating Joe's cabin would likely be his top priority. Despite the police already having searched it, that wouldn't stop him from doing a once-over. She removed her phone from her pocket, set it on the passenger seat, and voice dialed Bev.

"Hello, Olivia. I'm so glad it's you. I haven't been answering any calls from unknown numbers. Are you okay? What happened with the investigator?"

"I'm fine. I talked to Mack, and he won't be bothering you anymore. He knows you know he was lying to you."

"Did he say why he did it?"

"Not exactly. We can't trust him anyway. Did you tell him about your cabin?"

"We discussed it. He told me he liked the area and was thinking of building one for himself as a weekend getaway."

"Did you tell him where it was?"

Bev remained quiet for a moment and then spoke in a hushed voice. "Someone was passing by in the hallway. I'm in my office, but I closed my door. Not specifically."

Olivia would wager that the cabin's location was one of the key pieces of information he'd wanted to wheedle from Bev. "Have you spoken with Preston any more today?"

"Not so far," Bev said.

"Next time you do, tell him that all the Carters are in play as suspects in Stuart's murder."

Bev gasped. "His own family? I know they didn't get along, but I can't believe any of them would kill him."

"There's a lot of history and animosity among them. Tell Preston I talked to the family, and they confirmed that Stacey's fiancé threatened Stuart. The police spoke with the Carters, but I'm almost positive that's something they wouldn't have shared with them. I don't care if Preston gets upset this is coming from me, but he should know."

"Okay, I'll tell him. I'm also going to give him a piece of my mind about the way he spoke to you."

"It's no longer a concern of mine." She didn't mean

it by any stretch, but saying so kept her focused. "You told me neither you nor Preston have gone to the cabin often since Joe died."

"That's right."

"I assume Preston knew about Stuart's stay at the cabin."

"He wasn't living in Apple Station then. He didn't move back until Joe passed. My husband didn't even tell me everything about that night, and I never discussed it with Preston."

Olivia dialed down the heat and then cracked the window for a low flow of fresh air. "Preston has probably never searched the cabin or the surrounding area."

"If he has, he never said anything about it to me," Bev replied.

"Do you mind if I look around the cabin? I think there are others, Mack included, who want to do the same. I'd like to get there first."

"Do you really believe the necklace is there? The police already searched. Don't you think they would have found it?"

"I don't know. Someone believes it's still in Apple Station, and the only place we can pinpoint to search is the cabin. It may not be in the cabin itself. It could've been hidden in the woods or someplace close by. Who knows how thorough the search was three years ago. There's not much daylight left, and I'd like to look around before anyone else does."

"Okay. You'll need the key. I have a copy here at the inn, but I can't get away right now to bring it to you."

She checked her rearview mirror, and with no other cars coming in either direction, she U-turned and headed back into town. "I'm on my way."

As Olivia drove, Bev talked her through the directions to the cabin, adding that she would write them out as there were several turns and landmarks to keep track of. Without a GPS or a guide, anyone searching for it would need a lot of luck to even know where to begin.

She arrived in town, feeling a sense of déjà vu, and parked in front of the inn. As she walked into the lobby, Zoey greeted her with a sunny smile, pointing toward the back.

"Bev's in her office."

With a quick word of thanks, Olivia hastened through the lobby, weaving around guests like they were agility cones. She picked up the key from Bev and reviewed the directions again. The exchange took less than two minutes, and after promising to be careful, Olivia zipped back out into the lobby as Preston entered the inn. She slowed upon seeing him, and they met near the welcome counter.

Saying anything to him about her plans to search the cabin would be like throwing water on a grease fire. She'd leave it up to Bev to relate the suspicions surrounding the Carters. There was no time to debate any of it with him, knowing he'd only admonish her to stay away from his mother.

As for personal matters, she wanted to clear the air and take the temperature down between them. "I'm sorry for not telling you right away about the blackmail threat."

He glanced down, and then at her while avoiding her eyes. "What are you doing here now?"

She searched for a succinct answer that wouldn't mire her deeper in quicksand. Though she wouldn't lie, she felt no need to explain herself or seek his approval.

"Well, I guess that says everything," he said.

"I know that between Stuart's murder and what's happening with your mother, you don't have time. But after things get settled—"

"I can't talk about this now. If you need help with a police matter, call the station." He stepped around her and headed toward the back offices.

"Preston, please. Wait."

He stopped and turned as she stepped closer to him. "Look, Olivia. There are a lot of things I'm dealing with right now. It's hard enough handling the situation with my mother, let alone investigating a murder. I can't lose my focus. Please don't do anything that's going to make me worry about you too."

They held each other's eyes for a moment, and then he turned and walked away.

She stood still and watched as he opened the door leading to the back offices. His concern kindled some small hope that all wasn't lost between them. Or maybe the situation was about to get a lot worse once Bev told him about her suspicions arising from her visit with the Carters.

CHAPTER 25

Bev hadn't been kidding when warning Olivia that the cabin was tricky to find. The paved road off Somerset Turnpike gave way to a gravel lane, and by the fourth turn, she was driving on deeply rutted hardpack dirt. Dense brush from untamed thickets encroached on the narrow road, and she almost stopped twice, considering turning back.

According to Bev's directions, there was one last turn to make. If Olivia had followed them correctly, the cabin should be a short piece up ahead. She veered to the right at a fork in the road, spotting a landmark grouping of three pines. Just beyond the towering trees, a compact cabin nestled in the flourishing forest.

The bare-bones DIY project looked small but sturdy, designed as a simple rectangular box with a mossy, pitched shingle roof. The hunter-green front door was on the short side of the cabin facing the road. A tiny, white-framed window next to it served as an oversized peep-hole. A power line extended from the cabin's rear corner to a nearby lodgepole pine equipped with a transformer, and dead leaves, fallen branches, and unchecked weeds littered the ground. A wooden picnic table, rotted by rain, sat near collapse in the front yard.

She parked, got out, and paced around the cabin's perimeter, abandoning her plan to search the surrounding forest. The light was waning, and wading through the thick underbrush would be tempting fate. Twisting an ankle or surprising a sleeping snake weren't items on her to-do list today. After completing her walk around, she stood near the entrance and peered at the dirt road as it continued onward past the cabin.

She opened a mapping app on her phone. After dropping a pin at her location, she switched to view a satellite image of the area. The coordinates showed her standing in a small clearing in a clump of trees. She scrolled the map, tracing the road past the cabin to a larger nearby clearing surrounded by dense greenery.

With less than half an hour of daylight remaining, she got back behind the wheel and drove deeper into the woods, wondering if Bev had a neighbor. The first quarter mile rode as rough as the stretch leading to the cabin. Then, around a bend, the dirt lane became a wide paved road. Prominent "Private Property" and "No Tres-passing" signs were posted at frequent intervals. Two pole-mounted surveillance cameras warned that those who passed by were being watched and recorded.

A swing gate blocked the road ahead, and so she pulled up to it and stopped. Such extensive security this far back off the main road, in the middle of the forest, struck her as extraordinarily odd. This wasn't the rich rolling hills of Virginia's horse country with multi-million-dollar estates. Yet the paved road and surveillance spoke of someone who wanted privacy and had the means to ensure it.

After exiting her Expedition, she tramped through the brambly brush to circumvent the locked gate and then walked farther down the road. On her phone, the mapping app showed her location near the clearing on the satellite image. She continued onward for a short distance, quickening her pace upon spotting a large luxury cabin fifty yards ahead. Whereas Joe's cabin looked like a getaway man cave, this home would make the perfect cover photo for a country living magazine.

The house faced the road and had three distinct sections. The center featured an oversized, wood-framed bay window with an ornamental copper hood and a chimney. The large section to her left had steps leading to an open porch, which wrapped around the front and side of the cabin. The opposite end boasted a second porch, showcasing lavish stonework and a full-length wood awning. Strings of colored lights decorated the porch railings, and the dark honey-stained exterior conveyed warmth and coziness. Pine trees dotted the front yard, and dense forest surrounded the sides and back of the home.

With dusk descending, warm lamplight glowed through the uncovered windows. As she was reconning the house, watching for movement, loud, guttural barking made her jump. Pivoting a quarter turn, she faced a charging German shepherd a stone's throw away. She backpedaled a few steps but then stopped, knowing running would only incite the shepherd to chase. Doubting yelling "good dog" or "sit" would do the trick, her mind raced through self-defense tactics, most of which pertained to bear attacks.

Movement twenty yards behind the shepherd split her focus. A woodsman carrying a rifle was tramping through the dead leaves, trailing his canine companion. He was well-dressed, wearing a green barn coat over a collared shirt and khaki pants. Judging by his thinned gray hair and sagging jaw, she pegged him to be in his sixties.

"Who are you?" he snarled.

She homed in on the shepherd, who had stopped five feet from her. "My name is Olivia Penn. Call off your dog."

"Get off my property! You're trespassing."

"Call off your dog," she repeated without daring to move an inch.

He whistled. "Come here, Daisy."

The shepherd quieted, turned, and padded to his side.

"Now, get off my property."

After trekking all this way and facing down the shepherd, she wasn't about to leave without seeking the answers she'd come for. "There's a cabin a short distance from here, down that way. Do you know the owners?"

"What's it to you?"

"I'm a friend of Bev Styles and her son. Bev's late husband, Joe, spent a lot of time there. Did you know him?"

He gauged her with suspicion. "Yes."

It was a start, but she knew better than to ask yes or no questions when wanting elaboration. "How well did you know him?"

He bent down, running his hand over Daisy's head several times. "Why are you asking?"

"I'm trying to help Joe's family. Were you a friend of his?"

"Sometimes when he came to stay, he would drop by and say hello. I've never met his wife or son."

She glanced at the luxury cabin, guessing this was his residence and not a vacation home. He hadn't volunteered his name, but she let it go, betting Bev would know him. "Your house is far back in the woods, way off the road. You'd be a hard person to find if someone was looking for you."

"I like my privacy. Didn't you see the no trespassing signs?"

"I did. And the gate and the security cameras. This is a fortress you have for being so far off the beaten path. Have you lived here long?"

"Almost five years."

That put him in play for being in the area the night Stuart stayed at the cabin. "Can I ask you about a night three years ago? I realize a lot of time has passed since, but something happened at Joe's cabin on Christmas Eve back then. The next day, there was a lot of police activity at his place. Do you remember anything about that night or the following day?"

He grimaced, setting the rifle's heel on the ground. "Three years ago? How would I remember anything from then? I live here alone, and I don't bother anyone. I don't know anything about what happened then."

She doubted that. For someone so concerned with security, he almost certainly would've known about unusual activity at Joe's cabin, especially since it seemed they'd been friendly.

She looked at the rifle and then back at him. "On Friday, the police found a body a little way from his cabin. Did you hear any gunshots that night? Say, sometime between ten and midnight?"

"I think you should go now. Leave or I'll call the police."

She held up her hands. "Okay. I'm going. Sorry to bother you." She walked backward a few steps, waiting to turn until he did the same.

"And stay off my property," he yelled over his shoulder. "Come on, Daisy."

As soon as he headed toward his house, Olivia hastened away, peeking behind her a few times to ensure she wasn't being followed. Then she retraced the trampled path through the brush around the swing gate and climbed into her Expedition.

After several three-point turns, she was on her way, driving back toward Joe's cabin. With the light fading, she could now only do a cursory search of the interior. The fact that Joe had a friendly neighbor who placed a premium on privacy and security may be the most valuable information she would glean from this excursion.

CHAPTER 26

Olivia unlocked the cabin's front door, pushed it open, and stepped to the side, wary of scaring any critters who had claimed the seldom used hideaway as a home. Mice skittering to their holes, she could handle, but trapped bats and spooked raccoons were best left alone in the wild kingdom.

When the coast was clear, she entered the cabin and walked straight into a kitchenette furnished with counters, cabinets, and a table with two chairs. The refrigerator's low hum confirmed that Bev kept the electricity running, despite hardly ever visiting. Skimming her hand along the wall next to the door, she located a light switch. Flipping it up and down several times had no effect. Slivers of natural light from a pair of curtain-covered windows did little to illuminate the back half of the cabin.

She turned on her phone's flashlight function and

stepped through the kitchen toward an all-in-one room with wood flooring. Sweeping her cell from side to side, she spied a twin bed and a nightstand along the wall on her right. Across from it sat a sofa and a recliner, positioned in front of a large-screen TV. All seemed tidy, but a spring cleaning was in order, and the musty air hinted that the roof may be leaking.

The sparse interior offered few prime hiding spots, so a thorough search wouldn't take long at all. The worn floorboards cracked as she paced toward the back, where a door in the rear corner was partway open. In her initial walk around, she had noticed an addition built onto the cabin with a small window and a vent, betting it was a bathroom. Opening the door confirmed her guess, as the cramped room contained a toilet, sink, and mirror. She could understand Bev's ambivalence about staying here for any length of time. Though wired for electricity and with indoor plumbing, its rustic condition didn't inspire a cozy, romantic vibe.

Scanning around, she decided to search systematically, progressing from front to back. She strode to the kitchenette and opened the higher cabinets, finding them well stocked with plates, pots, and pans. After shuffling the contents and not spotting anything strange, she shifted to the lower cabinets, starting with the nearest end unit. She shoved aside a hodgepodge of cleaning supplies, spying a small hole, about the size of a hand, in the back. The cabinet was too deep from where she was kneeling to see into the gap. She would need to crawl inside.

Before committing to covering her coat in unknown grime, she stood, checking the space between the wall and cabinet for any hint of what lay on the other side. As she bent down, shining her phone's light at the slim gap, meaty hands wrapped around her mouth and waist.

Her phone thunked on the floor, and she twisted like a squirming worm in vain. With her arms pinned, she kicked back, aiming for a shin. Her heart pumped in quick, strong pulses, and she breathed in rapid, shallow puffs through her nose. Then her feet left the floor, and she lost all leverage, leaving a reverse headbutt as the best counterattack. Certain this would harm her more than him, she stilled, baiting the bullyboy to relax his hold. As he loosened his grip, a flashlight clicked on, and her eyes clamped shut, blocking the painful, blinding beam.

"Let her go," a woman said.

The cool white LED light turned off, and the beefy biceps holding her released on cue. She scampered away, nearly out of breath and cagey as a cornered cat. With a click, an overhead light came on, and she stared through spots in disbelief at the two familiar faces in front of her.

The last time she had seen the pair was in October at Whispering Meadows Country Club. Back then, Ms. Butler was a concierge, dressed in a prim pencil skirt, whose delight was providing the club's guests with exceptional service. Now, she sported a moto leather jacket with matching black pants, looking like an undercover operative from *La Femme Nikita*.

The bulging arms that had crushed her ribs belonged to the golf pro she well remembered for his sparkling smile, tight pants, and offer of private lessons. Rhett still looked like an A1 hunk, and at least now, she knew what it felt like to have his behemoth biceps holding her.

She looked back and forth between them, struggling to make sense of the scene. It was like the shock of seeing your kindergarten teacher in the real world for the first time, flummoxed that she didn't live at the school.

"What's going on?" Olivia demanded, in between gulps of air. "Where'd you come from? Why are you here?"

"Sorry about the manhandling," Rhett said with a wink. "You've got good core strength."

Such a compliment normally would've delighted her, but under the circumstances, it seemed like a bizarre thing to say. "Who are you two?"

"We're the security team Bev hired to look into the blackmail threat she received," Butler said.

Olivia stared at them, relaxing her stance and about ready to give up on making heads or tails of anything that had happened to her today. The spots were dissipating, and her mouth was desiccated, tinged with a hint of garlic thanks to whatever Rhett had eaten for lunch. She stepped over to the sofa and plunked down, needing a moment to take it all in.

She looked at Butler, gauging whether, in fact, she

had grasped the situation correctly. "You're not a concierge at Whispering Meadows?"

"Negative," Butler replied.

Then she pointed at Rhett. "And you're not a golf pro."

"No, ma'am. But I can teach you how to grip a club, swivel, and swing."

Butler groaned. "Put a sock in it, Cro-Mag."

That Rhett wasn't an actual golf instructor struck her as a shame, as she'd considered signing up for lessons from him in the spring. Now that dream was dashed, as was her fantasy of him with his comment.

"Are you two private investigators?" Olivia asked. "What are your real names?"

"My last name is Butler, but you can call me Rho. We're contractors, not PIs."

Rhett dropped onto the sofa next to her. "I'm good with Rhett, and you can call me anytime."

His two hundred plus pounds caved in the cushion they shared, causing her to lurch into his shoulder. She offered a thin smile, sliding away from him to the end of the sofa. When Bev had told her about hiring consultants, she'd pictured IT specialists, not mercenaries who looked like Spec Ops action figures.

"What were you doing at Whispering Meadows?" Olivia asked.

Rho went over, picked up Olivia's phone, and handed it back to her. "We were on a job."

"Cool location for undercover work," Rhett added.

"We were following a husband whose wife thought he was spending too much time there."

"Meaning what?" Olivia said.

Rho crossed her arms. "She thought he was having an affair."

"Turns out he spent almost no time there at all," Rhett said. "We tracked him to a hotel where he was spending *a lot* of time and money, if you know what I mean."

"Got it," Olivia replied before he elaborated far more than she wanted to hear. "What are you doing here now? And where did you come from? I didn't see your car when I drove up."

"Bev told us you were coming, so we wanted to check it out too. We've already been through the place. When we heard a car pulling up, we got out and hid to see who it was. We're parked down the road. Which reminds me …" She removed her phone from her jacket pocket and dialed. When the call connected, she said, "Bev, it's Rho. We did a once-over of the cabin, but we didn't find anything. We ran into your friend … Okay." She handed the cell to Olivia. "She wants to speak with you."

Olivia took the phone, and as Rhett moved closer, she stood and walked to the center of the room. "Bev, *this* is your security team?"

"I'm sorry. I should've warned you they were coming. I hope they didn't scare you."

"Other than the part about fearing for my life, all's dandy." She lowered her voice, even though doing so had zero discretionary effect. "Does Preston know about them?"

"Not yet."

Olivia grunted. "Bev!"

"We're all working for the same goal," Bev replied. "How about the three of you return to the inn, and then we can all get on one page with what we know."

"That page has got to include your son," Olivia said.

"Yes, of course."

"Fine. We're on our way. See you soon. Bye." She handed the phone to Rho. "Bev wants us to gather at the inn."

Rhett stood, and they all strode out of the cabin. As Rho lingered a minute to lock the door, Rhett followed Olivia to her Expedition. "Do you want me to ride with you?"

"Absolutely not," she replied before her next breath.

She got behind the wheel, fastened her seatbelt, and watched as Rhett and Rho walked down the road. *How could Bev trust these two out of the blue?* Dealing with their sort wasn't in Olivia's wheelhouse, and she had no way of knowing if they were legit or if what they were doing was legal. She needed her own backup with a more rele-vant skill set, and that meant calling Sam.

CHAPTER 27

On the twenty-five-minute drive to town, Olivia filled Sam in on the details of what she'd learned since Friday night's meeting with Mack. Then she asked Sam to lend her eyes and ears to help balance the wildcards of Rhett and Rho. Sam readily jumped on board, agreeing to meet them within thirty minutes.

Olivia arrived in town at six o'clock, followed closely by Rhett and Rho. The Sunday shopping throng had departed, leaving plenty of parking for the two black SUVs. They aligned bumper-to-bumper then walked together to the inn. Rhett opened the door for the ladies, inviting them inside with a sweeping-arm gesture. He shot Olivia his sparkling grin as she scooted by with a listless smile. Her focus zoomed past his protruding pecs and landed on Bev, who was speaking with Preston and Allen at the lobby counter.

Bev waved them over, and when they were within a

discreet distance, she introduced everyone. "Preston, Agent Allen, this is the security team that has been working with me. Except for Olivia." Bev eyed Preston. "Olivia is here strictly for moral support. She's not involved in any other way."

Super smooth, Bev.

Preston glanced at Olivia without betraying his thoughts.

"This is Rhett and Rho," Bev said.

Nobody shook hands, and Allen's furrowed brow signaled his displeasure. "Mrs. Styles has informed us of your involvement," he said. "Any information that you find gets passed on to me or the police department. Do you understand?"

Rho sneered. "We don't answer to you."

Allen closed the gap between them, facing up to Rhett. "If either of you interferes with the investigation, I'll have you arrested." His stare lingered for a moment, and then he brushed by them and left the inn.

Preston glanced again at Olivia and then spoke to his mother. "I'll call you later. Cole will be here when you're ready to go home. He'll have the first watch shift."

"I still don't think that's necessary," Bev replied. "I'll be fine."

"It's not up for discussion." He turned toward Rhett and Rho. "I expect your cooperation." Then he nodded once at Olivia, walked with a clipped pace through the lobby, and left without looking back.

Bev exhaled a weighty breath as if she'd just tiptoed

through a minefield. "At least everyone knows each other now. Let's go back to my office."

As Rhett and Rho followed Bev, Olivia tarried a moment and texted Sam about their location before joining the others in the office. Bev closed the door and invited them to sit. Ever the hostess, she had provided a platter of finger sandwiches and bottled water, as if this peculiar strategy session was a casual picnic.

Rhett picked up a pair of petite ham-and-cheese sandwiches and demolished his first sample in two bites. "I could eat all of these."

Olivia didn't doubt it. Biceps with such girth needed plenty of protein to build and maintain. Rho sat, grabbed a bottle of water, and dove straight into the business at hand. She recapped their search of the cabin for Bev, concluding that if Stuart had stashed the Star of Athens in the forest, nature had likely claimed it forever.

Olivia listened, keeping mum about her encounter with Joe's friend down the road. She wanted to discuss it in private with Bev before sharing it with Rhett and Rho.

Then Rho related their efforts to trace the blackmailer's IP address and decipher how Bev's accounts had been hacked. Their work had yielded no leads, which suggested they were going toe to toe with a seasoned pro. Their plan was to wait until the blackmailer's next communication and then try to pinpoint their location. They had installed security monitoring on all of Bev's phones, leaving Olivia silently questioning the legality of their tactics.

Olivia shared what she'd learned about the Carters, and then Rhett admitted to having already followed Dylan two days last week. They all agreed Ed was in play as a suspect, and there was a strong possibility someone else in the family was in cahoots with him to get money for Kaitlyn's treatment.

Knocking on the door interrupted the conversation. Olivia looked at the wall clock and stood, grateful for Sam's punctuality.

"Bev, I've asked Sam to come on board with us. You already know she was with me when I met Mack. She's up to speed on the details. I trust her, and I think having someone else involved for your safety can only help."

Then Olivia opened the door, and Sam walked in as all eyes turned toward her.

Rhett lit up with an amused smile, speaking as he chewed. "Sam! Long time, no see."

Sam assessed everyone in the room and then glared at Rhett. She clenched her jaw and stepped to within arm's reach of him. Then she drew her fist back and sucker punched his face. "That's for shooting me, you son of a—"

"Sam!" Olivia yelled. She shuffled between Rhett and Sam, aiming to prevent any retaliation. "He shot you?"

He grinned at Sam, rubbing his cheek. "It was a flesh wound, babe. And you're welcome for saving your life."

Sam bristled and postured as if about to fire her fist again.

"Whoa, Sam," Olivia said. "Everyone, stop."

Sam pointed a finger over Olivia's shoulder at Rhett. "I was doing fine until you showed up."

"Not from my vantage point. You were a sitting duck. How many rounds did you have left?"

Rho took a swig of water and smirked, unfazed by the out of the blue melee.

Sam seethed, looking down at Rho and then back at Rhett. "Who's your new little sidekick?"

"Rho," he replied. "Partner, meet my old buddy, Sam, who still packs a mean wallop. Good to see you always have the guns locked and loaded."

Sam stared down at Rho. "As in row, row, row your boat?"

Rho launched upward, and Olivia wedged herself between her and Sam.

"Her Christian name is Alice," Rhett added. "As for the Christian part, I can't comment."

"Shut your yap," Rho snapped back.

He held up his hands. "Go to it, ladies."

Olivia didn't know what was happening. Having never seen this side of Sam, she gave her the benefit of the doubt, thinking maybe this was how special op types sized each other up. Regardless, Olivia was ill-matched standing between them, so she stepped to the side in case things turned violent.

"Rho, I asked Sam to come because I think she can help the team," Olivia said.

"I'm cool with that," Rhett replied.

"Me too," Bev peeped from where she stood, cowering in the corner of the tiny office.

Rho stared at Sam for a moment more and then sat back in her chair. "Whatever."

The tension eased, and they talked for another twenty minutes, with Sam grilling Rhett and Rho on their efforts to date. When it was close to seven o'clock, Bev announced that she needed to attend to her hostess duties for the dinner service. They all agreed to cooperate and gather back sometime over the next few days, or sooner if circumstances warranted.

As they walked out into the lobby, Olivia was acutely aware of what an odd lot they must look like, especially with the fresh bruise blooming on Rhett's cheek. Bev left them to go to the dining room, then Rhett and Rho headed upstairs to the second-floor rooms where they were staying. Olivia strode with Sam toward the exit, dying to know exactly what Sam really did for a living and how well she knew Rhett.

CHAPTER 28

Olivia grasped Sam's forearm, stopping her as soon as their feet hit the lamppost-lit sidewalk outside of the inn. "What the heck, Sam? Rhett shot you? When? Are you okay?"

Sam waited until she loosened her grip and then zipped up her leather jacket, standing casually as if discussing the weather. "It's history. Rhett is right. He only grazed me, but I still didn't appreciate it."

Olivia stared at her, unable to fathom a response to her matter-of-fact answer. "Rhett intentionally shot you? What? Is that normal for you? Does your job involve getting shot at regularly? I haven't wanted to pry, and maybe it's none of my business, but seriously … what the heck?"

Sam looked at the inn and then back at her. "Not here. Let's get some distance. Come on."

They crossed the street and walked around the town square until they were on the opposite side along Blossom Avenue. Sam sat on a bench and leaned back. Olivia perched on the seat's edge and turned toward her, waiting for her explanation.

"I work as a security consultant for a private company."

Olivia already knew that. But under the circumstances, she pressed for details without worrying about overstepping her business. "What kind of security? Is being shot at a routine occupational hazard? Because, to me, that sounds like a deal breaker."

Sam shook her head. "Not normally. The situation was unusual and complicated. Rhett made the right call, and I would've done the same if matters were reversed. Although, I wouldn't have hit him. He's a lousy shot."

Olivia's work-related perils were limited to missing deadlines and receiving occasional angry e-mails about advice she'd given. Trying to wrap her head around Sam's nonchalance was like being air-dropped blindfolded in a foreign country.

"Were you and Rhett partners?"

Sam pocketed her hands in her jacket, staring straight ahead. "Not exactly. Sometimes we cross paths. When did you first meet Rhett?"

"In October at Whispering Meadows."

Sam nodded. "That's interesting. I was unaware he had been in the area all this time. But it's not like we're pen pals."

Now, what little Olivia knew about Sam was making sense. She often watched Sam's house and gathered her mail when she traveled for work, which sometimes extended for weeks. She never snooped for details of destinations. Sam's sparse job description had always dissuaded her from diving deeper into her private affairs.

"If it's not normal for you to be shot at, and thank goodness for that, then what *is* normal? Every time you leave on a work trip, do I have to worry about whether you're going to return?"

Sam slid forward, joining her on the edge of the bench. "No. Occasionally a situation goes sideways, but I can handle myself. My job normally is rather mundane. I find missing things."

"What sorts of things?"

"Items, money, people, information."

Of course. Things we all lose track of.

Olivia watched as a couple walked by an animated light sequence of Santa's sleigh taking flight. Scenes of Sam as the protagonist in a spy thriller flashed through her mind. She envisioned her dodging bullets, hanging from buildings by her fingertips, and parachuting out of planes.

Since Sam was being forthcoming, Olivia indulged her curiosity. "Is what you do legal?"

Sam stood, giving a thin smile. "Yes, but I think it's best left there for right now, for everyone's sake. I trust in your discretion. Where are you parked?"

Olivia pointed across the square, to near the inn.

"Over there. Of course, I won't say anything. I'm not exactly sure what I would even say, anyway."

"Thanks," Sam replied. "I'm parked down the block from you."

Olivia glanced over her shoulder toward Sophia's clinic on the other side of the street, about half a block down. She figured it had to be at least a quarter after seven, making her late for her dinner invitation.

"I'm past due at Soph's," she said. "Her mother and grandmother are having a casual get-together. Soph will be there, and maybe A.J. Why don't you join us? I'm sure they won't mind."

Sam shook her head. "I don't want to impose."

"They were already expecting my dad, and he's not coming, so I know they'll have extra space and food. When Josefina and Maria cook, there's always plenty to go around. They're happy to share with as many as can fit at the table." She pulled out her phone and texted Sophia about bringing Sam. The reply came in a snap. "See? Perfect. They're thrilled you'll be joining us."

Sam gave in without further arm twisting, joking about how Olivia could have a second career as a cruise ship coordinator. They walked the short distance to the clinic, where Sophia was waiting for them outside. After they entered, Sophia locked the door, and they proceeded through the hallway to the kitchen.

A festive linen cloth featuring boughs of holly and wreaths with red bows covered the table. All the serving bowls and platters were in place, ready to go. A.J. was sitting beside Josefina, complementing her on the food's sumptuous aroma and the tempting dessert trays on the counter under the cabinets. They all greeted one another, and then Sam, Sophia, and Olivia took their seats around the table. After Josefina said grace, everyone was free to fill their plates.

Holding a ladle, Maria offered each of them pozole rojo from a large tureen centered on the table. The traditional Mexican stew of pork, hominy, and red chilies was a staple for Sophia's family during the holidays. A platter of pork tamales and a side dish of apple salad were passed around, and all indulged in healthy portions.

The conversation meandered from holiday memories to New Year's plans. Josefina added her two cents, suggesting that Olivia, Sophia, and Sam make resolutions about getting married. Olivia silently thought that wouldn't do for Sam, as being tied down probably wasn't part of her long-term plans. Sophia and A.J. had seemed to be oddly buddy-buddy as of late, but she was probably making too much of that. As for her and Preston, that relationship had fizzled and stalled before it was even out of the starting gate.

She glanced at the dessert-covered counter under the cabinets. That typically meant Maria and Josefina had been baking for either a holiday gathering or a charity sale. They often used the commercial-sized kitchen when cooking large quantities. The single oven at the home they shared dramatically cut their productivity.

"It looks like it's been a busy day of baking," she said.

Sophia nodded, looking at the counter. "Abuela and Mamá made all that for the church bake sale tomorrow. The proceeds go to local charities."

"Everything looks great," Olivia replied. "I'm sure you'll sell out in no time." She swiveled toward Josefina. "My dad has been helping with the baking for the column in the *Times*. I'm thinking of getting him some professional lessons for Christmas."

"Send him to me," Josefina said. "I'll teach him."

"He'd like that," Olivia replied.

Maria removed a napkin from her lap and placed it on the table. "Sam, do you bake for the holidays?"

Olivia glanced at Sam, imagining any apron she owned would be black with a bullseye target emblazoned with the words "Mission Impossible."

"Not really," Sam said.

"Do you have any plans for the holidays?" Maria asked.

Sam shook her head. "I'm not a big holiday person."

"Come over to our house for dinner on Christmas," Olivia offered. "My dad is cooking ham, so you'd be doing us a huge favor. It's like what Dorothy Parker said: 'Eternity is a ham and two people.'"

"If Olivia and her father get you for Christmas Day, then you're with us for Christmas Eve," Maria said. "And I won't take no for an answer."

Sam accepted both invitations with profuse gratitude. As they continued eating, A.J. talked about the playground construction and Sophia's aid with the design and equipment selection. If all went well with permits and funding, the park should be ready by summer.

Maria offered Olivia the bowl of apple salad, asking if she would like a second helping. After she politely declined, Maria inquired, "How's work going for you? We've been enjoying your recipe columns in the paper over the past week."

"Thank you. My dad has been a huge help. At first, I felt suckered into it, but we've had a lot of fun. Work otherwise is fine. I've taken two weeks off over the holidays. My editor is running columns that were saved and batched for such occasions. I'll be back at it soon enough, but recently, I've been thinking of exploring some new options."

"I thought you enjoyed writing," Maria said.

Olivia nodded. "I do, and I have no complaints about the column or the paper. But I've been doing it for a while, and I'm thinking maybe it's time for a change."

"This is news to me," Sophia said.

"Nothing is imminent. It's not like I'm actively searching for something different, but I'm open to the possibility."

"What sorts of opportunities would you be interested in?" Sam asked.

Olivia shrugged. "Probably something writing related. That's easier said than done when the realities of retirement plans and health insurance need to be considered."

"We all go through seasons in life," Maria said.

"People used to stay in one job their entire career, even if it made them miserable. Changing your mind and doing something different takes courage and belief in yourself. I worked as a paralegal before Sophia was born, and my dream was always to be a civil rights attorney. When Sophia came along, I stayed home with her while my husband was completing his medical residency. I thought I'd never go back to school, but along the way, I changed my mind, and I wanted to teach. It wasn't easy, but I earned my graduate degree in education and then taught for over twenty-five years. I loved it, but then it came time for a change, and I happily retired. And now, I'm ready to become a doting grandmother once Sophia—"

"Whoa!" Sophia interjected. "Mamá, don't go there. You sound like Abuela."

"Escucha a tu madre," Josefina said.

"I do listen to her," Sophia replied. "And how did this become about me?"

"I'm teasing, mija," Maria said, consoling her daughter with a wink.

They all shared a good laugh and continued with dinner. After another half an hour, Olivia and Sam thanked their hosts and prepared to leave. Sophia walked with them out to the foyer and inquired about news regarding Bev. Olivia put her off, promising to fill her in on the details as soon as she could.

Sam and Olivia left the clinic and strolled around the square to where they had parked. Large flurries were floating down, dusting the road with snow. They parted ways and got into their cars. Olivia followed Sam past the inn and out of town, hoping that by tomorrow morning, the police and FBI would have come up with some leads to help Bev.

CHAPTER 29

Olivia greeted her father Monday morning in the kitchen, where he was sitting at the table working on the newspaper's daily crossword puzzle.

"You were an English major," he said. "I need a nine-letter word for scribe. Begins with an 'S' and ends with an 'R.' If I have the correct answer down, there's a 'V' in the middle."

She grabbed two containers of yogurt from the refrigerator and a banana from a crystal bowl on the counter. "Just because I was an English major doesn't mean I know every word in the dictionary." After grabbing a spoon from the silverware drawer, she sat across from him. "Scrivener."

He filled in the answer. "Yes! All that college education is finally paying off."

"Wow, Dad. That's endearing."

"How about this one? An anagram for 'elegant

man.'"

"Let me see." After he handed her the folded paper, she studied it for a moment while taking a bite of the banana. Then she slid the puzzle back across the table. "A gentleman."

He wrote in the answer. "Aha. That helps with the rest of this top section. The other day I heard a couple of good ones. 'The detectives' is 'detect thieves.' And 'Christmas' is 'trims cash.'"

"How timely," she replied. "Will you be trimming any more cash with last-minute shopping today?"

He set the paper aside, removed his glasses, and placed them on the table. "I have a few small things I want to pick up in town. Your car needs a state inspection, so I thought I'd take it to Jed's and get that done first. I'll check to see if it's ready for an oil change. You can use the Escape if you need to go anywhere."

"Thanks. I've been meaning to do both, but with all that's been happening with Bev, I haven't had time."

"Have there been any developments?"

"Many would be an understatement." She filled him in on the details while finishing her breakfast. "So, I hope either the police or the FBI have good news this morning," she finished. "Between Bev's private security team and the round-the-clock police watch, at least she's safe."

He pushed away from the table and stood. "I think it was a good idea to bring Sam on board. I'm willing to do anything to help. Especially if it involves stakeouts. I'll bring the snacks. Do you think Sam likes doughnuts? I'd probably have to pack carrots for you."

She grinned, finishing the last spoonful of her yogurt. "Hold your horses, dear Watson. Let's hope it doesn't come to that."

He slid the plastic bag containing her mother's broken pen next to his wallet on the counter. "I'll also go to the jewelry repair shop and see about getting this fixed."

She stacked the empty yogurt containers and placed the banana peel inside. "Thanks. If it costs a fortune, don't worry about it."

"We'll see what happens. We won't know until we try. What are you doing today?"

She stood and threw out her trash. "I have the final copy for the last column to tidy up. Did you transfer your pictures to your laptop?" After he confirmed that he had, she asked, "Do you mind if I use your computer? Mine's out in the office, and I can pull my draft down from the cloud, complete it, and attach your photos to the e-mail that I'll send to Ellen."

"My laptop is on the coffee table. I still don't understand where the cloud is. Are we all in the same cloud together?"

She kissed his cheek. "There are a lot of clouds. You're in a big fluffy one in a bright blue sky."

"Is that good?"

"Very good," she replied, walking into the living room.

After grabbing his laptop, she headed upstairs to her room with more than one mission in mind. The first order of business was to complete the column copy for the paper and send it to Ellen. For the vignette, she wrote about one winter when school had been closed for two weeks because of a nor'easter blizzard. She and A.J. had built an igloo in which they had a picnic, feasting on cookies and hot chocolate her mother made for them.

She sent the column copy and her father's photos to Ellen, then shut the door and retrieved a roll of wrapping paper and a bag of gifts from her closet. Over the next half an hour, she wrapped two shirts and a book for her father, along with his favorite coffee from Jillian's. Buddy would receive toys and treats. Last year, he'd been more interested in chewing the boxes and crinkling the shiny paper than in his presents.

Once the task was done, she piled the gifts in her closet and stashed the paper, tape, and scissors, removing the evidence of her secret endeavors. Then, using a private browser, she searched for cooking schools offering classes for amateur bakers. She found programs hosting everything from one-hour lessons to a month-long immersion in a bakery. Some focused on specific bakes in different sessions, while others provided general instruction on a wide spectrum of sweets.

She hadn't thought of extending her search beyond the local area until coming across a renowned baking school in Oregon. The program offered a variety of courses ranging from two to twenty days, including instruction on how to set up a bakery. The hefty price tag was more than she'd planned for, but the prospect was tempting. She had money saved from her canceled move to New York, and her only reservation was not knowing whether her father would want to travel that far. Deciding to mull it over, she wrote the name of the school in her notes app and planned to revisit her options before Christmas Day.

The last item on her agenda had caused her consternation. Before yesterday morning's blowup with Preston, she had wanted to get him a gift. The question now was whether he would even accept it. Despite their current shaky dynamic, she proceeded with her search anyway. She had something in mind, but finding both the exact item and guaranteed delivery by Christmas would be challenging.

As she was writing the names of several stores under the bakery school in her notes, her phone buzzed, displaying a call from Bev.

"Hey, Bev. How are you today?"

"They contacted me," she replied.

"Who are 'they'?"

"The blackmailer. They want the money tonight."

"Did you tell Preston?"

"Not yet. Rhett and Rho want to handle it. They have experience with this sort of thing."

Olivia stood, as if doing so would give her tone more sway. "Terrible idea. Contact the police and the FBI right away."

"The blackmailer said if I get the police involved, they'll tip off the media, accusing Joe of taking part in the heist. This is all happening too quickly. I need to keep this quiet."

"Absolutely not. Hang up now, and call your son." A knock on her door kept her from continuing. "Hold on a second." She lowered her phone. "Yes, Dad? Do you need something?"

"There's someone here from the FBI to see you. Agent Paul Allen."

Frak. "Okay, thanks. I'll be right down."

She held her phone back up to her ear. "I need to go, but I'll be in touch soon. You tell Preston, and I'll handle the FBI."

CHAPTER 30

Allen was sitting on the sofa, chatting with her father, when Olivia joined them downstairs. Dressed for business in a black suit, Allen appeared bright-eyed and relaxed, as if he'd slept seven hours on a pillow-top mattress. They were discussing who made the best all-weather tires and where to find good deals online. Her radar was up, though, as a personal visit on a Monday morning from an FBI agent surely wasn't to swap tips about traction and treads.

Her father rose from the recliner as she circled the sofa and stood next to him. "I'll let you two talk," he said. "I'll be upstairs if you need me." Then he left the living room and went up the steps.

"Your father is very kind," Allen said. "And you have a lovely home."

She took a seat in the recliner. "Thanks. Where's home for you?"

He shifted to be more in line with her and folded his hands, casually resting them in his lap. "These days, D.C."

"I hope your business in Apple Station won't keep you from your family over the holidays."

"It's only me there. I'm divorced and have two adult children who don't live in the area. My daughter is visiting for a few days, though, and I'm looking forward to seeing her."

"That'll be nice. I used to live in Georgetown before coming back to stay here."

A warm smile softened his cheeks. "Georgetown is such a beautiful area, especially when the cherry blossoms are blooming."

"Yes, but to see them in their full glory, you need to go to the Tidal Basin. I don't know every corner of Georgetown, but the only cherry blossoms I can remember seeing, in any number at least, are at Dumbarton Oaks. If you've never been, the gardens are beautiful to visit."

He nodded. "I'm acquainted, and they are stunning. On Christmas Day last year, my daughter and I took a trip there. It's such a peaceful oasis in the city."

"The museum is nice too," she replied. "How did you get in on Christmas? I wanted to do the same with a friend once, but the website said they were closed on federal holidays."

He lowered his eyes, trying to hide a bashful grin. "It's embarrassing to admit, especially since it's not condoned, but the badge may have greased some wheels. It was a brief visit, but I wanted to do something special with my daughter."

"Gotcha. I suppose being an agent has some pull."

"I've seldom done that, and since I'll be retiring soon, all such considerations will go away." His sheepish smile faded as his demeanor shifted toward official business. "I don't want to take up too much of your time this morning, so I'll get to the reason I'm here. I've been with the FBI for over twenty-five years, and much of that time has been working in the Jewelry and Theft Program. I've been tracking this thief—we call him Royce—who we believe has committed a series of high-end heists along the East Coast."

"Royce? As in Rolls Royce?"

He nodded. "Yes. Because with the value of the jewelry he's stolen, he could buy several of them."

Buddy ambled into the living room from the kitchen. He sniffed Allen's shoes, jumped over his feet, and lay on his belly by Olivia's feet.

She leaned down for a moment, scratching his head while looking at Allen. "He can be shy around strangers."

"Beagles are great hunting and tracking dogs."

"We try to keep his lifestyle a little less adventurous, but he's had his mischievous moments."

He glanced at Buddy and then returned to the business at hand. "I'm going to be upfront with you. We have good reason to believe Royce is in the area."

"That means you think Stuart hid the Star of Athens someplace."

"Yes, and we believe he had help doing it. Carter's release from prison has been on our radar ever since day one of his term. Our profilers feel Royce has been waiting and watching too."

"Even after three years?" she said.

"This heist for Royce is the score of a lifetime. We're dealing with someone who is in it for the glory and the money. Losing the Star of Athens is a blow to his reputation and legacy." He studied her for a moment before continuing. "I can see your doubt, but this is how criminal minds operate. I don't understand it either, but this is what our profilers have come up with after piecing together over a decade's worth of his crimes. The profile is the most we know about him. Royce is smart, and he's never left behind useful evidence."

"What about the video footage?"

He shifted in his seat. "Not conclusive. The Star of Athens heist was an embarrassment for us. He walked out of the hotel, maybe even right by me. Now, I'm confident he's someplace in the area. I don't know if we'll catch him, but if we can recover the Star of Athens, at least we could deny him the glory he wants and return the necklace to its rightful owners."

Buddy pawed at her shins, and she picked him up, setting him next to her in the recliner. "I understand the significance of your investigation, but why are you here talking to me about it?"

"For a couple of reasons. First, you're already involved, and we want to keep a tight rein on information. Second, you're close to Mrs. Styles and her son." He paused for a moment, allowing the silence to heighten the gravity of what he was about to say. "We believe Joseph Hills was involved in some capacity."

She reflexively shook her head. "But the police questioned him, and they searched the cabin. What's any of this got to do with me?"

"The FBI's role here is twofold. Apprehend Royce and recover the necklace. We're assisting with the murder investigation, but that's not our primary mission. Though we can't rule out a connection between Carter's death and the heist, there has been no history of violence in any of the thefts that we've connected Royce to. It's not his MO. Maybe you can see the conflict here. We're working with the local police department whose lead detective is related to suspects for the heist and murder. It's a delicate balance. We must consider the possibility that Detective Hills may be protecting his mother by controlling the investigation."

"But she's being blackmailed. How do you explain that? You can't possibly believe she was involved in Stuart's death."

He rested his arms on his thighs, looking like a coach giving her a pep talk. "We have multiple working theories. I'm here today to ask for your cooperation."

"With what?"

"We want you to be a fly on the wall. Let us know if Mrs. Styles confides anything to you or if you notice she does something out of her normal routine."

She couldn't help but smirk. "You want me to spy on her for you?"

"Spy is a strong word. We're asking you to report anything that raises a red flag, particularly about this security team she's working with. We haven't been able to uncover any information about them, and for all we know, they could be involved. Has Mrs. Styles told you anything about them?"

She glanced at Buddy and stroked his head several times. Though far from investing her full trust in Rhett and Rho, she wasn't about to offer any details that may be detrimental to Bev or Preston.

"Not much," she replied.

"Okay. If anything comes to light, please let us know. We're also looking into John Mack in relation to all this. Have you been in further contact with him?"

She shook her head without answering, allowing her silence to shroud her lie, and then redirected the conversation. "Do you think anyone in the Carter family is involved?"

"We're looking into every possibility. Outside of the family and law enforcement, there are few people who know about the connection between Carter and the heist."

Marco Esposito was one of those people. Without

Royce's identity or his capture, she figured Marco's editor would be reluctant to go to print with his investigation.

"What about the reporter who visited him in jail?" she asked. "It seems odd a reporter would visit someone like him. He had few friends, and his charges were hardly sensational enough to attract media coverage. Do you think it's possible she was looking into the heist?"

"What reporter?"

"Mack told me only a handful of people visited Stuart in prison, one of whom was a female reporter."

He shook his head. "I reviewed Carter's visitor log myself, and there was no such person."

"But Mack said—"

"He lied to you, which begs the question why." He stared at her for a moment before continuing. "Can I expect your cooperation?" When she didn't provide an immediate answer, he straightened on the edge of the sofa, adding a touch of intimidation to his demeanor. "I'll remind you that withholding information could make you an accessory, which may result in criminal charges."

"Are you threatening me?"

He backed off, holding his hands up. "Not at all. I'm asking for your cooperation."

Saying no wasn't in her best interest, and landing in hot water with the FBI had failed to make her bucket list again this year. Still, she wasn't about to say anything that could implicate anyone in Preston's family. Playing along, she threw him a bone. "Of course. You should know that the blackmailer contacted Bev this morning. They want the money today."

Allen took out his phone. "What else did she tell you?"

"Nothing else. I told her to inform Detective Hills. I'm sure you'll be hearing from him soon."

He wrote and sent a text and then returned his phone to his pocket. "This could be the break we need. I'll gather my team, and we'll strategize a plan." He stood, readying to leave. "Thank you for your time. If you think of anything else or find out something that could help, call me." He pulled out a thin case from inside his suit jacket and placed a business card on the table.

She picked up the card, scanned the contact details, and nodded. "Of course."

After she showed him out, her father came downstairs, meeting her in the living room.

"I wasn't eavesdropping," he said. "But I heard him leave. What was all that about?"

She plopped down on the sofa, needing a breath of fresh air. "That was the FBI agent leading the investigation of the heist. He wants me to spy on Bev and Preston, which I'm not doing. He thinks Joe was involved." She continued to recap the conversation as he stood listening.

"I think you handled it well. Cooperate, but don't volunteer what you don't have to."

Knocking on the front door interrupted their discussion.

"I'll get that," he said.

She watched as he opened the door and then turned toward her.

"It's for you," he said. "Looks like it's back upstairs for me."

CHAPTER 31

Olivia rose upon seeing Preston standing on the porch. The odds of him showing up right after Allen's visit gave her pause, mostly to consider playing the lottery or avoiding open spaces should lightning pop up. As there was no cover from the incoming storm, she bit the bullet and joined them by the door.

She flashed her well-practiced, polite but wary smile for the second time on this young day. "Hi. I didn't expect to see you here today."

"Good morning," Preston said. "Do you have a moment to talk?"

She glanced at her father as he turned and walked back into the living room, heading for the stairs.

"Sure. Do you mind if we speak outside? I could use some fresh air."

"That works."

She grabbed her coat off the hook rack, slipped it on,

and stepped out onto the porch. After closing the door to a crack, she gestured at two rocking chairs aligned side by side. "Do you want to sit?" After they both settled, she took the lead. "The blackmailer contacted your mother this morning."

He nodded with a narrow smile, placing her more at ease. "Yes, she told me and made sure I knew it was at your insistence. Although, she swears she was going to tell me. Thank you for that."

A red cardinal landed on the porch railing and then flitted over to a bird feeder hanging from a pole in front of the azalea bushes. Seconds later, a brown cardinal perched on top of the tube feeder, prompting her mate to cede his position.

"I want to apologize to you," Preston said. "When I learned my mom was being blackmailed, I was upset. I'm sorry I took it out on you."

She nodded, welcoming the faint whiff of pleasantness between them. "I understand. I would've felt the same way if it was my dad."

He rocked the chair a few times. "At least your dad wouldn't have hired a private security team behind your back."

She thought of her father and Sam geeking out over guns on Friday night. "I don't know about that. Your mom is afraid, especially for your sake. She thinks if the blackmailer makes the allegations against your father public, it could affect you. She's concerned about you losing your job."

"That would never happen."

"The threat was enough to put the fear in her. Everything I did"—*and still am doing*—"is because I'm worried about her and you."

He nodded with his head bowed. "I know. You probably can't help yourself. Would you like an application to the police academy?"

She laughed at the thought of herself in uniform. "No, thank you. I'm more suited to PI work."

"I don't doubt that. Lord have mercy on anyone who finds themselves the target of your investigations."

The teasing compliment of her formidable nature hinted that the tide was turning in the right direction for them. "I think I'll stick with writing for now until I come up with a better Plan B."

She shifted on the rocker's cushion and grabbed a loose thread hanging from a side seam. After wrapping it around her finger a few times, she tugged sharply, only to pull the thread out farther.

"I hate it when that happens," she said. Trying again, she anchored the string near the cushion. After a quick yank, it was an inch longer.

He reached into his jeans pocket and pulled out a knife. "Here, let me get that." Holding the thread, he tried a quick cut, but it failed to sever. He added more oomph, and then the string separated. "Looks like I need to sharpen my blade."

"Or maybe these cushions are made of kryptonite," she joked.

"Now that would make more sense."

"Is that knife like the one your father had? Your mom mentioned it to me the other day."

He turned it end over end. "Not exactly. His had a burlwood handle with a satin-finish blade. It wasn't anything fancy by today's standards."

"Your mom told me he wanted you to have it."

"Yeah. I wish I would've kept it. My dad said you should always carry a pocketknife with you. I have ever since I was ten when he gave me my first one for my birthday."

"You carried it even when you went to school?"

He grimaced. "I know that sounds bad, but it was a different time back then. Do I have to bribe you to keep my secret?"

She flattened her smile, mustering her sternest judicial tone. "Detective, this is a serious offense. As an officer, you are to model lawful behavior to the impressionable youth of Apple Station. To keep this matter off-the-record, I'll require coffee and a pastry next Saturday morning at Jillian's."

He sighed with repentant eyes. "I accept those terms, and I thank you for your leniency."

They shared a laugh, then sat for a moment in silence as the cardinal pair alternated flying back and forth from the bushes to the feeder.

"Thanks for coming all the way out here," she said. "I know you have a full plate, and you could've just called."

"I wanted to see you. I didn't like how I left things between us."

"I'm glad you came. What's happening with your mom's situation?"

"I have a call scheduled with Allen in about an hour to discuss a plan."

"He was here a short time ago." She paused, carefully choosing her words, not wanting to create any inter-agency conflict. "I have to tell you he thinks your dad was involved in the heist."

"He had nothing to do with any of it. He was trying to help Stuart, that's all."

"I believe you. Why do you think Allen has it out for your family?"

He shifted forward to the edge of the rocker. "I don't think he does. He's following the evidence. I would do the same. His team is investigating the heist. Our department is working on Stuart's murder and dealing with the blackmail threat. We're cooperating, but our agendas are different. We've had little interaction."

That made sense if the FBI was trying to keep tabs on Preston without tipping their hand. She stopped short of telling him about Allen's request for her cooperation, afraid it would spur Preston to confront him. For now, it was best to maintain eyes and ears in the FBI's camp. By doing so, she could relay inside information to Preston if the threat to him or Bev worsened.

"I'll be fine," he continued. "There's nothing you need to hide from the FBI."

She nodded, wanting to wipe Allen from her thoughts for the rest of the day. "Do you have any leads in the murder investigation?"

He shook his head and chuckled. "I wondered when that was coming. You know I can't discuss any details with you, but we're looking into several angles."

"Do any of them involve the Carter family, or perhaps Ed Graham?"

"You won't stop," he teased. "Are you sure you're not an investigative journalist?"

She held up her hands, surrendering the inquiry. "I had to ask." She paused for a moment. "Did your mom tell you I was at your dad's cabin?" When he nodded, she asked, "You never go there?"

"Not really, other than to check up on it. When my dad was alive, I would spend a weekend there with him sometimes. But you've seen the place. It needs work, and I don't have the time. My mom should sell it as a hunting cabin. She'd find a taker."

"I met the man who lives up the road from the cabin. His home looks quite luxurious from the outside. Do you know him?"

"Must've been Henry Zimmerman. He's the only person I know of who lives close by. I've never met him."

Now armed with the neighbor's name, she would be sure to ask Bev about him the next time they saw each other.

The screen door flew open and they both startled,

turning toward her father as he stepped out onto the porch.

"Detective Hills, a word with you in private, please," he said.

She stood in slow motion with her sixth sense on high alert. "Dad?"

"Give us a few minutes, sweetie."

She peeked at Preston, who appeared as confused as her.

"Dad, what's up?"

Her father pointed at Preston, keeping one hand behind his back. His mouth was moving, but no words were coming out, as he seemed to be making something up on the spot. "I … would … like to know what your intentions are regarding my daughter."

She gasped, shaking her head. *What the*—*?* "Dad, no. What are you doing?" She stepped to the screen, opened it, and tried to usher him off the porch. "Inside. Now!"

He stood firm. "I'm sorry, honey. It's time I had a man-to-man talk with Preston."

She drew in close to him with her heart hammering as her stomach dropped to her feet. Clenching her teeth, she spoke low and stern. "Stop it." Then she turned, eyeing Preston, certain that she was redder than Nolan's Jeep. "I'm sorry. My dad appears to be having an episode."

Preston stood with an accommodating smile she'd seen him give Bev on more than one occasion. "No. It's okay. I have a few minutes."

Her father stepped to the side, gesturing as if Preston needed to be shown the way. "Great. Take a seat in the kitchen. I'll be right in."

Preston walked between them, catching her eyes in passing as he entered the house.

Once he was inside, she tugged her father out of view of the doorway. "What on earth do you think you're doing?"

He whipped his arm out from behind his back and thrust her wallet and phone, and his car keys into her hand. "Sam called your cell. I answered it, thinking it could be about Bev. She wants you to meet her at the inn as soon as possible. Take my Escape. I'll run interference with Preston."

She shook her head, grasping the get-away accoutrements as her father released his grip on them. "No. He and I will go together."

"Find out what this is about first. I'll tell him I sent you to the store for some baking supplies. I have it all figured out."

Her stomach somersaulted, petrified and horrified about what he was planning to say to Preston. "Please, don't do this. Don't say anything to him about me. This won't help matters."

He backed toward the door, shooing her away. "Go. I'll take care of this."

She stepped after him and put a hand up, holding the door open before he closed it the whole way. A two-inch gap was all that remained between her and absolute catastrophe. She cocked her head, trying to look him in the eye through the narrow opening. "I beg you. Please, Dad, whatever you're about to say to him—don't."

"Trust your old man, sweetie. I've got this."

With that, he thrust the door shut, jolting her back a step. She stood upended, with the wreath's red bow inches from her nose. Moments ago, she and Preston had rekindled a connection, and now a sinking rumble screamed that ship was about to be set aflame. Preston had apologized to her, but how could she ever make up for what her father was about to say to him?

CHAPTER 32

Gray clouds blanketed the noontime sky, dulling Olivia's hope of seeing any more sun today. She drummed her thumbs on the wheel to the clicking beat of her turn signal, waiting for a coupe to maneuver out of a parking space in front of Carol's Comforts. On the drive to town, she had attuned to every bit of white noise the Escape offered, distracting herself from thinking about what her father was saying to Preston. To maintain her focus now, and maybe forever, it was best to pretend like the conversation between the two never happened.

After parking, she hustled to the inn, glancing through the newspaper office window in passing. Several of her colleagues were in the workroom, but she kept walking by without breaking her stride. Friendly chitchat would have to wait until she had a less pressing agenda.

"Liv, hold up," Cassandra called from behind her.

She turned as Cassandra jogged a few steps, catching up.

"Hey, what's up?" Olivia said. "You must be freezing."

"It's like a pizza oven in the office. I had to take off my sweater before I started sweating. I was about to text you, but shazam, you zoomed right on by. Guess what? Ed Graham has an arrest record for an assault charge from two years ago. He received a fine but no jail time. I looked through his social media, and most of his posts are hunting related. Lots of photos of the game he's tagged. No surprise, in almost all of them, he's holding a rifle. I found him in a club forum for hunters of the Shenandoah Valley, and he's written detailed threads about weapons and ammunition."

"Many people hunt around here, so that doesn't surprise me," Olivia replied. "Dylan and Darcy defended him, insisting the threat he made against Stuart was all bark and no bite. But an assault charge proves he's otherwise capable."

"When people show you who they are …"

"Believe them," Olivia said, finishing the sentiment.

Cassandra vigorously rubbed her arms. "Anything new from your end?"

"You should get back inside and warm up. I'm on my way now to speak with someone. If anything comes of it, I'll let you know." Though she couldn't yet share any details about the blackmail, having Cassandra on board to bounce ideas off was like having Paige's ear. "I hope all this isn't interfering with your official work."

Cassandra unwrapped her arms and blew on her hands. "Not at all. This is always a slow week for us. Why do you think Ellen is devoting so much space to your recipe column?"

"Because I'm a natural-born baker," Olivia deadpanned.

"Dream on, Penn. I hinted to Ellen—don't worry, I didn't give her any specifics—that I had a lead on something big, and she told me to run with it."

A sensational story was brewing. The question of which way it would turn for Preston's family twisted the knot in Olivia's stomach.

"Thanks. Get back inside. I'll be in touch."

After sharing a brief goodbye, they parted ways, and Olivia walked to the inn.

As she entered the lobby, she spotted Zoey perched on her stool at the welcome counter, bobbing her head to a lively rendition of "Carol of the Bells." Zoey simply smiled and pointed. "They're waiting for you in the back."

She offered a wave of gratitude and proceeded to Bev's office. There, she found Sam and Rho sitting on opposite sides of the desk, discussing the strength of cell signal transmission.

"Hey, what's happening?" Olivia said.

Sam nodded toward Rho. "She's mining through

data trying to determine the cell that called Bev with the blackmail demand."

Olivia shut the door. "How are you doing that?"

Sam glanced at Rho and then said, "The dynamic duo has MacGyvered their own cell site simulator."

Olivia sat in the seat next to Sam and selected a soft ginger cookie off a silver serving tray. Ever since the office had morphed into a makeshift command center, Bev ensured snacks and beverages were available to keep her team's blood sugar operational. "What's a cell site simulator?"

"It spoofs a cell phone tower so calls or texts sent within a certain radius direct through the simulator," Sam said. "The user can mine metadata from the caller's cell."

Olivia finished chewing before speaking. "What data?"

"It depends on how sophisticated the simulator is and whether it's passive or active," Sam replied. "It can catch the IMSI—those are unique identifying numbers for phones."

"And help locate a cell and scrape messaging data," Rho added.

"That doesn't sound legal," Olivia said.

Rho looked up from her laptop. "It's a technology that law enforcement agencies, including the FBI, are using, but keep quiet about. Some feel its use doesn't jibe with the Fourth Amendment's protection against unreasonable searches and seizures."

Rho's loop the loop of her question about the device's legality revealed all Olivia needed to know. "How is it that you have one? And I'm guessing this isn't something you're sharing with the police or FBI."

"Bev hired us to do a job," Rho replied. "We use whatever resources are at our disposal."

"It's best you leave it there, Liv," Sam said. "You're already straddling the fence of plausible deniability."

Trusting Sam, Olivia dropped it for the moment and addressed the reason she had come. "My dad gave me your message. So why am I here?"

Sam slid her cell off the desk and slipped it into her jacket pocket. "I've been checking into Mack's background. It seems he has a mixed reputation."

"How so?" Olivia asked.

"I talked to two PIs who know him, and they were both critical of his tactics."

"What does that mean?" Olivia said.

"Most of what I heard involved questionable surveillance methods. Things that extend beyond legal and border on stalking. Some of his clients aren't quite citizens of the year. You wonder what jobs he gets hired for when those paying his bills have a nefarious reputation. I wouldn't put blackmail outside of his code of conduct."

"If you're implying that some of his clients have criminal associations, what would we even be talking about?" Olivia asked.

"It could be anything," Rho chimed in. "Drugs, guns, extortion. Any avenue where money can be made."

"She's right," Sam said. "The bottom line is that we can't trust Mack, and we should consider him dangerous." She side-glanced at Rho. "His work isn't limited to chasing down cheating husbands. Clients with deep pockets come with high stakes. That's a recipe for doing whatever it takes to get the job done."

Using questionable surveillance tactics may point to Nolan as the one responsible for Mack's reputation. Not quite knowing whether Rho was trustworthy, Olivia kept that theory to herself.

Rho shook her head, pounding her fist on the keyboard. "There's nothing useful from this data. The cell that called Bev's phone must've been out of range of the simulator. It was a long shot, but I thought it would work." She picked her cell up off the desk. "I'm calling Rhett."

Sam rose and adjusted her jacket, preparing to leave. "I'm going to dig deeper into Mack's background. I'll contact you when I know more."

Rho raised her hand as a goodbye and swiveled in her seat, turning away while waiting for her call to connect. Sam lingered by the door for a moment, caught Olivia's eye, and subtly nodded toward the hallway.

"I'm going to the restroom," Olivia said. She stood, stepped out of the office, and partially closed the door. Then she skedaddled, quiet as a church mouse, to where Sam was waiting by the exit to the lobby.

Sam drew in close, wasting no time. "I talked to Rhett, and he confirmed the details of their operation at Whispering Meadows. What he was less forthcoming about was why the Wonder Twins have been holed up here at the inn all this time."

"Bev said they come and go, and I thought they were using it as a home base for whatever other operations they're conducting."

"Maybe," Sam said.

"Are you thinking they're involved in this somehow?"

Sam glanced over Olivia's shoulder. "Cell site simulators are expensive. It's possible Rhett has the backing for it, but they're using a DIY model. It's plausible, but it would require hacking know-how. Rhett isn't a genius, and I don't know Rho that well to say whether she has those chops."

Olivia paused at Sam's slip about Rhett having financial backing. She had assumed, much as Allen had, that Rhett and Rho were guns for hire and not operatives of an organization offering logistical support. With the relevancy uncertain, she let it go for now.

"Dylan Carter," Olivia said. "He might have the expertise. Mack's assistant, Nolan too."

Sam nodded. "Both possible. Watch yourself. I'll be in touch."

With that, she opened the door leading out into the lobby and walked away. Olivia paced back toward Bev's office and waited outside, listening for any tidbits of one-sided conversation coming from Rho. After half a minute of silence, she tapped on the door and cracked it open a bit more.

"Are you finished?" Olivia asked.

Rho looked up from her laptop. "He's not answering. I'll try again later."

She stepped inside, closed the door, and sat across from Rho.

"What are you planning to do about the blackmailer's demands?" Olivia asked.

Rho rested her forearms on the desk. "We wanted to handle the drop, but Bev told the police and FBI, so we're sidelined. We have other avenues we're exploring."

Olivia selected a Linzer cookie from the tray. "Like your cell site simulator. You have quite the skill set."

Rho followed suit, picking up a peanut butter blossom cookie. "It comes in handy."

"These are much too tasty," Olivia said. "I'll have to limit desserts in January to make up for all the sweets I've been eating this week. Is spending time with family over the holidays even a consideration in your line of work?"

"The blackmailer's demand for the money has pushed up our operational timetable. If the police don't botch it up, our role may be over. I could use some downtime. Apple Station is quaint in a small-town, charming way, but we've been here for a while. I'm ready for warmer weather."

"Where's home for you and Rhett?"

"Rhett is a nomad. Home for me is Florida." She looked at her screen and continued typing.

"Whereabouts? I was in Tampa once."

Rho paused and then closed the laptop. "I lived in Tampa a few years. St. Petersburg, Miami, Jacksonville too. My parents separated when I was very young, and when I was old enough, I went to live with my dad. He was in property management and moved around a lot, depending on where his company needed him."

"Is Rho a family nickname?"

She softened with a glint of a smile. "Not quite. My parents named me Alice after my grandmother. I like the name, but it doesn't fit the image I'm going for with my clients."

Olivia matched her grin. "I get that. My middle name is my grandmother's first name. Rose."

"Olivia Rose. That suits you."

"So, where did the nickname come from?"

She leaned back in her seat. "The origin is geeky. When I was in the army, I always volunteered for night patrols because I have strong low light vision, which is helpful for detecting movement or potential threats. Our unit's physician joked I must have a mutant form of rhodopsin. That's a protein found in the rods of our eyes that helps us see in the dark. A few dolts in my unit thought it was hilarious, and because rhodopsin isn't all that catchy, it got shortened to Rho. See, super nerdy."

"That's kind of cool," Olivia replied. "It suits you. Was Rhett one of those dolts?"

She picked up her phone. "I should try to call him again."

Cue the cone of silence.

Olivia pushed her chair back and stood. "Right. I'll let you get to that. Thanks for all you're doing for Bev. It was serendipitous that you and Rhett were on hand when all this started."

Rho's brief congeniality flatlined as she nodded without saying a word.

Olivia offered a friendly wave, turned, and exited the office. She couldn't blame Rho for her evasiveness, given her line of work. But it raised the question of whether Rho was protecting their identities or hiding the real motivation behind what they were doing.

CHAPTER 33

"Psst! Olivia, hold up."

Olivia stopped on her way to the exit and turned back to see Bev standing at the bottom of the lobby's staircase. Having caught Olivia's attention, Bev spun around and hustled up the stairs to a landing halfway between the floors.

I guess I follow you? Not needing to devote much brainpower to the hunch, she reversed direction and trudged up the stairs. "Rho is in your office. Sam left a short while ago."

"He's back," Bev said. "I wasn't sure what to do."

"Who's back?"

"The private investigator who told me his name was Joseph."

"What? Where?"

"He's in the dining room, eating. After you told me who he really is, I asked Zoey to be on the lookout in case he ever returned. I was talking to a guest on the second floor when she texted me he was here. I was afraid to go back downstairs. What should I do?"

Olivia's cheeks heated, fueled by Mack's audacity to show his face at the inn again. She stared at the dining room entrance for a moment, improvising a plan. "Let me handle Mack. Don't talk to him."

Bev bobbed her head. "Thank you. Should I tell Preston?"

"You can, but Mack has done nothing illegal that we know of yet. Preston can't stop him from coming in here." She waited for an older gentleman to pass by, walking downstairs one step at a time. After Bev exchanged pleasantries with her guest, Olivia continued. "This morning, Preston told me about the neighbor who lives close to your cabin. Henry Zimmerman."

Bev's worry lines unfolded. "He was a friend of Joe's."

"When I was at your cabin yesterday, I drove down the road and spoke with him for a few minutes outside of his home. Did you tell Rhett and Rho about him?"

"No. I haven't even thought about him in years."

"Do you know anything about him?"

She nodded. "A little. He has a tragic past. His wife and daughter were killed in a car accident during a winter storm a week before Christmas, about ten years ago. Joe was still working back then, and he was the one who informed Henry about the accident. Joe drove him to the hospital, but his wife and daughter both died before they arrived. They're buried at St. Luke's. It's such a sad story. His wife was killed on her birthday. That's something you don't forget."

"He seems to be well-off."

"He patented an aerospace device and then sold it. After his wife and daughter died, he became a recluse. Joe would check in on him occasionally, but I've never met him. Why are you asking about him?"

"I'm not sure yet." Henry's all-too-quick denial about the night of the heist almost certainly implied he knew more than he was saying. The question of where Joe had been during those missing hours may have its answer half a mile down the road from his cabin. "Keep Henry's name out of this for now. Don't mention it to Rhett, Rho, or the FBI."

Bev agreed, and then darted upstairs to her second-floor hideout.

Olivia stepped under the mistletoe hanging over the entrance to the dining room and spotted Mack sitting alone at a table for two by the fireplace. He appeared at ease, eating his lunch while reading a newspaper. She zigzagged between the tables, pulled out the rustic wood chair opposite him, and sat.

His head shot up, and then he beamed a wide smile, gesturing with an open hand toward her. "Please, join me. There seems to be space."

"You have some nerve showing up back here."

Mack beckoned a server over to the table. A young man dressed in black slacks and a white shirt responded quick as a whip, carrying a pewter pitcher. He overturned a goblet in front of Olivia and filled it to the brim with ice water. Then he pulled a petite menu from the pocket of his waist apron and presented it to her.

She politely waved him off. "No, thank you. I'm not staying."

Mack leaned forward. "Come on. Get something. It's my treat." He stabbed a piece of ham with his fork and then placed it in his mouth. "How about a glass of Merlot? Or maybe you're more of a whiskey drinker."

She glanced up at the server. "Nothing for me."

Mack set his fork down, removed his napkin from his lap, and wiped his mouth. "Have you ever tried moonshine? The legal kind, of course."

"What are you doing here?"

He swept his hand in front of him, highlighting the country ham, roasted potatoes, and white corn on his plate. "Besides enjoying a scrumptious down-home meal and being joined by lovely company?" He tapped the folded copy of *The Apple Station Times*. "This is a charming paper. You can learn so much about a town by reading the local rags. I saw your special feature. I think it's wonderful that a syndicated columnist is writing recipes for her hometown. Odd, but fabulous nonetheless."

Her impatience was mounting, as was her dislike of Mack for having researched her background. She dug deep, doubling down on her calm veneer.

"I was hoping to speak with Bev to give her my

compliments on another fine meal and to clear the air," he said. "I wanted to apologize for misleading her about my identity. After our last conversation, I felt horrible, so I came to say I'm sorry and to offer her my services—at a discounted rate, of course."

"What could you possibly do for her?"

Mack looked at his plate and then shoved it away from him. "I'm stuffed. I never eat this much for lunch. What can I offer? The answer is anything she would need."

How very convenient during a blackmail scheme.

Not trusting a bone in his body, she put Sam's revelation about his reputation to the test. "Why did you lie to me about Stuart's visitor log?"

He lifted his water goblet and took a large gulp. "What are you talking about?"

"You told me a female reporter visited him in jail, and that's not true, according to the FBI."

Mack narrowed his eyes and sneered as if she was the liar. "My source is solid."

The server dropped by, setting a basket of buttermilk biscuits on the table.

Mack grabbed his phone and blankly waved at them. "Please have one." After half a minute of tapping and scrolling, he turned the screen toward her. "See. Said person identified themselves as a member of the press."

She took the phone from him and perused the short list, homing in on the only unfamiliar name. "Carie Bullet. Really? That seems like a name you made up."

Mac nodded. "I know. Ironic, given how Stuart died. It's probably French. I'm sure it's pronounced *boo-lay*. I told you a female because I assume Carie is a woman. I suppose it could be a man's name. I apologize insomuch as there was no attempt to mislead you regarding gender." He waved the server over to the table.

When the server arrived, Mack took out his wallet and handed him a fifty-dollar bill. "I'm sure that covers my meal. Keep the change."

The young server's eyes widened, and after he profusely thanked Mack, he removed the plate and silverware from the table.

Mack extended his hand toward her, and she returned his phone.

"I'm not the bad guy here," he said. "I'm a treasure hunter. That's all." He stood and donned his coat. "Please give my compliments and offer of help to Bev." With that, he forced a smile and bid her a good day.

She remained sitting, staring at three framed black-and-white photos of the inn arranged on the wall by the fireplace. Mack and the FBI were spinning different tales. Mack wasn't to be trusted, but what if he was telling the truth? Why would Allen deny the validity of the visitor log? Could it be that Carie Bullet was working with Royce, making her or him a person of interest in the FBI's investigation?

Her cell buzzed with an incoming call. She slipped her phone out of her pocket as a photo of her father popped up on the screen.

She hit accept and fired away. "Dad, what did you say to Preston? Please tell me you didn't discuss his *intentions* toward me. Who even says that anymore? We haven't even been out on a date. That's what you came up with? His intentions. I swear, if you said anything embarrassing ..."

"Honey, don't worry. Everything's okay. I'll tell you about it later. We've got bigger problems right now."

Her switch flipped. "Are you okay? What's wrong?"

"It's your car. I'm at Jed's, and after he inspected it and changed the oil, I told him to rotate the tires."

Her DEFCON level dropped a notch. Car issues she could handle. Annoyance tinged her tightened lips over repair costs piling on top of her looming problems. "Okay, so what's the issue? I haven't noticed anything wrong with it."

"The Expedition is fine, but Jed found a tracker attached to the undercarriage."

"What?"

"A tracker. Jed says he's seen this happen before in stalking cases. He did a quick search online but couldn't find a match for the device."

She shot up, leaving her chair orphaned from the table, and hurried out of the dining room. "What does that mean?"

"That it's a more sophisticated tracker than any Joe Blow can buy for a few bucks online."

Once out in the lobby, she stood by the unoccupied welcome counter and out of earshot of two women milling around the balsam fir. She dismissed coincidence and unwanted admirers in a blink. Her digging had struck someone's nerve, and she wanted to know who and why.

"Tell Jed to leave it on," she said.

"Are you sure? What if it's some nut job following you?"

"I don't think it is. We can use this to our advantage. Do me a favor. Take a picture of it and send it to me."

As she was waiting for the photo, Preston and Allen entered the inn. Of all the eight billion plus people on the planet, the very two she'd rather not see at this moment were walking toward her as a team.

"Got it. Thanks, Dad. Gotta go. Preston and Allen are here, and neither one looks happy."

She ended the call, and then forwarded the photo to Sam with a text. "Tracker found on my car. Ever seen anything like it?" Then she pulled up her last thread with Cassandra and wrote, "Carie Bullet. Possible reporter or an accomplice to the heist. Any information?"

She pocketed her phone and turned as the two men stood in front of her—one she wanted to wrap her arms around, and the other who had asked her to spy for him.

CHAPTER 34

"Agent Allen, Detective Hills," Olivia offered as a greeting. "I was on my way out."

Preston glanced over her shoulder, and she turned, following his focus to Bev, who was descending the staircase.

"Excuse me," Preston said. "I'll be right back."

After he stepped away, Olivia's phone buzzed once. She slid her cell out of her pocket, keeping the screen from Allen's eyes. A two-sentence reply from Sam informed her that the tracker appeared high-end, but specifics couldn't be determined without a closer study.

Allen removed his overcoat and draped it over his arm. "If it weren't for official business, this inn would be a charming place to spend the holidays. Ms. Penn, I want to apologize again if I came across as heavy-handed this morning."

She peeked back at Preston, who was engaged in a

conversation with Bev. "I understand the importance of your investigation."

"After we spoke, my team informed me they uncovered troubling background information regarding John Mack. He's not quite who he says he is." Allen's focus shifted away from her as he straightened his posture, cutting short his disclosure.

"Agent Allen, if you're ready, we can go over things privately in the back," Preston said.

"Okay, Detective."

Olivia wanted to pull Preston aside to apologize for whatever her father had said. But under the circumstances, she opted, instead, to make herself scarce. "My cue to leave. Good to see you all again." She took a step away from the counter.

"Ms. Penn, if you don't mind, I would like you to stay."

She'd rather not. Allen was maneuvering her like a piece on his chessboard, and she didn't appreciate being a pawn in his game. Glancing at Preston, she hoped for and expected a protest, but he nodded instead, confirming that it was okay by him.

Allen and Bev walked ahead, and before Preston followed in line, she lightly grasped his forearm, holding him back for a private word.

"I'm sorry about what happened this morning with my dad. Whatever he spoke with you about, I had absolutely no part in it."

That triggered a captivating smile. "We had an interesting talk. You know how much I like your father."

She was certain that he'd deduced by finding her here that the grocery run was a ruse. That he didn't call out the father-daughter hocus-pocus charmed her even more. "What did he say to you?"

He watched Allen and Bev walk through the doorway to the back. "We'll talk about it later."

She released his arm. "But are we … okay?"

He placed his hand on the small of her back, sending a tingle up her spine. "We're good, but let's join them before Allen thinks I'm conspiring with you."

He gently propelled her forward, and they walked in step to Bev's office. When they entered, Allen was perched on the corner of the desk, speaking with Bev about the logistics of the blackmailer's demands. Olivia sat, and Preston stood with his arms crossed beside his mother.

Allen tossed his overcoat onto the empty chair next to Olivia. "Mrs. Styles, do you have questions about the operation?"

"They said no police," Bev replied. "What if they find out and never show or get away?"

Allen folded his hands on his thigh, speaking with the confidence of a commander-in-chief. "I assure you they won't know we're there, and they won't escape."

Since Olivia's role was to be a fly on the wall, she buzzed about, pressing Allen to share details that were none of her business. "How's the drop being handled?"

He didn't miss a beat. "The blackmailer requested Mrs. Styles leave the money at a designated spot behind the Turner Mill House."

"The historic site?" Olivia said.

"Yes. Are you familiar with it?"

"I am. Is there any significance to that location?"

Allen stood, removed his suit jacket, and laid it over the back of the empty chair. "We're not sure. Our tactical team scouted the area using satellite imagery. There are difficulties in establishing surveillance positions. There's a lengthy lane leading to the property with open ground for at least one hundred yards on three sides. The rear of the house faces a tree line about fifty yards back. The only vehicular approach is from the front."

Preston widened his stance. "That means the only one getting close to the site is the person doing the drop."

Bev looked at Preston. "They said it had to be me."

He shook his head. "We've been through this. That's not an option. We'll have Deputy Stone do it."

"But Jayden screams cop," Olivia said. "Whoever is behind this probably already knows who she is. Jayden is the only female officer in your department, and you have to assume they're aware of that."

Allen nodded. "She's got a point."

"What about Rho?" Bev asked.

"This operation is need-to-know only," Allen said. "This could be the break that leads us to Royce's capture and Carter's killer."

"Does that mean you think Royce is behind the blackmail and the murder?" Olivia asked.

Allen loosened his tie. "We have multiple working theories."

Her own theory kept coming back to the same through line: two linked crimes committed by two people from a murky, cramped suspect pool. The timing and demands of the blackmailer made little sense unless they were trying to serve up someone in the Carter family on a silver platter. The blackmail demand seemed like a diversion, but from what and from whom, she couldn't quite put her finger on.

"I'll do it," Olivia said. All eyes turned toward her. The room went pin-drop quiet until she clarified, "I'll deliver the money."

"Absolutely not," Preston said.

She scooted forward, directing her argument to him. "It's a simple drop, right? In and out. If they're watching, and they already know who I am, it won't blow Bev's cover that she told the police. I'm just the concerned friend. Not an undercover cop."

"No," Preston said.

Allen picked up his overcoat and then sat next to Olivia. "We don't believe there would be any threat to you."

"She's not doing it," Preston interjected.

Allen swiveled in his seat. "We don't have much time, and she has a valid point about using your deputy."

"Get someone from your team," Preston barked.

"We have one female agent, and she's needed for tactical support."

"I'll call the Winchester PD for an officer to come down," Preston countered.

"There's no need. I'm already here, ready, and willing," Olivia said.

Preston locked in on her. Then he stepped to the door and swung it open. "Olivia, a word."

She stood and circled her chair. Once they were out in the hallway, he closed the door to a crack, and they walked a few paces away from the office.

He softened a bit but remained resolute. "I can't allow you to do this."

She looked up into his fiery, cognac-brown eyes. Telling him about the tracker would only solidify his determination, so she withheld the not so itty-bitty development for now. "I'm not asking for your permission."

"This is dangerous. We don't know who we're dealing with. I don't want you in harm's way."

Acting on instinct, she reached forward and gently grasped his hand. His skin was warm and somewhat rough from the combination of manual labor and the arid winter air. He curled his hand around her fingertips. They stood frozen for a moment, silently confirming all that had been building between them over the past months.

She swallowed hard, quelling the frenzied fluttering in her throat. "I know you're worried, but we both agree your mother can't go. Let me help." Before he could protest, she squeezed his hand. "I'll be fine. You'll be nearby."

Though longing to stay in his hold, she loosened her grip and brushed her fingers along his hand as they separated. She walked backward a few steps toward the office, unable to break the spell of his alluring eyes.

"Come on," she said. "Let's do this. It's going to be okay."

CHAPTER 35

Turner Mill House was a once privately owned property twenty miles southwest of town. The original owners had donated the land and buildings to a local historical society, which now oversaw its preservation and upkeep. The site included a museum and gift shop, and it received funding from donations and the proceeds from an annual gala held at Whispering Meadows.

The instructions for the drop were succinct. Bev was to deliver the money in a non-bugged duffel bag at 10:00 p.m. on the back steps of the outbuilding behind the mill house. Allen, along with Preston and several deputies from the department, had established a staging area a mile from the site. Olivia was waiting for showtime in Jayden's cruiser as all the law enforcement personnel conferenced.

In the hours that had passed between the breakup of the afternoon's strategy session in Bev's office and now,

Olivia cooled her heels at home. Trying to ease her restlessness, she watched the first ten minutes of a British crime drama and then read a chapter of a mystery novel. The tone of both hit too close for comfort, so she zoned out, viewing a steady stream of cat videos in anticipation of Willow's three-month stay.

She had related her role in the sting to her father and was equally surprised and disturbed by his enthusiasm over her participation. Seven months ago, he would've grounded her if he could've for investigating Paige's murder. Now, he wanted to be the Watson to her Holmes. He tried to guilt-trip her into bringing him along as a spectator, but she had learned her lesson on Friday night and vetoed his entreaties. He had given in, harrumphing and calling her a killjoy, but still lovingly insisted she have dinner before a deputy picked her up at eight.

Now, as she was biding her time in the cruiser, she checked her e-mail, reviewing three purchases she'd made before Jayden had arrived at the house. She had splurged, dipping into her savings for a twenty-day baking course for her father at the school in Oregon. Crossing her fingers, she had completed the purchase, hoping he was up for traveling in the spring. The red silicone spatula set was an easy-peasy click and buy, coming with two-day free shipping. And a small, family-owned outdoor store in southern Virginia had the exact present she'd been seeking for Preston. She didn't mind paying a premium for expedited shipping to guarantee his gift would arrive by Christmas.

Three knuckle taps on the window spurred her to look up from her screen. Jayden, decked out in tactical gear over her regulation uniform, opened the door for her. "We're ready for you."

Olivia checked that her phone was set to silent before dropping it into her coat pocket. Then she exited the cruiser and followed Jayden to the gathered team. Preston dismissed the deputies, giving them the go-ahead to advance to their assigned positions.

"Are you ready?" Allen asked Olivia. When she nodded, he said, "Let's review the plan. You'll drive Mrs. Styles' car on the access road to the site and park in the lot. The duffel is in the front seat. The outbuilding is twenty yards behind the house and to your left. Proceed to the drop site, place the bag on the steps, and hurry back to the car. You'll drive out and meet us here. Keep your head up and on a swivel. If you notice anything unusual or see anyone, get out of there. We'll have visual on you when you approach the mill house, but once you go behind the outbuilding, you'll be out of our sight. Don't stop. Move quickly. Questions?"

"No."

"Don't worry," Allen said. "You'll do fine. Detective, I'll set up at position two while you finish with her." With that, he turned and walked to his car.

Preston and Olivia stood alone by his F-150.

"What do you have to finish with me?" she asked.

He opened the driver's side rear door of his truck and grabbed a black tactical vest from the backseat. "Can you remove your coat?"

She did as he asked. "I take it that's a bulletproof vest."

He pulled apart the wide straps on both sides. "It's ballistic body armor with polyethylene plates. Nothing is truly bulletproof, but this is the highest level of protection we have at the station." He lifted the vest and slipped it over her head.

The heft hit her by surprise. "How much does this weigh?"

"About nine pounds. I need to adjust it."

He started on her right, bracing his hand on the portion of the vest covering her ribcage. Then he wrapped the back flap around her, securing the halves together. After he repeated the procedure on her left, he ran his hands all around the bottom half, checking for fit.

She was scarcely breathing. If it weren't for the ballistic vest and protective plates, his touch would've been downright intimate.

"How does that feel?" he asked.

You have no idea. "Snug."

"Perfect. Now for the shoulder straps."

He unfastened the wide band over her left shoulder. "Your shirt got bunched up here." He pulled the top of the vest out, placing his hand over her collarbone.

There was no way to silence the breakneck whumping of her heart. She breathed in deep, willing her eyes not to focus on his lips that were a few inches from hers.

His hand lingered as he suppressed a smile, but the emergence of his dimple hinted at what he was thinking. "That's a strong heartbeat."

Her quick-to-blush nature left her with nowhere to hide. "It betrays me." At that, his lips parted, and she matched his flirtatious grin. "Are you going to finish, Detective?"

He ran his hand over her shoulder, smoothing out her shirt, and then tugged the two halves of the vest together so hard, she almost toppled into him. After he finished with the other side, he gently freed the lengths of her hair trapped between her shirt and the vest. He checked for fit one more time and then helped her put her coat back on.

She opened the car door and sat behind the wheel, eyeing the duffel bag on the passenger seat. "I would've thought you'd need something larger for ten thousand dollars. Where's the money from?"

He bent down, leaning in toward her. "Allen provided it."

"Where's his team, anyway? Shouldn't they be around?"

"I don't think he's got much of a team, maybe only a few others working with him. He's the lead and our only contact person. Don't worry about them. We're the point on tactical, and I have deputies in position as close as we can be." He reached forward, taking hold of her hand.

"Olivia, if you sense anything is wrong, promise me you'll get out of there."

His touch tickled the butterflies in her stomach. "Liv," she replied. "You should start calling me Liv. And I know, bob and weave. Be unpredictable."

He straightened, releasing her hand. "That I know you can do."

She nodded while reaching for her seatbelt. "I'll see you in a few minutes."

"Thank you for doing this, Liv."

He closed the door as she started the engine. Within seconds, she took off, glancing in the rearview mirror as he watched her drive away.

The last time she had visited the Turner Mill House was on a field trip during elementary school. The outing was etched in her memory only because she tripped on a gravel path while running, bloodying both of her knees. Now, the earlier thick cloud cover had thinned, allowing black gaps to color the evening sky. The nearly full moon peeked brightly through, making the streaking gray clouds appear like phantoms haunting the night.

She drove into the unlit lot, parked, and left Bev's car with the duffel in hand. She hastened, scanning in all directions, but there wasn't even a hoot from an owl to hear. After walking around the side of the mill house, she paused at the rear corner and surveyed the tree line. Though it was too dark to see if anyone was there, she felt a smidgeon better for having checked before making herself an easy target.

The outbuilding was larger than a shed, but not big enough to be a barn. She hurried across the twenty-yard gap, beelining for the steps behind the building. Arriving in a jiff, she turned her back to the woods. The moment she set the duffel down, a green laser dot appeared on her hand. She spun like a top, and the dot jumped to the center of her chest. Her eyes shot up, focusing on a thin, green laser beam shining from the forest. She took a shallow breath, and before her exhale, it vanished.

The message was loud and clear. She turned and bolted to Bev's car, adding a few zigzags in case the threat targeted her again. After peeling out of the parking lot, she floored it down the access road and drove to her rendezvous.

Preston and Allen were waiting, and when she told them of being sighted by a scope, they argued about whether to move in. They finally agreed to hold their positions after conferring with Jayden, who confirmed a visual of the bag, which was still sitting on the outbuilding's steps.

Though the laser targeting had kicked off Olivia's flight response, it hadn't rattled her, as she took it more as a show than a threat. Someone was making a point, and she was merely the pawn in play. Maybe, too, her uncanny calm had to do with Preston's trust in the vest to protect her in the worst-case scenario.

Preston waved a deputy over as Allen stepped away to make a call.

"Let me help you get the vest off," Preston said.

She removed her coat, and then he ripped open the straps and lifted it over her head.

"The deputy is going to take you home."

She wanted to stay but knew he wouldn't allow it. He was all business, and now wasn't the time or place for personal conversation. So they parted with barely another word as the day neared its end. Settling into the front seat of the deputy's cruiser, she prayed that by morning, the police would have the blackmailer in custody. Then she could move on with her life and start over with Preston, minus the need for a ballistic vest.

CHAPTER 36

Last night, after detailing the sting to her father, Olivia had dropped into bed, and it was lights out within minutes as best she could remember. Now, diffuse morning light and Buddy's rhythmic snoring gently nudged her to start her Tuesday.

All was quiet on the message front, but perhaps she'd been wrong to assume Preston would contact her if the police had made an arrest. After taking a shower and getting dressed, she walked downstairs with her cell in hand and found her father reading the newspaper in the living room. The twinkling tree and cheery Christmas tunes streaming from his laptop buoyed her weary mood.

He paused the music, folded his paper, and placed it beside his coffee mug on the table. "Did I wake you?"

She bent down, greeting him with a kiss on his cheek. "No. I've been up for a while."

"Have you heard any news from last night yet?"

She perched on the sofa's arm as Buddy padded down the stairs. "No."

"Maybe no news is good news. Why don't you call Preston?"

And ask his intentions?

She refused to think about what the two had discussed, still preferring to pretend it didn't happen. Given their flirtations yesterday, it must not have been life-altering, horrifying, or humiliating. Small comfort, but that's the story she was sticking with now, and perhaps forever.

"It's a little early," she said.

"It's nine o'clock. I think he'll already be working."

"Good point."

She first tried his cell but got ushered straight to voice mail. Then she dialed him direct at the station, and after two rings, the call connected.

"Apple Station Police. Deputy Stone at the desk of Detective Hills."

"Hi, Jayden. It's Olivia. Is Preston there?"

"He's speaking with the chief in his office. Wait, it looks like they're done. Hold on ... Detective Hills, I've got Olivia Penn on the phone."

She heard him thanking Jayden, and then he came on the line.

"This is Detective Hills, but I'm not sure I know an *Olivia*. I'm acquainted with a *Liv*, though."

The silly quip sparked a smile, and she stood and turned away from her father, hiding her amusement.

"I use Olivia as my pen name." That earned her a chuckle. "I don't want to take up too much of your time, but I was curious about what happened after I left last night."

"Dylan Carter showed up."

"Dylan is the blackmailer?"

"He swears he knew nothing about it. He told us he had received an anonymous text saying someone had information regarding Stuart. The sender instructed him to come to the Turner Mill House at midnight."

She paced around the coffee table and glanced at her father, who was unapologetically listening to her side of the conversation. "Do you believe him?"

He sighed. "I don't know. He's in custody, but we can't hold him long without charges. We're getting a warrant to search his phone and computer. I have deputies rechecking his alibi for the time of Stuart's death."

"I'm sorry last night didn't work out the way you wanted."

"There were no guarantees, and it doesn't take away from the bravery of what you did."

"It helped to be wearing body armor," she joked. "How's your mom holding up?"

"She's hanging in there, but she's worried about the blackmailer's threat of contacting the media."

Scratching at the back door prompted Olivia to step around the sofa to let Buddy out to do his business.

"I'll get him," her dad whispered.

She waved him off and then walked into the kitchen. "Do you think that's even an actual threat?"

"No, and the demand for the money last night may not have been real either."

She let Buddy loose, watching for a second to ensure he was heading for his normal spot, and then closed the door. "What do you mean?"

"Early this morning, I drove to my dad's cabin and found it ransacked. Somebody went through the inside and ripped it apart."

"Oh, I'm so sorry. That can't be random or coincidence. Do you think that means the blackmail drop was a setup?"

"Yeah. I think whoever targeted you with the laser was aiming to tie up our resources. They knew we'd send deputies to search the woods at some point, and we did. Meanwhile, they had hours to go through the cabin."

She leaned against the countertop. "It was all a diversion. Do you think it was Royce?"

"It's the most logical conclusion. Liv, I can't overstate my gratitude for what you did last night. Having a citizen take part in an operation like that usually isn't even a consideration. If it hadn't been about my mother, there's no way I would've allowed you to be involved. You've done more than enough to help my family, and I don't want you to take any more risks. Going forward, leave the case to the police."

She nodded, not having a solid angle to pursue, anyway. "I hear you."

"Okay, I need to go. Can I call you later?"

After she gave him the green light, they said a brief goodbye and ended the call.

She opened the back door, and Buddy barreled inside, scampering straight for a vent blasting warm air near his dog bed in the corner.

Her father joined her in the kitchen, carrying his empty cup. "I think I got the gist of it."

"You missed the part about Joe's cabin being torn apart."

He shook his head. "Poor Bev. She's got to be worried sick. Maybe you should keep a low profile today and get that tracker off your car. The same whacko who put it there could be the one who trashed their cabin."

"You're right about Bev. Maybe about the tracker too."

Whoever had deemed her of enough interest to keep tabs on was still out there, and the tracker kept them connected. She decided to give it the day before telling Preston, knowing he would sideline her after finding out.

Her father set his cup on the counter and then stepped over to the pantry and removed an airtight storage container of Buddy's dry kibble. "It seems like you've done all you can do."

She grabbed an apple and a cup of yogurt from the refrigerator, setting both on the table. "Maybe." After plucking her coat off the hook rack, she donned it, dropping her keys and cell into one of its pockets. "I'll be out in the office for a while." She gathered her breakfast and a spoon from the drawer, leaving through the back door as her father poured bite-sized morsels into Buddy's bowl.

A bluebird sky hung over her brief stroll through the backyard. The cottage lights were still shining from last night, though their colors lacked dazzlement in the day. She had thought very little about the holidays since Friday afternoon. Other than ordering the gifts yesterday, the season's spirit had been in short supply from the moment she spotted Nolan's Jeep blocking in her car. Normally, she'd be making lunch plans with Sophia or A.J., relieved not to be like others in a frenzy, dashing about town. Now, she ixnayed the thought of any more shopping. They could make do with the groceries already in the house until next week. At least with all her father's baking in the freezer, dessert was just a matter of thawing from now until February.

She unlocked the office, stepped inside, and turned off the outdoor lights. Though the two windows helped cool the cottage in the summer, chilly air seeped through them during the winter months. A pair of portable heaters combated the drafts, making the one-room building cozy within minutes of being turned on.

She sat at her desk, booted up her laptop, and dug into her breakfast, distracted by Dylan's arrest. He was Mensa material, and it seemed implausible that an anonymous text would have duped him. Perhaps more likely, he'd set himself up as a victim, diverting the police's attention away from his family. He hadn't been shy in sharing his scorn for Stuart and his loving devotion to Kaitlyn. Of all the suspects in her pool, he had been the most forthcoming.

There were two others circling the edges of the spiraling narrative, whom she knew little about. Henry Zimmerman and Carie Bullet were both mysteries, and the question was whether they were minor or major characters.

Armed with what Bev had told her about Henry, she opened a browser and searched for his name, curious about what would come up first. The top results highlighted his aerospace engineering background and the device he had patented.

Switching tactics, she entered "Zimmerman obituary" and "Apple Station, Virginia." She struck pay dirt with a link to a tribute to his wife and daughter on the website of the funeral home responsible for their arrangements. A caption under his wife's photo listed her birthday as today.

Adding her name to a long tail of keywords, Olivia fished for information about the accident. A local paper from her hometown detailed the events of that horrible day. The accident had occurred at noon when her car hit a patch of black ice and collided with a tractor trailer.

She cringed reading the details, unable to imagine Henry's sudden tragic loss. His withdrawal from life spoke to a devotion that had left him both unwilling and indifferent to moving on. She knew grief was something one never gets over, though you become better in time.

Between the deaths of her mother and Paige, she had to trust that a heart heals from sorrow, whole and complete, given space and love.

Every year, on the anniversary of her mother's passing, she and her father would visit the gravesite around the time of her death. It was a special way of memorializing the day and celebrating her mother's life. She glanced at the laptop's screen. It was thirty minutes before noon, and she wondered whether Henry may do the same. She wanted to speak with him again, especially now, after the ransacking of Joe's cabin. As forthcoming as Dylan had been, Henry was equally reticent.

Olivia turned her attention to Carie Bullet. She fired off a text to Cassandra, inquiring if her research had yielded any leads. Then she opened the photos on her phone and reviewed Paige's notes about the burglary. Scrolling through the pages, she focused on the words Paige had circled: Marco, Tuxedo Bandit, Star of Athens, partial print, Stuart Carter.

Cassandra replied, "Nada, zippo, zilch on Carie Bullet. Is she a ghost?"

A ghost. That was the same word Allen and Mack had used to describe Royce. She dialed Cassandra and placed her on speaker.

"Hey, Liv. Did you see my text?"

"Yes. I'm looking through Paige's notes from when she spoke with Marco. She wrote that the police found a partial print at one burglary."

"That's what Marco told me too," Cassandra said.

"Did he say what his source was on that?"

"An off-the-record interview with a detective investigating the theft. Why do you ask?"

She silently read Paige's circled words again. "Ghosts don't leave evidence."

"What does that mean?" Cassandra asked. "Is there something you'd like to share?"

"I'm working on it. Thanks, Cassandra. I'll get back in touch with you later."

They ended the call, and then she swiveled in her seat while finishing the last bites of her apple. Two people, two ghosts working together. One to create the distraction and the other to recover the gem. She would bet on the theory that one of the two had murdered Stuart.

"Carie Boo-lay," she said with an exaggerated French accent. All the other Caries she'd ever known spelt their name with two *R*s. "Boo-lay, Bullet, bull. But you're missing an *R*. But you're not real. But who are you? But, but, but …" She rubbed her eyes and then leaned forward, resting her arms on the desk and her chin in her hand. "But, but, but … Butler … Butler. Rho Butler. Alice Butler. Alice. Alice Butler … Alice … Butler."

She shot up straight, snatched a notepad out of a drawer, and scribbled "CARIE BULLET" on it. Her focus tap-danced between the first and last names, and then she wrote "BUTLER" underneath. One by one, she crossed off the letters from above, leaving her with "CAIEL." A shake and a stir of what remained confirmed her suspicion. Carie Bullet was an anagram for Alice Butler. One ghost no more.

Though it would be criminally naive to consider it a coincidence, the alias wasn't evidence of wrongdoing. Someone could've hired Rho to wheedle information out of Stuart about the night of the heist. Without something meatier, Olivia lacked a solid motive to relay to the police. For now, keeping all the moving pieces in a holding pattern was the best strategy. As long as her cover remained intact, Rho would continue playing her part. If Bev knew the truth, she'd be a wreck around Rho and surely tip her off. Where Rhett fit in, Olivia was unsure. Sam had vouched for him, but secrets, mystery, and deception shrouded their business. Whether they could trust Rhett remained in question.

Olivia glanced at the time as the hour ticked closer to noon. Then she launched from her seat, turned off the heaters, and threw her coat on. Acting on a hunch, she left the office and raced across the lawn to her car, scheming to scare up a lead on the second ghost by poking around at the graveyard.

CHAPTER 37

Seasonal speckles of red and green adorned the dormant, brown grass on the grounds of St. Luke's cemetery. Poinsettias, wreaths, and potted trees prevailed as gravesite memorials. But cards, chocolates, and balloons were always scattered among the mementos, along with random pinwheels. Between the regular visitors and those that only came during the holidays, the cemetery was never livelier than at Christmas.

Olivia pulled into the lot in front of St. Luke's Church a few minutes before noon, joining three other parked cars. Scanning the grounds from behind the wheel, she was second-guessing her hunch. Finding Henry here was a long shot, but only time would be lost if he didn't show. She'd still track him down by trekking out to his cabin, crossing her fingers he didn't tote his rifle around during the day. There was no guarantee he would be any more forthcoming in meeting her here, but trying again on neutral ground, where they both had buried loved ones, at least gave them something in common.

She walked down a gentle slope through the cemetery and stood for a few minutes at Paige's grave. Two years ago, Paige had stayed with her in Georgetown over a weekend near the holidays. They attended *A Christmas Carol* at Ford's Theater and then staged their own head-to-head bake-off challenge at her condo. Paige made her laugh throughout the visit, imitating Scrooge's "humbug" using an exaggerated southern drawl. A framed photo of them together from that weekend sat on Olivia's dresser. It was one of the first sights to brighten her eyes every morning when she woke.

Then she strolled a short distance to where her mother was buried. Last week, she had placed a bouquet of fresh holly by the memorial marker, cut from shrubs her mother had planted in front of the house. The hollies were older than Olivia and may still be alive after she was gone. Maybe one day, if she ever had a child, they would do the same for her. After a few quiet minutes recalling the last Christmas that her family had shared, she turned to visit Joe's grave.

A car door's closing clunk caught her attention. She looked over her shoulder at the parking lot as Henry walked toward the cemetery section designated as "The Garden of the Blessed Mother." She reversed course, bowing her head while keeping her distance. Not wanting to disturb him at the graves of his wife and daughter, she'd wait to approach until he was finished. She took her time, weaving her way through the memorial stones, and paused twice to pray at random sites. At each, she spent ten minutes, paying respects to those who were helping her stall without attracting his attention.

She glanced his way as he closed a small book and made the sign of the cross. Then he touched a fingertip kiss on the top of each grave marker, stepped onto the sidewalk, and strode back toward his car.

She moved to intercept him, meeting him halfway along the length of the church with a smile and a warm wave.

"Mr. Zimmerman, can I speak with you for a moment?"

He stopped on a dime, eyed her, and sparked with recognition. "What do you want?" he growled.

"I'm sorry about your wife and daughter. Bev Styles told me about your loss. I know today must be a tough day for you."

"What would you know about that?"

She gestured toward where her mother was buried. "My mom's grave is over there."

He looked behind him and then back at her, ratcheting down his gruff demeanor. "I'm sorry to hear that. You look too young to have lost your mother."

She inched forward. "Every year, on the anniversary of her passing, my dad and I come up together around the time she died. I had a hunch you may do the same."

He nodded. "I wasn't with them when they died, so

coming here when they did makes me feel closer to them."

"I can understand that." She paused, ensuring no one was around. "Mr. Zimmerman, I need your help."

He pocketed his prayer book, looking at her as if she was speaking Greek. "With what?"

"Joe Hill's wife and son are in trouble."

His expression shifted, resembling that of her father whenever she needed aid. "I don't know how I can help them. I've never even met them."

"Late last night, an intruder ransacked Joe's cabin. It wasn't random. They were searching for something specific. Did you hear or see anything unusual?"

He shook his head. "No. Who would do that?"

"Three years ago, on Christmas Eve, Joe let someone he knew stay at his cabin. On Friday, that man was murdered not far from it. I know you and Joe were friends. Did he visit you that Christmas Eve night?"

His disposition about-faced. "I've gotta go." He took off, hurrying past her.

She spun and jogged a few paces to catch up. "Please, Mr. Zimmerman." He stopped when she got ahead of him and held up her hand. "Two crimes have been committed that are related to that night three years ago. Joe's wife and son need your help. If Joe was still alive, he would do anything to protect them. But since he's not, if you know something about that night, will you help them now?"

He glanced at his watch, and then twice started and

stopped himself from speaking. His vacillation confirmed she was onto something, and his wavering hinted that a part of him was willing to share. If he didn't volunteer what he knew, though, there was little else she could do.

"Joe was a good man. He spoke highly of his wife and son. They were what mattered the most to him—like my wife and daughter to me." The weight of the day tipped the scales as he swatted the air in front of him, sighing with the bitter loneliness of someone who had given up on life. "What the hell does it matter now, anyway?" He peeked at his watch again. "My dog and cat need feeding. If you want to know what happened that night, you'll have to follow me home."

CHAPTER 38

Dark-honey-stained walls complemented maple hardwood flooring, infusing Henry's home with a soothing, affluent air. In the living room, two saddle-brown leather sofas faced each other, separated by a walnut table with scalloped legs. A floor-to-ceiling stonewall fireplace anchored the spacious room, primed to provide cozy warmth on a wintry night. Olivia imagined curling up on the sofa and losing herself in a novel, lulled by the calming charm of the rustic, romantic hearth. Though artfully designed and arranged with taste, the sparse interior lacked life and flare. No photos or mementos were displayed, holding personal meaning or sentimental value.

Henry invited her to sit and then excused himself while he fed his cat and shepherd. She sunk into the comfy cushions on the sofa, musing that it was a shame that he didn't have someone to share his beautiful home with. The disparity between Henry's house and Joe's cabin couldn't be more dramatic. This spacious chalet made Joe's one-room man cave seem like an outpost shelter.

Henry returned, shadowed by a sleek black cat with a high, curled tail. He sat on the opposite sofa and glanced at his feline companion. "I rush home to feed her, but she'll eat only when she's good and ready."

"She's so cute. What's her name?"

He leaned forward for a moment and brushed the cat's cheek. "Bella. Because she's my beauty."

"That suits her. I'll be cat sitting for three months to help a friend. I live with my dad, and he has a beagle puppy. The cat is staying in our home, and I'm worried about how they'll get along."

Henry settled back, resting his elbow on the sofa's arm. "Don't believe the nonsense you hear about cats and dogs fighting all the time. Daisy and Bella are best friends. You need to give cats space and respect their boundaries, but they'll return all the love you show them in their own way."

"Thanks for the encouragement and advice. I've never taken care of a cat. I'm hoping the temporary arrangement doesn't stress her too much."

"You'll both do fine. I bet you won't want to give her back." He reached toward an end table next to the sofa. After picking up a bottle of amber liquor and a thick glass tumbler, he poured himself a drink. "Would you like some bourbon?"

Being neither a day drinker nor a whiskey aficionado, she politely declined. Though eager to get to the reason for her visit, she waited for Henry to tell his story in his own way and time.

He sipped his bourbon and then held the tumbler in his lap. "I met Joe the day my wife and daughter died. He's the one who came to tell me about the accident. I was in shock and in no condition to drive, so he took me to the hospital and stayed until I was ready to come home." His eyes lowered for a moment, as if drifting through memories of that day. "He kept in touch afterward. When I lived at my old house, he'd check in on me from time to time. We'd get together once a month at the tavern in town for a drink. Then he started inviting me to his cabin sometimes when he stayed for the weekend. That's how I found this property. I liked the isolation, so I sold my house and built this place."

She gazed at the fireplace's stately stonework. "You have a gorgeous home."

"I had nothing to do with the design of it. I hired a young man who did all of this. It cost a fortune, but I didn't care. I wouldn't know the slightest thing about what goes with what. I relied on my wife for that." He swirled his bourbon and then took a sip. "What kind of trouble are Joe's wife and son in?"

She outlined the heist and the blackmail threats while he listened without saying a word or giving away his hand.

"Who was the man murdered Friday night?" he asked.

"Stuart Carter. He was local and had family in the area. His ex-wife, two children, and granddaughter live in Apple Station. Stuart had several run-ins with the law. Three weeks before his murder, he had been released from a prison near Richmond after serving time for stealing a car and violating his probation."

"He sounds like a real prince. How old is the granddaughter?"

"Five."

"Are kids in school at that age these days?"

She nodded. "She'd be in kindergarten, but she can't go to school because of a medical condition."

"What's wrong with her?" he asked matter-of-factly.

Because Darcy had already publicly discussed Kaitlyn's diagnosis, Olivia felt okay about sharing the big picture. "She has a respiratory condition that makes her susceptible to infections. For her to be in an environment like a school where there are always colds going around isn't ideal. There's a medication that could help her, but her mother's insurance has denied coverage, and the family can't afford it, otherwise."

He downed the rest of his bourbon. "Damn insurance companies. That's not right. That little girl is just an algorithm to them."

Whether it was the alcohol or the friendly, listening ear, Henry seemed comfortable enough for her to press him on the reason she was here.

"There are some who think Stuart found the necklace in the car he stole, hid it that night three years ago, and then came back looking for it after his release from prison. Someone told me Stuart had a plan to turn his life around. They think the plan was to retrieve the necklace, sell it, and buy back his family. But nobody even knows for sure whether he knew about the necklace or if he hid it someplace."

Henry grabbed the bottle of bourbon and poured himself another drink. "This Stuart … If he came back looking for that necklace, he wasn't ever going to find it."

That got her attention like a tornado siren when bluebird skies turn ominously green. "Why would that be?"

He breathed in deep and quickly exhaled. "You're right. Joe came to my place that Christmas Eve night. It was after eleven, but I was still awake. He apologized for showing up late and unannounced, but he needed a favor. He told me someone was staying at his cabin for at least a day, but maybe longer. He asked if I would keep an eye and ear out for anything unusual. If I drove by there and saw other cars or people, he wanted me to call him. I said sure, no problem. Then we spent some time talking right here on these sofas."

The mystery of Joe's missing hours finally had been solved. She sat rapt, waiting for Henry to fill in the remaining gaps of the story that Joe and Stuart could no longer tell.

"It was after one in the morning when he left,"

Henry continued. "About half an hour later, I drove down the road, parked my car a short distance from the cabin, and walked the rest of the way to look around."

"Why?"

"It was apparent to me that whoever was staying there—this Stuart fellow—was trouble. Joe wouldn't have asked me to watch his place if he didn't have concerns. Joe had a big heart, and I didn't want his cabin to get trashed because he was doing someone a favor."

"So, you went to check it out, and then what?"

"The front door was partway open, and there was a Mercedes parked outside. I peeked in the window, and I saw a guy with his head down on the kitchen table with a bottle of whiskey and a gun beside him. This lowlife looked like he didn't have two pennies to rub together. Nothing looked right about the situation. I used to own a Mercedes, so I know how much those cars cost. The guy was out like a light. I didn't want to risk waking him by walking inside, especially with the gun sitting there and him probably all sauced up. So, I decided to look through the car. I figured I'd find drugs or more guns. When I popped the trunk, I saw a duffel bag."

Bella jumped onto the sofa and rubbed her head along his arm. He went silent for a minute, as if he had finished telling his story.

"What was in the duffel?"

He took a slow sip of bourbon. "A bunch of tools, and a jewelry box that held what must be this necklace you're talking about."

Her pulse thumped as she connected the dots with the ramifications of the revelation. All the disjointed pieces of the puzzle came together with Henry as the missing link.

"What happened to the necklace?" she blurted.

He stared squarely at her. "I took it."

She launched to the edge of the sofa. "That's stolen property. The Star of Athens is worth fifteen million dollars."

The words had no effect on him. "What kind of arrogant fool spends that much on a necklace? That's a vanity piece. Useless. For someone with that kind of money, that necklace is a trinket. It's not their retirement plan."

Mack, Allen, and Royce were all right in their estimations. The Star of Athens had been hidden, but not where or by whom they expected.

"Do you still have the necklace?" After he nodded, she clarified, "You have it here, in this house?"

"No. It's in a storage unit."

Her thoughts leapt to the closest facility she knew. "The Stuff and Go off Somerset Turnpike?"

"Yes. That's where I stored my wife's and daughter's things. I didn't want it here, so I took it there."

She slid back on the sofa. "Why did you take it? And why didn't you tell Joe or go to the police with it?"

He sipped the last drops of bourbon in his tumbler and then picked up the bottle. Bella swatted his arm, and he frowned, returning both to the table.

"The next day, I went to see if the guy was still there, and when I got close enough, I saw police cars everywhere. I turned around and came home. I didn't know what was going on. I wanted to talk with Joe first. He let this man stay at his cabin, but I didn't know the whole story. I gathered the guy stole the necklace and probably the car. I'm sure Joe knew nothing about either or he would've never let him stay. But I thought if I went to the police, Joe could get in trouble."

"You were trying to protect him," she said.

"That's right. I thought Joe would come the next day and tell me what had happened, but he didn't. I decided I'd wait until the next time he visited, and I'd bring it up then. But I never saw him again. I learned a few months later that he had died of a heart attack. What was I going to do with the necklace at that point? It wasn't like I could take it to the police and say I found it in the woods. I figured that's why all those cops were there that day. I looked to see if there was anything in the papers about it, but I couldn't find a single mention of it. With Joe no longer here to tell his side of the story and nobody missing it, I thought it best to let it be."

"You never thought of getting rid of it? If you believed it was stolen, weren't you afraid of being caught?"

He shook his head. "I could tell it was worth a lot. I never would've guessed fifteen million. I wouldn't trash it, and I don't need the money." He paused as his eyes watered. "I'd sell everything I have in a heartbeat, including that damn necklace, if it would give me my wife and daughter back."

Her shoulders lowered, feeling the weight of his pain. He had been a loving husband and father who now lived trapped by his grief. A door had been closed, and he stood still on the other side, unable to walk away. To break through his isolation, he needed to find meaning in his life that was larger and outside of himself.

Henry's reason for taking the Star of Athens was the same motivation fueling her actions to protect Preston and Bev. What he did to safeguard Joe, she now had to do for them.

"I understand why you did what you did," she said. "But the necklace needs to be returned to the rightful owners. I don't know what this means for you legally, but I think if the police hear your story, maybe they'll show some leniency. There are no guarantees, but I have to tell the police what I know."

He leaned forward, folding his hands in his lap. "I took it to protect Joe. I never thought a man would die because of what I did."

"Stuart's murder is not your fault. That's not on you."

They shared a few quiet minutes. As Henry sifted through memories, she mapped out the puzzle pieces in her head. The blame fell on whoever was working with Royce. Allen had been adamant that the thief always had been a loner, but something had changed in this case. He had to bring in a trusted ally with a certain skill set for his scheme to recover the necklace.

Her pulse spiked as the fog lifted and the flywheel broke free. The misdirection and the connection between the criminal duo became clear as day. The score of a lifetime and the thief's legacy would be denied, thanks to Carie Bullet's visit with Stuart in prison. Both needed to be caught red-handed, and now she had the right bait to hook them.

"Can I get the necklace from your storage unit?" she asked, as her thoughts raced, hatching a plan.

"I'll take you."

I have to get them there together first and then have the police come.

She shook her head. "I need you to stay here and help me."

"How can I help you from here?"

The timing has to be just right. Thirty minutes? No. Forty-five. Might not be enough.

"Do you have paper and a pen?" she said.

He rose and took a pad and pencil from a drawer in a side table, then came back to the sofa and handed them to her. She wrote Preston's cell number on the top sheet, ripped it out, and gave it to him.

I just need one of them to bite.

"What's a good number to call you on?" She entered the number he gave her into her phone. "Once I leave your house, if you don't hear from me in one hour, call Joe's son, Preston, and tell him I'm in trouble at the storage facility. Tell him I asked you to do this. One hour."

"If you're in danger, I can't let you go there alone."

She slid forward and then stood. Though her skill set didn't include executing stings with known criminals, it was Sam's bread and butter. "I'll have backup there, but I need you to be my backup here."

He sighed, hesitating and debating while shaking his head.

"Time is of the essence," she urged. "I have to know you'll make the call. Please."

He pushed up from the sofa, wincing but giving in. "Okay. I'll do it."

He retrieved the key to the unit and told her where to find the necklace inside. After promising to be careful, she left his house and raced to her vehicle. If correct, she could bring down two birds with one fifteen-million-dollar stone. Everything hinged on timing—sixty minutes, and Henry's call.

The Expedition jostled about at the hasty pace once its tires hit the rutted dirt road where Henry's paved entry ended. In less than five minutes, Olivia shifted into park in front of Joe's cabin and grabbed her phone, allowing the engine to idle.

She opened her photos to the first sheet of Paige's notes, focusing on the circled words "Tuxedo Bandit" and "partial print." Running one last time through her suspect pool, she arrived at the same conclusion. Two among all had been less than forthcoming, misdirecting her with their motivation. Had it not been for Paige's circled clues, the thief and the murderer may have gone unnoticed.

She knew what she was about to do went against Preston's wishes for her to stay out of trouble. Twice before, she'd pursued cases when he warned her not to. Now, again, she'd have to rely on his quick response and understanding. She didn't fancy herself more capable than the police, but she was in a unique position to recover the necklace and trap the thief and the murderer. To clear his family's name, she was willing to take the risk, even if it drove a wedge between them.

With precious time ticking by, she called Preston's cell, though not to tip him off. For her plan to succeed, she had to ensure he was in town and ready to respond to Henry's call. He would be more likely to believe and react to an SOS than the dispatch monitoring the station's emergency line. The slightest delay in sending the cavalry could leave her up a creek, cornered by two criminals. If she couldn't rope him into his role, her scheme would need rapid recalibrating.

After two rings, he answered. "Hi, Liv. Do you mind if I call you back? I'm in the middle of something."

Me too. "I'm going to be tied up for the next little while here. Can we meet in an hour?" Seconds of silence stretched into an eternity, and she scrambled, pressing him for an answer. "You owe me a coffee."

"Yeah, sure. I can break away for a bit. Allen is here, and we're meeting before he leaves."

"Where's he going?"

"He's returning to D.C. The FBI raided a jeweler's shop in New York yesterday, and they found stolen goods related to one of his cases. Since the leads have dried up in his investigation here, he's taking off."

Her pulse ramped its pace as the clock ticked. She couldn't hint at her ploy, but keeping Allen in town was key to entrapping Royce and his accomplice. "When is he leaving?"

"When we're done."

"Okay. I'll see you soon."

They exchanged a hasty goodbye without making specific plans. She opened her notes app to where she'd stored Allen's contact information, copied the number, and texted him. "Located evidence you're looking for. Meet me at St. Luke's Church ASAP."

Though not expecting a reply, she'd ignore it if one came through. Then, putting the last piece in play, she scrolled through her directory, crossed her fingers, and called Sam.

"Hey, Liv," Sam answered. "We have a problem. Rhett is missing."

"What do you mean?"

"He's gone. So is all his gear. I went to see him this morning, and instead, I found Rho in his room. She hadn't seen him since last night. She's out now looking for him."

Olivia's thoughts were whirling as another minute drained away. "But you vouch for him, right?"

"Yes. It's not like him to flake out on a job, despite everything else that's eye-rolling about the man, myth, and legend."

She shifted the Expedition's gear into drive, readying to peel away. "Okay. Listen to me. I don't have time to explain. Rho is involved in all of this."

"What? How?"

"I've got to get moving, and I—"

"What's going on?" Sam demanded.

"I need your help immediately. You're the only one I can trust right now. Meet me at the Stuff and Go self-storage facility on Somerset Turnpike. Unit eight. Bring firepower. Don't tell anyone what you're doing."

"Whoa, wait. Are you in trouble?"

Olivia disconnected the call with a silent "sorry" to Sam. There was no time for an explanation. She needed Sam to act, not try to talk her out of the plan.

After pocketing her phone, she sped away from the cabin, a small cloud of dust visible in her rearview. She prayed her ten-minute stall was long enough for the tracker on her car to pin her location and signal her stalkers, luring them straight into her trap.

CHAPTER 40

At two-thirty in the afternoon on the day before Christmas Eve, the self-storage facility was a ghost town. Sorting through old things wasn't on people's agendas when new, shiny gifts were waiting for many of them under their trees.

The outdoor complex housed four rows of drive-up units separated by lanes large enough to accommodate midsized moving vans. All the site entrances lined up like soldiers, fronted by ten-foot-wide blue doors. Olivia readily found Henry's unit and parked along its neighbor. After exiting her car, she opened the lock and rolled up the door.

The unit stretched about twenty feet back, but it wasn't even a quarter full. Henry had organized everything toward the rear, leaving plenty of room up front to stash a car and his sofas, if he wanted to.

The site had no electricity, but there was enough natural light for her to make out the contents in the back. She stepped inside, heading for a shelving unit stacked with several rows of labeled cardboard boxes. Personal items belonging to Henry's wife and daughter occupied most of the storage space. She scanned from top to bottom, stopping at a box on the middle shelf marked as "Autumn's Memories."

She slid the box out, set it on the floor, and removed the lid. A framed picture of Henry's family lay on top of his daughter's belongings. Even in the low light, the resemblance between Autumn and her father was evident. In the photo, she wore a Sweet Briar sweatshirt and appeared to be in her early twenties. She stood in between her parents on the steps of the town square's gazebo during Apple Station's annual fall festival.

Olivia removed the photo and several notebooks, placing them all on the floor with care. She pushed aside pint-sized stuffed animals, a stack of greeting cards rubber-banded together, and a baby blanket covered in cartoon butterflies. Underneath everything, at the very bottom, Henry had hidden the Star of Athens. She grasped a white ceramic piggy bank with a round plastic closure on its belly that he had glued in place. As she turned the bank upside down, a faint clink sounded from within.

There was only one way to get the necklace out, and that meant breaking the bank. She took two steps forward, turned her head, and slammed it on the floor. It shattered, scattering a debris field of chunks, fragments, and chips. A black velvet pouch dotted with ceramic dust sat amidst the carnage.

She bent down, picked up the pouch, and unknotted its drawstring tie. Then she opened her palm and slid the hidden contents into her hand. Even in meager light, the Star of Athens sparkled bright, dazzling her eyes with wonderment. The faceted sapphire spanned the length of her pinky, and it glinted as she tilted it from side to side. Any of the necklace's forty brilliant diamonds could've shined as the showcase of a stunning engagement ring. She had neither seen such an exquisite piece of jewelry nor held something worth so much in her hand.

Her phone buzzed once. She dropped the velvet pouch into her coat pocket, pulled out her cell, and flipped it over to view the screen. The text was from Sam. She had to return home but would be at the complex in half an hour. Thirty-five minutes had passed since Olivia left Henry's house, keeping her timing intact.

There was no guarantee the thief or the murderer would show, but she bet the bait in her hand would be too tempting to forego. If neither came, she at least had recovered the necklace to turn over to the police. But if she didn't get the proof she was seeking, the criminal duo could and probably would abscond and disappear like ghosts without a trace.

She stashed the necklace in her coat pocket, placed Autumn's belongings back in the box, and returned it to the shelf. After waiting ten minutes, she heard a car approach and stop nearby. Then the engine cut off, and a car door clunked closed. She opened a voice recorder app, put the phone in an empty coat pocket, and slipped back into the shadows, letting the recording roll.

CHAPTER 41

Allen inched around the edge of the unit's entrance, keeping close to his cover. As Olivia emerged from the shadows, his vigilance eased, and he stepped into the open, greeting her with a relieved smile.

"I'm glad it's you," he said. "I was concerned I wouldn't make it in time."

"You were expecting someone else?" He had no ready response, and before he could conjure one, she proceeded. "What are you doing here? You were supposed to meet me at St. Luke's."

He nodded once, tightening his lips. "I received your text." After stepping a few paces into the unit, he scanned the storage boxes and shelves behind her.

"Did you get lost?" she said.

He looked back at her but didn't counter.

"But you knew I wasn't there. The tracker on my car led you here."

This he seemed primed for, holding his hands up in surrender. "You got me. I admit I placed that on your vehicle on Sunday morning when I came to your house. I'm sorry, but I didn't know if I could trust you. This is the best opportunity we've had in years to capture Royce, and I had to use every means available to make that happen."

"Royce. Not the Tuxedo Bandit? It's a catchier name and more appropriate given how he conned people into believing he was someone else."

Allen glanced behind him and then locked in on the remains of the piggy bank off to her side. "You texted that you found evidence."

Ignoring the diversion, she continued. "Multiple sources confirm that investigators dubbed the serial jewel thief the Tuxedo Bandit. He's profiled as a charming chameleon who blended in with the social circles he targeted. Yet, you call him Royce. At first, I thought it was an inside joke amongst the agents involved. Strange to double up on the pseudonym, but maybe."

"Yes, that's all correct," he offered.

Which was to say nothing. "Then there was the story about using your badge to grease wheels to tour Dumbarton Oaks with your daughter. That struck me as odd. It's not a federal property, and how would you even access the grounds on Christmas? And why would an FBI agent admit to doing so to a practical stranger? The thing is—I don't believe that happened. I do believe, though, that you have a daughter."

Allen kept his distance, assuming the same flat expression of authority as when she first met him. "I'm not sure where you're heading with this, but if you found the Star of Athens or evidence leading to it, you'll need to turn it over."

Please be watching the time, Henry.

"Where's your team?" she asked. After he shook his head, as if not understanding the question, she carried on. "Your team was only one other person. You insisted Royce was a loner, but the diversion of the blackmail scheme suggested two actors. I wondered who the famed Tuxedo Bandit would trust enough to help him recover a fifteen-million-dollar necklace. It would have to be someone extremely close, someone like family. At first, I didn't understand why you misled me about Stuart's visitor log. Why were you so adamant that Mack had lied about a female reporter seeing him in prison?"

"John Mack is a liar," he interjected.

"Then, when I figured out Carie Bullet is an alias for Alice Butler, aka Rho Butler, it became clear."

Allen held up his hand. "Stop, Ms. Penn. You're wasting my time."

She stepped forward. "You didn't want to confirm evidence of her—your accomplice—being involved. You were trying to protect her. Could there be a special reason for that?"

His voice grew louder as he loosened his tie. "I'm not sure what game you're playing. If you have the Star of

Athens, hand it over now before I change my mind about charging you with obstruction."

Make the call, Henry.

She estimated they'd been talking for ten minutes. Needing more time, she stalled, staring in silence for a short while until playing her last card. "You gave yourself away when you described Royce as a ghost. Somebody said the same to me about Carie Bullet, but she wasn't really a ghost. The thing is—ghosts don't leave evidence."

"I don't know what you're talking about."

She reached into her pocket and tilted the phone's microphone toward him. "You insisted there was no evidence left at any of the crime scenes."

He looked over his shoulder again and then back at her while rubbing his chin.

"Except you did leave something behind," she said.

He pointed at his chest. "Me? Let me get this straight. You think *I'm* the thief? Do you have any idea how absurd that sounds? I'm an FBI agent. I'm not Royce or the Tuxedo Bandit or whatever cutesy name you want to use."

"In your hubris, you thought you were so careful and cunning in your execution that you got away clean every time. What you don't know is that you left a partial print at a heist in Miami. I assume anyone deeply involved in pursuing Royce would know that, Agent Allen."

He smirked, placing his hands on his hips. "Why would I share evidence of the investigation with you?"

"You couldn't share what you didn't know."

"What you're proposing is preposterous. You believe I somehow fooled the entire police department, and I've been working with the very people who want to capture me?"

She nodded. "It is an impressive feat. But you've had decades of practice in convincing others you're somebody that you're not. You wouldn't need to fool everyone in the department up front. Just the one person who verified your credentials, if anyone even did." She removed her phone from her coat pocket. "Let's clear all this up now. I'll call the police, and they can run your prints against the partial print in evidence. As an FBI agent, I'm sure your prints are already in a database, anyway, right?"

"Put it down," Rho said as she stepped around the corner of the unit with a gun drawn, pointed at Olivia. "Now."

Gotcha.

"Easy, Ali," Allen said. "She found the necklace."

Rho kept the gunsight locked on her. "Phone down, now."

Olivia's heart pumped wildly as she stared at the gun, but she was trapped along with Allen and Rho, and that was the endgame. All she could do now was to stall and trust in Henry, Sam, and Preston to play their roles. She bent forward as if to set the cell by her feet, but then slid it back toward the shelving unit. She gambled that they would be more concerned with retrieving the necklace than the phone.

"Sorry. My bad."

"Don't worry about it, Ali," Allen said. "Just get the necklace from her, and we'll leave."

"We can't let her go, Dad. She knows who we are."

"Nobody else is getting hurt," he replied. "Follow the plan. They won't ever find us."

Olivia raised her voice, hoping it would carry to her phone. "What is true is that you avoided violent altercations during your heists. The Tuxedo Bandit—a gentleman who had a misguided perception that if he could steal without violence, then the jewels were rightfully his. I didn't believe you would turn against your legacy by killing Stuart. Murder isn't your MO." She eyed Rho. "You, on the other hand ..."

"Keep quiet, Ali," he ordered.

"You killed Stuart," Olivia said. "Why? Did you think he was returning to the cabin to retrieve the necklace? You didn't realize that he probably never once laid eyes on it."

"Ali, get the necklace," her father said. "Let's go."

Rho kept her aim on Olivia as she stepped forward. When she was within arm's reach, she lowered her gun while scanning Olivia from head to toe. Then she reached into Olivia's coat pocket and removed the necklace.

"You should've stayed in your lane," Rho said, while admiring the sparkling sapphire. She closed her hand, securing the necklace, and raised her gun while backing away.

Olivia's focus darted to Sam as she stepped into the unit, aiming a gun at Rho. *Thank heavens. Be careful.*

"Drop it, buttercup," Sam said, standing several feet behind the father-daughter team.

Rho's head spun as she kept the gun's barrel targeted at Olivia.

"You drop it," Rho replied. "You know I'll shoot her."

"Ali, we've got what we came for," Allen said.

"I've got this, Dad."

Allen reached under his suit jacket, drew a gun, and pointed it at Sam.

"No!" Olivia cried.

Sam glanced at Allen while keeping her crosshairs on Rho.

"Nobody needs to get hurt," Allen said. "We have what's ours. We have no interest in either of you."

"Sam," Olivia pleaded, shaking her head. "Don't."

Sam glared at Rho and then lifted her hands in surrender. After she set her gun on the floor by her feet, Rho quickly closed the distance between them and kicked it away.

"Get over there by your friend," Rho said.

Sam turned, walking backward until she was beside Olivia. Rho picked up the gun and then stood next to her father.

Olivia's pulse was galloping as she shifted her feet,

readying to spin and bolt for cover behind the boxes. She peeked at Sam and whispered, "I'm sorry."

Sam kept her eyes locked forward, lowering her hands. "Don't be. I'm glad you called."

"We can't let them go," Rho said.

Anytime, Preston. Please, Henry. I hope you made the call.

"Ali, follow the plan. I'll take care of them and then meet you at the rendezvous."

"What are you going to do?" Rho said.

"Don't worry about it. You need to get out of here with the necklace."

Where are you?

Rho lowered her gun and backed away until she was near the entrance. Then she abruptly pivoted, turning her attention outside. "Dad, sirens. Let's go."

"Get out of here, Ali!" Allen said, raising his gun toward Olivia and Sam. "I'll take care of them. Go!"

In no time flat, Sam reached behind her back, swept Olivia to the ground, and fired two rounds from a pistol toward the entrance.

Allen crumpled, crying out in pain. "I'm hit."

Sam ducked down and covered Olivia, holding her fire but keeping her aim steady.

"Dad! Are you okay?"

"Stay down," Sam ordered Olivia.

"I'm okay," Allen groaned. "It's only my arm. Go, Ali! Quick!"

"No, no. I'm not leaving you!"

As the sirens grew louder, Sam scrambled off Olivia, staying in front of her and low to the ground.

"Sam!" Olivia shouted. "Watch out!"

"Get out of here, now!" Allen yelled.

As Rho dashed out of the unit, Sam popped up to her feet and sprinted toward Allen. "Drop it!" she commanded.

He surrendered his gun to the floor and then wrapped his hand around his wound. She kicked the gun out of his reach as the sirens silenced and whirling red and blue lights lit up the unit.

Thank you, thank you.

Olivia stood as Jayden launched out of her vehicle and dashed across the front of the doorway with her gun drawn.

"Get out of the car, Butler!" Preston yelled from outside the unit. "Hands up! Out! Now!"

Sam looked back at Olivia, keeping Allen guarded. "Liv, you okay?"

Thank you, Henry. She nodded while taking rapid, shallow breaths. "You?"

Sam beamed a wide smile as if she lived for this. "Never better."

CHAPTER 42

"Do you have her, Detective?" Olivia heard Jayden yell outside.

"She's secure," Preston shouted back. "Check inside."

Jayden and Cole rushed into the storage unit with their firearms drawn.

"Drop it!" Jayden called out to Sam.

She complied immediately, setting her gun on the floor and stepping back with her hands up.

Allen winced, holding his hand over his wound. "That woman shot me. Arrest her."

Preston entered the unit, rapidly surveying the scene. "What happened here?"

"She tried to kill me," Allen said, pointing at Sam.

"No," Olivia countered. "That's not true, and he's not an FBI agent. He's the thief. Rho is his daughter, and she has the Star of Athens."

Allen rolled over onto his knees, readying to stand. "Don't listen to her. She's lying. Those two conspired to steal the necklace, pin it on Butler, and kill me to cover up their crime."

Preston holstered his gun. "I highly doubt that. Jayden, search and secure him and then call an ambulance." He pointed to Sam. "Cole, take her outside. Stay with her." Then he hastened over to Olivia. "Are you okay?"

After looking around the scene from the shelving unit to the ceramic debris, she nodded. "Yeah, I ... ah ..." Now that the crisis was over, the adrenaline had left her foggy. Though she was sweating, chills set in, and she started to shiver.

"Take your time." He wrapped his arms around her, holding on tight until she steadied. Surprised by the embrace, it took her a second to reciprocate. Her hands glided across the yoke of his denim shirt, coming to rest on his shoulder and back. She eased into his support, stealing a short-lived intimate moment before they separated.

Then he grasped her hand. "When EMS comes, I want them to check you over."

She shook her head. "No. I'm fine. I'm not hurt." Her daze lifted as she thought of Sam. "Allen drew his gun on us, and Sam acted in self-defense. He's been lying this whole time. He's not an FBI agent. Who verified his credentials?"

Preston locked in on her eyes as if piecing together in

fast-forward what she was suggesting. "Deputy Simmons. He's a rookie. Henry Zimmerman called me and said you were in trouble. He told me you came here to retrieve the necklace."

"Did he tell you everything?"

"Enough to make me believe him."

Olivia glanced behind her. "My phone." She turned back toward him. "Thanks for coming and believing in Henry—and me." She squeezed his hand, then released her hold and stepped to the shelving unit. After searching the floor, she found her cell, woke it, and stopped the recording. Then she went back to Preston and handed it to him. "This will prove that what I'm saying is true."

She gave him a short version of Allen's and Rho's duplicity and criminal activity. After listening to the recording, he switched gears, fully resuming his official role.

"We'll talk later," he said. "Are you sure you're okay?"

After she nodded, they walked out of the unit and met Jayden, who was waiting for him by her squad car.

"Detective, I found an alternative ID on Allen," Jayden said. "It's a Florida driver's license issued to Mason Andrews."

Preston glanced at Allen, who was leaning against another patrol vehicle, guarded by a deputy. "Okay. Get him in cuffs until EMS arrives. Run the name through the system. Call Simmons at the station and find out how he verified his identification. Then have him contact the

FBI field office in Richmond and run the credentials he showed through them."

"Yes, sir," Jayden said. She turned, removing handcuffs from her duty belt as she walked toward Allen.

Olivia glanced up and down the lane between the units, gathering the police had entered from both ends to box in whomever they would find. Preston had parked his F-150 two doors down, facing off with a gray sedan with an opened driver's side door. Chief Raymond Payne had angled his vehicle toward Preston's truck, blocking off the avenue. Rho was sitting in the back of Payne's cruiser while Sam was speaking with Cole in front of the storage site opposite Henry's unit.

Preston brushed her arm. "Are you okay to wait for a few minutes while I speak with Payne?"

"I'm fine. What about Sam?"

"I'll take care of it. You should sit while you're waiting. My truck is open."

"I'll wait in my car."

"A deputy will photograph the scene, and your vehicle is part of it. Best not to have you in it when he does that." He reached into his pocket, pulled out his keys, and handed them to her. "Turn it on and get the heat running. You may have to be here for a while. I'll ask Jayden to take a statement from you, and I'll see what Payne wants to do. We may release you from here without you having to come to the station, but for now, you'll have to sit tight. Can you e-mail me a copy of the audio recording?"

She opened the app on her phone and sent him the file.

"Thanks. There's bottled water in the backseat," he added. "If you need some energy, there are peanut butter crackers in the glove box."

She couldn't help but chuckle at the thought of having a snack after being held at gunpoint. "The orange cheesy ones?"

"Yeah. A guilty pleasure."

"A true gourmet. That works for me."

They parted ways for the moment. He strode to where Payne stood by his cruiser, speaking on his cell. She walked to Preston's truck and gave Sam a thumbs-up, hoping they would both be free to go soon.

Settling into the driver's seat, she started the engine and warmed the cab. Preston spoke with Payne for several minutes before the chief erupted, yelling and pointing at every deputy on the scene. She figured Preston had just told him about Simmons' mistake and knew the rookie would probably face serious repercussions. One deputy was rolling out crime tape while another was photographing the scene outside Henry's unit. She reached for a bottle of water, eased back in the leather seat, and allowed gravity to take over.

The silence in the cab was soothing. Until now, she hadn't spared a second to think about what could've been. When bullets are flying, it's not a time to ponder or get emotional. She was relieved it had all worked out, whether thanks to her backup support, luck, or divine intervention—it didn't matter. But her somber mood drowned out any spirit of celebration. The risk she'd taken had led to staring down a gun, and that was sobering. Preston would likely be upset, and she couldn't blame him. Thoughts of her father weighed on her. What would've happened to him if Allen or Rho had killed her? Then there was Sam. None of this involved her, but she hadn't hesitated to help Olivia from beginning to end.

There would be time enough in the coming weeks to process all that had happened. Dwelling on the what-ifs, though, would be akin to having a conversation with her imagination. What if she'd gone with Paige the day she was killed? And what if Sam never showed today, and Preston came too late? But she hadn't gone, and she wasn't killed. That's what was real, not some made-up story in her head. There was nothing she would've done differently today, given a second chance, even knowing things may not have turned out as they did.

Her thoughts drifted to Henry and his heroic sacrifice. Accepting the consequences, he had told the police about the necklace so Preston would believe she needed help. She pulled out her phone and called him, letting him know that everything had gone well, and then offered to speak to the police on his behalf should he face charges. After she accepted his invitation to visit between Christmas and the New Year, they said a gracious goodbye and wished each other happy holidays.

Preston stepped over to where Sam was waiting with

Cole and discharged his watch. They spoke for a minute, then Sam turned and walked toward his truck. Olivia cut the engine, popped the door, and left the cab. She met Sam halfway and embraced her.

"Thank you for saving my life," Olivia said.

"Let's not be dramatic," Sam teased.

They released each other, mirroring relieved grins.

"When Allen pointed his gun at us, I feared for my life and yours," Sam said. "I defended myself. It's as simple as that."

"Just how many guns do you carry?"

Sam widened her smile. "I always have a backup. When you told me to bring firepower, I knew we wouldn't be playing in a sandbox."

"Do you think there'll be any legal issues with the shooting? I used to date a defense attorney, if you need representation. I can call him."

"No, I've got people, but it won't be necessary. With your witness account confirming the events, self-defense was justified. Allen's intent was to kill us and then make up a story, painting us as the bad guys. Meanwhile, Rho escapes with the necklace, and in the ensuing melee, he slips away, never to be seen from again."

"He was willing to forsake his nonviolent MO to protect his daughter," Olivia said. "You're pretty good at what you do, *security consultant.*"

"So are you, *writer*—if that's what you really do." They shared a laugh, then Sam said, "I think we'll be here for a while."

"Preston said Jayden would take our statements, but we might not have to go to the station." Olivia paused, watching an ambulance arrive, and then turned back toward Sam. "Seriously, you saved my life. You put yourself in harm's way to protect me. How can I ever thank you enough for all that you've done over the past few days?"

Sam shook her head and dramatically sighed. "Jeez. Don't get all sappy on me. I'm not a crier. Besides, I know you would've done the same for me a thousand times over."

"Yeah, but I think you're a better shot."

"We'll work on that."

Olivia glanced up and down the lane. "Where's your car?"

Sam pointed toward the far end. "I parked on the other side of those units. Without knowing what I was walking into, I didn't want to drive up, announcing myself."

"I should've given you more of a heads-up, but there was so little time."

Sam waved her off. "Your plan was solid. Risky, but well executed. Never hesitate to call me if you're in trouble, no matter what."

Then Jayden came over to take their statements. Sam went first, and while she was answering Jayden's questions, Olivia hopped into the passenger seat of Preston's truck. Feeling peckish, she opened the glove box and claimed a pack of his crackers. She needed the rest of her water to wash down the dry, gluey snack, but they tasted as good as ever. Eyeing the driver's seat, she imagined how sharing peanut butter crackers with him in front of a fireplace on a winter's night would be just about perfect.

Jayden completed her interview with Sam and then waved Olivia out of the truck for her round of questioning. They talked for fifteen minutes, and then Jayden gave her and Sam the green light to leave. When Jayden went back to her patrol car, Preston came over to them.

"Did Jayden tell you that you can get out of here?" he asked.

"She did," Sam replied. She glanced at Olivia. "I'm off. We'll talk later."

"Tomorrow," Olivia said. "Drive carefully."

"Hey, Sam. Thanks again," Preston added. "I meant what I said."

Her eyes wandered Olivia's way as she nodded, suppressing a smile. "I know." With that, she turned and walked away.

"You can take your car now," he said. "There's a lot we need to do here. I'll be busy the rest of the day, but can I call you tomorrow?"

"You have my number. By the way, you're down a pack of crackers."

"Did they help?"

"They gave me some pep. They're just like I remembered them. A girl could get used to sitting in your truck.

Comfy seats, gourmet food, and water. What else could I want?"

"I'll be sure to always have a stash for you." He bowed his head slightly, and then lifted his eyes, holding hers in place. "Liv, when Henry called and said you were in trouble … I …" He let out a deep breath. "If something would've happened—"

"We don't need to talk about this now. Later. You gotta go. You still owe me that coffee, anyway."

"That I do."

After they exchanged their goodbyes, she headed for her Expedition as he continued his official business. If it were under different circumstances and with no prying eyes around, perhaps they would've parted with a kiss. Another day, in its own time and place, what had sparked between them would find its way.

CHAPTER 43

Olivia woke at her leisure on Wednesday, without an agenda or any concern for the time. It was the type of morning she'd planned ever since putting in her two-week leave for vacation at the start of November. With half of her R & R down the drain, she'd have to double her efforts to kick back over the rest of the holiday season and rejuvenate her new year.

Last night, she had stayed up late, telling her father all about the takedown. She did most of the talking, and by eleven, the conversation meandered to her plans for staying in Apple Station for the foreseeable future. He listened with a patient ear, adding his two cents about the danger she'd put herself in. Even this, though, he tempered with love by jokingly bemoaning his exclusion from the capture. Teasing her, he suggested they open their own private investigation agency. That's when she realized fatigue had fogged them both, and it was time to hit the hay. Before turning in, he advised her not to make any hasty decisions about her job or personal life that would keep her from pursuing her dreams.

Now she selected a black sweatshirt from a drawer in her dresser and lingered for a moment, looking at the framed photo of her and Paige. That day in D.C. seemed like so long ago. Life had thrown them both a curveball, landing them in far different places. Paige's years had been cut too short, and Olivia's plans had seen upheaval. Still, Paige remained always in her heart, and caring for Willow was the best gift she could both give to and receive from her dear friend this Christmas.

After getting dressed, she grabbed her cell off the nightstand and went downstairs. Her father had left a note on the kitchen table informing her that he had driven into town for one more gift. Last night, he had composed a list of self-defense gear she should carry, including a stun gun, pepper spray, and a Swiss Army knife. When she expressed no interest in stuffing her pockets with weapons, he had decided a tactical pen would do for now until she saw things his way. By this time tomorrow, she'd probably be the proud owner of a weaponized pen that could write, ward off attacks, and break glass in an emergency.

She made a cup of coffee and carried it into the living room, planning to relax for a few minutes by the tree. After turning on the twinkling lights, she selected a seasonal playlist from a streaming app on her cell. Then she kicked back with her feet up on the sofa and covered her legs with a red fleece throw.

An incoming text buzzed over the soothing melody of a classical guitar strumming "Silent Night." She opened the message from Cassandra and read, "Gathering details on what happened yesterday. You'll give me your exclusive, right? Marco is coming into town on Monday, and we're co-writing the story for his—your—paper. Insert giddiness here!"

Amused by Cassandra's delight, she replied, "My story is yours. Congrats on collaborating with Marco. You deserve it. Thanks for all your help. How about we all meet on Monday?"

Cassandra's answer arrived in a beat. "Deal. We make a good team, Penn. We could do something with this. Cagney and Lacey? Rizzoli and Isles?"

Olivia thumbed, "Thelma and Louise?"

That earned a shocked face emoji along with, "That didn't end well for them. We'll work on the branding. Glad you're okay."

She nodded, replying, "Me too. Merry Christmas. TTYL."

Cassandra reciprocated, sending her a meme of three reindeer dancing the cancan.

She set her phone next to her coffee cup on the table, rose from the sofa, and went over to the front bay window. The morning sun shone through patchy clouds that were forecasted to thicken and settle in overnight. With freezing temperatures in place and the skies primed for a storm, there should be snow on the ground for Christmas.

She grabbed her coat, slipped on her shoes, and went out onto the porch. A cardinal hopping along the railing flitted over to the feeder for a safflower seed snack. His mate joined him on a higher rung, and both ate together unbothered by her presence. Looking across the yard, she spied Rhett come out of Sam's house and stand by the hood of a black SUV.

Olivia descended the porch steps and crossed both yards as Sam came out of her front door and joined him in the driveway.

"Hey, Liv," Sam said. "How are you this morning?"

"Rested and relieved. How about you?"

"Same. Even more so after finding this blockhead safe," Sam jested.

"Hey, now. I still have a headache from yesterday. Cut a guy some slack."

Olivia wasn't sure whether to ask or if she even wanted to know.

Sam jumped in, preventing any misunderstanding. "His buddy Rho drugged him."

"Not my buddy, and she stuck me with a needle," he corrected. "That's not cool."

Olivia cringed. "Ow. What happened?"

"Late Monday night, she came to my room to go over a few things. I turned around to grab my laptop, and then I felt a prick in my neck. I was out in a blink. The next thing I know, that chirpy front desk girl is shaking me awake in a utility closet down the hall from my room. I didn't know how I got there, but my head was pounding. When I returned to my room, all my stuff was gone. I called Sam, and when I heard about what had happened at the storage facility, we pieced it together."

"Why would she drug you?" Olivia asked.

"My guess is that she and her father were scheming to make their getaway sometime early yesterday," Sam said. "After coming up empty at the cabin Monday night, they probably decided to cut bait before somebody caught on to them. Rho took his laptop, phone, and everything else he may have used to identify and track her. But when you found the necklace, it changed their plans." Sam glanced at him. "You should keep better company."

He winked at Sam. "How about you and me—"

"Never. Need I remind you that you shot me?"

"Here we go again."

A delivery truck drove past Sam's house and pulled into Olivia's driveway.

"It sounds like you two have some negotiating to do," Olivia said.

Rhett rubbed his hands together as if in expectation. "I'm willing to compromise now that she has a cop in her back pocket."

"What's this?" Olivia asked.

"It's nothing," Sam replied, shaking her head at him.

"Your detective friend says he owes Sam a favor.

That's going to come in handy someday. I'm one of the good guys. Can I glom off your halo?"

Sam playfully shoved his shoulder. "I don't think so, Popeye. Preston was just grateful that everything turned out like it did."

Olivia nodded, having learned over the past few days that there was a lot about Sam that she would just have to trust her on. Sam had saved her life, and that earned her the benefit of the doubt always and forever.

"I'll let you two do what you do," Olivia teased. "I saw you over here, and I wanted to come over and say hello. I'll see you tomorrow for dinner, Sam. Merry Christmas, Rhett. Good luck in all your future endeavors."

"Same to you," he replied. "Hey, the offer of the golf lessons was legit. If you're interested, I'm available."

She flashed back to when they first met at Whispering Meadows. *What was I thinking?* "Taking up golf was going to be more of a spring fling for me, but I've got something better in mind now."

They exchanged parting pleasantries, and then she turned and walked back across the yards. The delivery truck was on its way out as she neared her porch. After picking up two small packages from the top step, she stepped inside, almost tripping over a partially unwrapped gift that had been relocated by their resident rascal. Buddy was pawing at her buzzing cell on the coffee table. A peek at the picture ID had her hotfooting around the sofa before the call shuttled to voice mail.

"Hey, Preston. Good morning."

"Same to you. How are you doing?"

"Relieved everything is over. I bet you had a long night."

"Yeah. Andrews has been staying at a hotel in Winchester, so I went out there with some deputies and searched through his things. It was late by the time we were done. His daughter, whose real name is Alice Andrews, seemed to have all her stuff in her car. Between the two, we found fake IDs, a lot of cash, and a small armory. It'll take a while for ballistic results to come back, but I'm confident we'll find a match for the round recovered from Stuart."

"Did either of them confess to his murder?"

"They both did."

"How does that work?"

"Mason Andrews confessed immediately. He passed on having an attorney present and wanted to sign his life away as soon as we could get a pen and paper in front of him. When I questioned Alice and told her about his confession, she copped to the killing. She gave us details of what had happened, which are consistent with our investigation."

"They were trying to cover for each other?"

"It looks that way. But all signs point to Alice being the shooter."

"Why did she do it?"

"We're still piecing it together, but it seems she'd been

following Stuart, and for some reason, he ended up near my dad's cabin Friday night."

"Why do you think he went there?"

"I don't know. Maybe he wanted to revisit where he took the last wrong turn in his life to exorcise his demons or to forgive himself. You know how hard it is to find without directions. He probably got lost along the way, turned around, and unfortunately ran into Alice. She thought he'd recovered the necklace, and they had a confrontation."

She set the delivered packages on the table and then shimmied out of her coat, letting it fall behind her on the couch. "That's brutal. Maybe he had turned his life around but never got the chance to prove himself. What about Mason Andrews? How did he pull off posing as an FBI agent?"

"Payne gave Simmons the task of verifying his credentials. Andrews gave Simmons the contact information that supposedly belonged to his supervisor. That name is real and belongs to an agent in D.C. All the information checks out, except for one of the phone numbers listed on the business card. Andrews included an office and a cell number. The cell is the general line for the D.C. headquarters. The office number is what Simmons called, and we believe this was a burner phone set up with another accomplice, probably one of his fences, for the express purpose of verifying him as an agent. The number was dead when I tried to call it."

Rummaging by the door prompted her to look back

at Buddy as he pawed at the package of treats he'd triumphantly left for her. "Andrews provided his own verification. That's bold and took planning."

"He didn't lack confidence, that's for sure. We were all fooled."

She went over and picked up the package and set it on an end table, giving Buddy a look. "Is Simmons in trouble?"

"He won't face any official repercussions. Payne tasked him with developing an outreach program aimed at protecting the community from scams and fraud."

"At least something good will come of all this. Do you think the Andrews are responsible for the blackmail threat as well?"

"We do. Among the many burner phones, we accessed one that shows the text sent to Dylan Carter about meeting at the Turner Mill House. It'll only be a matter of time before we find more evidence to connect both to the blackmail. This was quite a takedown scheme you came up with—on your own."

She knew this was coming. "I imagine you're a little —a lot—upset about that."

"It's hard to argue with the results. I'm not even going to weigh ends and means. I don't know anyone outside of law enforcement who would've done something as brave and foolish to help my family. I don't want there to be a next time, but if you're ever in trouble again, no matter the circumstances, call me."

"Deal. For what it's worth, I'm not planning on there

being a next time." Buddy braced his forepaws on the table's edge, trying to snatch the treats with his mouth. She guided his legs to the ground and vigorously petted his chest to distract him. "I bet your mom is relieved."

He chuckled. "She's thrilled, and still on me about what I said to you on Sunday."

"You know I understand. You don't have to apologize to me for feeling the way you did."

The line went silent for several breaths, spurring her to glance at her screen to see if the call had disconnected.

"Can I make it up to you once and for all?" he asked. "If you're available this evening, would you like to take a walk together through the Festival of Lights?"

Her unbridled smile sparked a bark from Buddy. "That sounds perfect. I'd like that."

After they set up a time to meet, they said their good-byes and ended the call.

"What do you think, little bud? Can you make room for Willow and Preston in your life? Two big changes. Are you going to be nice to both?"

He barked again, trotted over to the tree, and sniffed around the gifts.

"Keep looking. You've got some new red b-a-l-l-s, and now I have to rewrap your t-r-e-a-t-s for tomorrow."

He crawled over a box and then lay down on top of another. She picked up his treats and glanced at the packages on the sofa. On this, the first day of her *real* vacation, all she had to do was a little wrapping and a little prepping for strolling through the lights tonight.

CHAPTER 44

After an early dinner with her father, Olivia arrived in town half an hour before her date with Preston. All the stores were now closed until Friday. The inn, though, was still open, serving Christmas Eve fare for revelers or those attending midnight church services. The sidewalks in front of the shops were quiet and clear, as the hub of activity for the evening was the Festival of Lights on the town square.

She parked near the inn, exited her Expedition, and crossed Cider Lane. The lamp posts' amber light seemed to glow especially bright, as if energized by the banter and laughter from all who passed by. Carolers carrying candlelit lanterns strolled around the square, serenading visitors enjoying the lights. Applewood burning in the firepit by the gazebo spread its sweet, smoky scent strong and wide. She took her time enjoying the scene, and glanced at A.J.'s office and

Sophia's clinic in passing. She was looking forward to meeting up with them both to exchange gifts tomorrow, as was their custom.

Kaitlyn's infectious giggle caught her attention as she neared the living nativity by the start of the trail walk. The Carter family stood gathered around a pony that was posing as a donkey, and three shepherds dressed in bathrobes. She waved to Dylan and mouthed "hello." He let go of his niece's tiny fingers and said something to Stacey and Darcy. Then he jogged over to Olivia, meeting her by three Fraser firs wrapped in blue-and-green lights.

"Ms. Penn, do you have a moment?" he asked.

"It's Olivia, and of course."

Kaitlyn gleefully screamed as a little lamb nipped one of the wise men.

"It looks like your niece is having fun."

He peeked back at her. "She's so excited about Christmas. We all are, and we have you to thank."

She shook her head. "Me?"

"Yesterday, Henry Zimmerman called my mom and talked to her about the night Stuart stayed in Joe Hill's cabin. He also said you had told him about Kaitlyn's medical condition."

She winced. "I'm sorry for speaking about something so personal and private to someone outside of your family. There were extenuating circumstances, and for what it's worth, I don't believe Henry is much of a gossip. I hope you can forgive me."

His smile grew, resembling Kaitlyn's effervescent grin. "Forgive you? No, thank you."

The carolers neared the nativity scene, singing "O Come, All Ye Faithful."

"He told my mom about losing his wife and daughter, and then …" Dylan's eyes glistened, and he took a moment before continuing. "Henry insisted he pay for Kaitlyn's medication for as long as she needs it."

"Oh, Dylan, that's wonderful and so generous of him."

"Our family isn't the type to accept charity, but we can't refuse the offer for Kaitlyn's sake. She'll start the medication before the weekend."

"That's such great news, and a true Christmas miracle. I hope it's what she needs."

"I know I didn't make the best first impression, and I'm sorry for that," he said.

She held up her hand, stopping him from going further. "No need to apologize."

"My mom and sister were so overwhelmed that they invited Henry to Christmas dinner tomorrow."

"I think that's exactly what he needs. Henry has lost a lot in his life, and he's been alone for a long time. Being around a loving family will do him good."

He nodded. "Him doing this for Kaitlyn is more than Stuart ever did for her, so it's the least we can do." His smile thinned as he placed his hands in his coat pockets. "Stuart's employer in Winchester contacted us. He had been working in a warehouse out there. When he took the job, he signed up for life insurance, making my mom the beneficiary. Even though he worked there for only three weeks, the policy doesn't have a waiting period, so it'll pay out as soon as the claim processes. It's not lottery money, but it'll help my mom out."

She glanced at Kaitlyn, who was waving to the actors playing Mary and Joseph. "Maybe that'll give you some peace about your father."

"I may have been wrong about him," he replied. "I thought he couldn't ever change. I didn't believe him when he said that he'd turned his life around. I've done bad things, and I changed because of it. But I never had faith that he could do the same."

"Maybe it was because of you."

"What do you mean?"

"Maybe you inspired his change. In my experience, where there is a will to change, there is a way. But where there is no will, there is no way."

"Uncle!" Kaitlyn yelled, jumping like a pogo stick while swinging Darcy's hand.

"It looks like you're being summoned," Olivia said. "You better go."

His cheeks softened as he removed his hands from his pockets. "She'll only get louder if I don't. She's getting her picture with Santa, and that's all she's been talking about the entire day. My whole family thanks you." He held out his hand, and after they shook, he said, "If you ever need anything, call me. I'm pretty good with tech."

"Well, I'm not. So maybe I'll take you up on the offer sometime."

They wished each other happy holidays, and then Dylan rejoined his family. Olivia glanced at the gazebo, where Preston was waiting. She waved and went toward him, wondering whether her heart would always giddyup every time they got together.

CHAPTER 45

"I hope you haven't been waiting too long," Olivia said as she neared Preston.

"No. I just got here," he replied. "I saw you talking with Dylan, and I didn't want to interrupt."

"I ran into him on the way over. His family has received good news, and it looks like things might turn around for them. Maybe for Henry too." She glanced at the Carters as they headed for the backdrop display set up for night pictures with Santa. "This is the most crowded I've ever seen it on Christmas Eve for the festival. The sky is so clear, and the moon is so bright, it's hard to believe we could have snow on the ground by morning. Are you off duty, at least for tonight?"

He nodded. "And tomorrow. We'll pick back up with the Andrews investigation on Monday. We've transferred them to a more accommodating holding facility, and *real* FBI agents will come in next week to help process the evidence. We've already matched Mason Andrews' prints to the partial found at his heist in Miami, so his thieving days are over."

"And no more private security gigs for Rho-Alice-Butler. I don't even know what to call her."

"That's for sure. Turns out only half of my mom's so-called security team was useless."

"What does that mean?"

He waited until a family with two tykes, bundled up from head to toe, passed by. "Rhett located the lawyer who dealt with my great-uncle's estate. My guess is that Alice hacked into my mom's financial records and used the two-hundred-thousand-dollar deposit as a ruse in their blackmail scheme. They had to be researching my parents for months. Rhett helped us with one of Alice's laptops, and he pieced together a little of what she'd done. It seems my dad cashed the inheritance check instead of depositing it straight up. But an untraceable cash deposit leaves room for speculation, and the Andrews leveraged that for their scheme."

"Maybe that's what Alice had been up to since I first met her in October. The undercover job at Whispering Meadows was an excuse for her to be in the area. I don't get why she partnered with Rhett."

"There's a lot we don't have a handle on yet."

She thought of Sam's reference to Rhett's financial backing, wondering if Alice had targeted him to leech from his resources. But she let it go, as her role was done and she'd probably never see or hear from Rhett again.

"The blackmail threat was an inroad for Alice with your mother."

"The Andrews set the scheme in motion, and then Alice was conveniently available to offer her services to help. It gave them access to my mom, which I'm sure they were trying to exploit to locate the necklace. It was a recovery operation three years in the making. But then, you got involved and ruined their plans." After they shared a laugh, he asked, "How did it feel to have fifteen million dollars in your hand?"

"Surprisingly light," she joked. "What's going to happen to Henry? Will he face any charges?"

He slipped his fingers into his jeans' front pockets and shrugged. "I can't say for sure, but I don't believe so. I spoke yesterday to an FBI agent who's been working the Andrews case for years. He contacted the owners of the necklace, and they were overjoyed that it had been recovered. They want to give Henry a reward. Given the circumstances, I don't think any prosecutor would see any reason for, or benefit from, going after Henry. I think he'll be okay."

"That's a relief. He was only trying to protect your family."

"Like someone else I know."

She glanced toward the entry for the light trail, feeling her cheeks warm despite the thirty-degree chill. "Should we get going?"

"Let's," he replied.

They took their time along the trail, admiring the

festive displays and chatting about what they used to do on Christmas Eve as children. The roaming carolers spread out on the gazebo's steps, singing a medley of the season's most popular hits.

They strolled past elves in a toy shop wrapping gifts, and Santa driving a jeep full of safari animals through the Sahara. At the far end of the square, a cat and dog embraced in front of a roaring fireplace. She took a picture of the animation, hoping it was a sign of smooth relations between Willow and Buddy.

They neared the displays closest to the inn and stepped off to the side, allowing a family with five kids to pass by. Two older girls joshed their three younger brothers about who had been naughty and nice. A young couple emerged from the inn, crossed the street, and playfully bumped shoulders. Then the fellow picked up his date and spun her around three times.

"I take it you'll be dining at the inn with your mother tomorrow," Olivia asked Preston.

"Yeah. Before she owned it, she'd make a feast at home for me and my dad. But the restaurant gets packed for brunch and dinner on Christmas. She likes to be there with her staff and greet those who come."

"That sounds like your mom."

"Can I ask you something?" After she turned to face him, he said, "I was wondering … do you have plans for New Year's Eve?"

She dipped her eyes for a breath and then raised them along with a smile. "I have a friend who's throwing a hoedown of sorts at his father's ranch in Berryville. If you're interested, he encouraged me to bring a plus-one."

He nodded, matching her grin. "That sounds like fun. Can we call it a date?"

"I think we can."

He pointed at a nearby bench softly lit by a lamppost wrapped in pine. "Do you mind if we sit for a minute?"

They went to the bench and sat close to each other, facing a light display of seven swans a swimming. He reached into his coat pocket and pulled out a rectangular box wrapped in metallic-silver paper. He held it in his hand for a second and then angled it toward her.

"I got you something. I didn't know when I would see you next, so I brought it tonight." He handed her the present. "Merry Christmas."

"Oh, gosh. Thank you. I wasn't expecting this, and I would say you shouldn't have, but I have something for you too."

He gestured toward the box. "You go first."

She turned her attention to the neatly wrapped gift, lifting the tape on both ends. Then she slid her finger down the center fold, revealing a sturdy, sleek, hinged black box. She opened the lid, and was taken aback by the contents.

An exquisite turquoise fountain pen was nestled in a luxe velvet lining. Though not a collector, she knew the brand name stitched on the inside lid was a high-end designer. She removed the pen and pulled off the cap, uncovering a rose-gold nib that matched the clip. A cobalt-blue lacquer ring wrapped midway around the barrel, engraved with images of the sun, the moon, and a lake. The gorgeous pen balanced perfectly in her hand, but she knew it must have cost a fortune.

She placed it back in the box. "This is too much."

He winced. "You don't like it?"

"Oh, no. I mean yes." She shook her head, laughing at herself. "That came out all wrong. Let me start over. It's stunning, but I know how expensive it had to be."

He braced his hands on his thighs, leaning in toward her. "On Monday, after you left the house, your father and I spoke in the kitchen. He talked about your mother and how much you mean to him. He told me how your mom never had the chance to do what she wanted with her writing. Your dad knows how much writing means to you, and he doesn't want anything in your life to stop you from pursuing that."

Water welled in her eyes, and she wiped the corner of one to prevent a tear from running down her cheek. She, like her father, could cry at the drop of a hat, especially when reminded of the love they had for one another.

Preston smiled tenderly and lightly placed his hand on hers. "He showed me your mother's broken pen and told me he was going to have it repaired. I know you'll want to get it fixed because it was your mother's. But I thought you should also have a special pen of your own to write the stories only you could tell."

She didn't know what to say, but it all made perfect sense. Unable to control her smile, she let her heart lead the way. "Thank you. I love it." Then she leaned over, hugged him, and brushed his cheek with a gentle kiss.

He broke into a mile-wide grin, breathing a sigh of relief. "I'll tell you what. I've had people shoot at me, taken part in high-speed chases, and almost been attacked by a bear—twice. But I'm not sure that I've ever been so nervous as I was in hoping that you'd like it."

"I really do. I've never seen such a beautiful pen. Now, it's my turn, but mine isn't nearly as extravagant."

She pulled a small box, wrapped in embossed gold-foil paper, out of her pocket and gave it to him.

His eyes sparked, matching the shine of the package. "You didn't have to get me anything, but thank you."

He unwrapped the gift, shooting her a quizzical glance upon seeing the brand logo emblazoned across the top of the box. After he removed the lid, his smile grew two sizes as he turned the box over, letting a penknife drop into his waiting palm.

"Oh, wow! This is like my dad's. It looks identical." He unlocked the blade and held it up to the light, admiring the satin finish of the stainless steel and running his finger along its edge. "That's sharp. It feels perfect in my hand. I can't believe you found this." He closed the blade and held the penknife in his palm.

"I know it's not the same as having your father's knife, but maybe it'll remind you of him, and someday, you can pass it down to your son or daughter."

He grasped her hand, leaning in closer, and caressed her wrist with his thumb. "I love it. Thank you. That's really thoughtful of you. I've looked for something like this before, but I could never find anything as close as this." He curled her fingers in his palm. "Your hand is freezing. Would you like to get a hot chocolate to warm up?"

She glanced toward the end of the trail walk, where two local restauranteurs were selling snacks and hot drinks. "Let's."

They both slipped their gifts into their coat pockets, then stood and moseyed hand in hand down the home-stretch. They passed a row of candy canes and a four-car train chugging along a track, before pausing for a moment at the newest display of a butterfly fluttering in a field of swaying daisies.

The cheerful chatter and the exuberant chorus singing "We Wish You a Merry Christmas" faded into the background as she thought about how far she'd come in a year. Much had changed in its own time and season. Her heart was now in Apple Station, and she couldn't imagine ever leaving. As she and Preston strolled through the sparkling snowflake tunnel, she looked up through the arches at the night sky. She smiled, holding on tight and embracing her new life, walking under the light of the cocoon moon.

The End

ACKNOWLEDGMENTS

I'm deeply grateful for all those who have supported me in the writing of this book.

Thank you to my brilliant editor Serena Clarke for all of your work in making this story the best it could be. Your encouragement, guidance, and support are appreciated beyond words. Thank you to my wonderful proofreader LaVerne Clark for your painstaking attention to detail, instruction, and insightful feedback. As my last line of defense, you've saved the day on countless occasions. Thank you to Robin Vuchnich for your beautiful cover design.

Thank you to the welcoming and supportive community of Sisters in Crime.

Thank you to all my readers. Your support makes these stories possible.

A LETTER FROM KATHLEEN

Dear Reader,

Thank you for reading *Under the Cocoon Moon*! I loved being able to share this holiday mystery with you. The season is such a natural fit for coziness, connection, and a touch of magic, and I hope you felt all of that while following Olivia's latest case.

If you'd like updates on new releases, a peek into my writing life, and the occasional special promotion, you can sign up for my newsletter on my website. I'll never share your e-mail address, and you can unsubscribe at any time.

If you enjoyed *Under the Cocoon Moon*, I'd be truly grateful if you left a review on your favorite retail site or review platform. Reviews are one of the best ways to help other mystery lovers discover my books.

For me, one of the best parts of writing is being part of this warm community of readers. Please don't hesitate to connect through my website, email, or social media. Your messages always brighten my day.

With gratitude,
Kathleen

www.kathleenbaileyauthor.com
Instagram: @cozycrimewriter

WORKS BY KATHLEEN BAILEY

OLIVIA PENN MYSTERY SERIES

Where the Light Shines Through

Silence Says the Most

Under the Cocoon Moon

When the Carnival Came

Without a Shadow of Doubt

The Case of the Broken Heart (Prequel short story)

ABOUT THE AUTHOR

Kathleen Bailey is the award-winning author of *The Olivia Penn Mystery Series*. She writes mysteries with heart and humor that keep to the traditional and cozy sides of crime. For over twenty years, she worked as a pediatric physical therapist with children who have special needs, drawing on degrees in English, psychology, and physical therapy. She now writes in Virginia with her feline assistant, who insists on supervising every draft. When she's not writing, Kathleen can usually be found covered in cat hair, surrounded by far too many sticky notes, and plotting new twists to keep readers guessing. She is a member of Sisters in Crime. Visit her online at kathleen-baileyauthor.com.

9 781956 270099